NOT ALWAYS BLU SKYES

I0643185

NOT ALWAYS BLU SKYES

SECRETS HAVE A WAY OF COMING OUT

GABRIELLE MCMASTER

ZENITH PUBLISHING

Dedicated to Nanny—
I hope you're proud of what I've achieved

AUTHOR'S NOTE

I came up with *Not Always Blu Skyes* when I visited Llandudno, Wales for the first time. The place was magical to me, and I wanted others to know about its beauty. I just needed characters and a realistic storyline that I hoped would capture the hearts of my readers. Then, the basis of *Not Always Blu Skyes* had formed.

With my debut novel, I wanted to have a story that featured mental health issues, the dilemmas of high school life, and realistic romance. It was a pleasure to write this novel, and without travelling, music, family, and friends, this would never have happened.

Life can throw things at you when you least expect it and you can make so many mistakes. But it's what you do with it and how you fix your life that's important. All too often, we agree to things and we regret the choices that we previously made. But we can let all of that go and change our lives for the better— only if we let the past go and let go of what other people tell us we need to do, too. That's a tough lesson to be learnt, but it's a lesson that all of my characters experience.

Not Always Blu Skyes is a novel about letting the past, and your mistakes, go. It's about letting people into your life to change it and letting people go, even if it hurts, to make the most out of your life.

Secrets have a way of coming out. They always will because life is *Not Always Blu Skyes…*

Happy reading,
Gabrielle McMaster x

FIRST SEMESTER

"A woman's heart is a deep ocean of secrets."

Titanic (1997)

One

"This is your year. I'm sure we tell you that every year, but we're repeating it again."

This was apparently the start of our super-inspiring motivational talk about the new year ahead. The new school year that also happened to be our last year at high school— the year before we all go our separate ways. Or, in most cases, end up at the same university but never speak to each other again.

The talk kept going on. "To those in their last year, may the Buddha or whoever help all of the future people you'll be under the authority of. The community knows how much we've suffered."

Believe it or not, we weren't a religious school at all. Our headmistress just detested our year that much. It wasn't like we were a handful— most of the time. Sniggers travelled along our rows in the assembly hall. We were the type of class that the head liked to bring to the first year school assemblies in order to show them the example of what not to become. Of course, there were innocent ones, too. But some of us were worse than others. As they say, we were all tarred with the same long, sharp bristled brush.

We made our way back to the common room after assembly to find half of our year hiding there to avoid going to assembly. I slumped down on one of the black leather sofas. My friend Molly sat down beside me. She flicked through her phone and groaned.

"Did you see what she posted under our photo? A puking emoji! How childish," Molly complained, running a hand through her black hair. She turned her phone around and showed it to me. Over summer, we had gone on a trip to Scotland to see some universities with our other friend, Louise. The photo was from our trip. Clearly Lola, the most popular girl in our year, didn't approve.

"Just ignore her," Louise said as she flumped down beside me. The whole sofa moved. The school liked to give us broken sofas because they didn't trust us with new ones. It wasn't as though we were going to steal them. Auction them on eBay, maybe, but definitely not steal them. "We've got more important things to focus on this year."

Funny, that. That's exactly what my mum reminded me of this morning when she checked over my appearance before letting me go out the door. The year before you go off to university, you're always told that it's so important to focus on your studies throughout the whole year ahead. Sometimes it's hard not to. From here on in, our focus was getting a university place, exams, and interviews. It seemed impossible to live normally. To me, it didn't matter if I did or didn't get in. But, to my family, university was everything— it was the one thing that defined you as a person.

Louise and Molly began to discuss their university options. I hadn't even fully thought about it yet. I had a top ten list, but none of them were anything I truly wanted. No one, especially my parents, seemed to understand that.

When the bell rang, we all went to our first class of the new semester. Molly and I got off extremely lightly by only having study room first thing. With nothing to study, what could possibly go wrong? As we walked into the room, it was obvious what could go wrong. It appeared as though every pupil in the room was wrapped up in their own heads. Heads were firmly planted on desks, girls were checking their makeup aimlessly in mirrors, and others were on their phones. No one was speaking to each other. Each person was so consumed in his or her own little bubbles that they didn't feel the need to, nor did they realise that they could, converse with the person at the desk next to them. Miss Harshaw walked into the study room. It was then that everyone put away the things they weren't meant to be doing and sat up straight at their desk. Molly and I swiftly found seats beside each other and got out a writing pad and a pen.

Everyone hated study room. The reason? Miss Harshaw. She wasn't a teacher. She just minded us in the study room— she was essentially our babysitter. We all presumed she had been in the army, because she treated us all like cadets that needed to be whipped into shape. "Glad to see we have all learnt from last year. Sign-in sheet is going around now. Write your name, don't write other people's names, and most certainly do *not* write fake names. The headmistress and I were not pleased to have a 'Willie Isbald' on the last sign-up sheet we took before summer. It was utterly disgraceful," Miss Harshaw called out in her usual curt voice.

People were trying not to laugh. Their shoulders bounced up and down in an attempt to contain their laughter. Eventually, a bunch of people burst out laughing.

"Shut up and get on with your work!"

That was it. Silence. The Harshaw Cadets were firmly whipped into shape for the new semester. It took her less than five minutes—longer than her usual three minutes. Miss Harshaw could silence people with only a look. She could also detect a phone from a mile off like she had X-Ray vision or something. I gazed to my right and noticed Molly had her phone in her pencil case. She acted like she was trying to find a pen when she was actually texting.

"Are you crazy?" I whispered. Molly didn't hear me. She kept grinning into her pencil case like a constipated Cheshire Cat—believe me, that's not a pretty sight. I moved to the side on my chair and saw her chatting up someone. My chair began to tip, and it slammed down on the floor.

"Miss Bernard, haven't you got any work to be getting on with?" Miss Harshaw called. She wasn't even looking at me. She was pinning up a notice at the front of the room, with her back to me.

I sighed. "No, Miss. It might have something to do with the fact we haven't had any classes yet."

Miss Harshaw glared at me when she turned around. I smiled innocently, but of course that didn't work with her. "Well, Olivia, you have university choices to make. Plus, if you're really stuck, we can get you some Geography questions to do."

"I failed Geography AS. You know that."

She smirked slyly at me. "Precisely why you would benefit from it."

I rolled my eyes and wrote my name on the sign-in sheet before passing it to Molly. I looked at the blank page in front of me. University choices… That was probably a bigger insult to me than the Geography dig was.

My parents advised— no, wrong word— desired, demanded, almost filled out the UCAS application for me, in order for me to apply to Oxford. I couldn't lie to myself. Oxford had been a dream of mine, as well as my parents, since I was in Year Six, when I was almost ready to go to high school. I was the top student of my class, but when I got to high school, things changed as I met people who were significantly smarter than me. Suddenly my top-of-the-class status dropped down to being average. Yeah, I could still get into Oxford with hard work and dedication; but I didn't know if I could manage that pressure at every exam I was going to take in June. I knew if I didn't put it down, my parents wouldn't be proud. They wanted me to go to Oxford, and eventually, I just began to go along with it. It was drummed into me so much that it became my dream as much as theirs.

Miss Harshaw began to walk around the room. Her feet thumped, shaking the whole classroom with every step she took like an earthquake. I grabbed a pen and began to write the one word I dreaded on the first line of the page: *Oxford.* After that, I didn't know where I wanted to go. It was only because it's what my parents wanted. My Oxford dream was well over— I knew that anyway.

"Do we seriously have an hour of this?" Molly whispered. I looked at her and nodded. She groaned and took her purple-rimmed glasses off. I smirked.

"Who were you texting?" I asked.

Molly looked up to see Miss Harshaw coming closer. "Tell you later."

We put our heads down and began to think of our choices again. Our minds seemed to be filled with nothing else. University and exams— what a joy. I gazed over at Molly's page as Miss Harshaw passed us by.

She had got down her five choices with the grades beside them. At least she knew what she wanted to do.

Miss Harshaw managed to make her way to the back of the room and picked up the sign-in sheet. Everyone heard her sigh. We turned around in unison to look at her. She scanned around the whole room to spot someone being suspicious. No one gave themselves up. "Fine. I'll ask then. Who put down 'Dick Cumming?'" Miss Harshaw asked. We all began to laugh. Rage engulfed her face as her jaws ground together and the vein on her temple pulsed. "Who put down 'Willie Hardigan?'"

As everyone laughed, one person stood up. It was a boy we had never seen before. With his red hair and freckles, he had quite the Irish look about him. "Me, Miss. I'm Willie Hardigan... or William, as my parents call me. I'm new to this year," he said in a thick Irish brogue.

Miss Harshaw was shocked that the name had turned out to be a real person for once. "What an unfortunate name, and how unfortunate that you're Irish, too."

It was well known that Miss Harshaw had dated the old caretaker. He was Irish, and everyone loved him. Mr. O'Neill had three jokes, and by the Halloween break, you knew all of them by heart. He broke Miss Harshaw's heart when she caught him and his Irish girlfriend having it off in his office. Since then, she had had a thing against the Irish. She sighed. "Sit down, Willie."

We all burst out laughing again as he sat down. Miss Harshaw tried to silence us, but this time it just didn't work. She knew she was in for hell this year. We all knew she was.

The first proper class was Spanish. I couldn't do Spanish for the life of me, and most of the people in the class couldn't, either. They just enjoyed winding up Señora Stone. How do I even begin to describe

Señora Stone? Well, she's in her fifties, can't handle a class, and every year we drive her mad. That's probably one of the reasons why we were given the title of 'The Worst Year of Willow High.'

We poured into the classroom like a gushing tap. Señora Stone just looked at us over the top of her silver-rimmed glasses. The fear was obvious in her eyes, especially when it looked as though she might burst out crying. She pushed stray black hairs out of her face. The hairs had fallen out of her messy bun, which I presumed was a neat bun before she had first year pupils this morning.

"Let me get one thing clear, I will not be driven crazy this year," she announced, banging her fist on the desk to get everyone's attention. That was when Roger pulled out a takeaway tub of nachos. "No eating in class! No comes en clase!"

"But it's nachos. It's Spanish," Roger said. We all groaned. Roger was put in our group. We were the lower class set of Spanish because none of us could grasp it well. As I'm sure you can tell, Roger wasn't the brightest colour in the crayon pack.

"Ha!" Señora Stone said as she caught on. She pointed a finger at him, wagging it in a mad fashion that was so typical of her. "Nachos are Mexican, not Spanish! You see, I'm on the ball this year. Now put the nachos away and get your books out!"

We all did as we were instructed. Señora Stone began to run through how our exam and coursework would be marked. I tuned her out.

All I wanted was to live a normal teenage life, but Molly and Louise held secrets that had happened over summer, and in fact, happened right in front of my eyes. It felt almost like they were drifting from me. Almost.

Two

The common room smelt delicious as I walked in after a library session for lunch. I somehow managed to balance a lever-arch folder, a notepad, a textbook and my pencil case all on my arms without dropping any of them. It seemed impressive to the physics nerds of the year, but to me, it was a pure example of how dysfunctional my life was. I dumped my stuff on the sofa beside Louise. She looked up at me as she jumped in surprise at the large *thud* that had resounded beside her. "Liv! You scared the crap out of me," Louise commented, a hand on her chest in a dramatic fashion— oh, how typical of her. I threw my bag down on top of the whole pile and pulled out a curry chip I had bought earlier on the way to school. Thankfully, it hadn't spilt. Señora Stone would not be impressed if I got curry all over her first homework for us.

"I'm going to heat this up. I'll be back in a minute," I told her. She just nodded and mindlessly scrolled through her phone. In our common room, they somehow trusted us with a sink, toaster, and a microwave— along with a kettle. I put my tub of curry chip into the microwave and waited for it to heat for two minutes. In the meantime, I looked over to see Molly sitting beside Louise. They began to talk between themselves.

The microwave dinged, and I took out my curry chip. When I carried it over to the others, I sat down with them, shoving my stuff onto the floor.

"That smells amazing," Molly commented. I nodded and ate a chip off the fork.

"It really is."

Molly smiled. She brought out her sparkly, neon, pink-covered phone. Anyone who knew Molly knew she was a massive girly girl. It seemed strange that she would associate herself with me. I preferred to lounge in a pair of jeans whereas Molly preferred a skirt. Everything Molly owned was pink, including her Fiat 500. I owned a Polo, which was a boring black colour. Molly was lucky that her parents were *filthy* rich.

Her father was an accountant and her mother was a top lawyer. Everyone knew that her parents planned for her to go to Cambridge or Oxford and would pay her full three-year university fees in one payment. It was so unfair; it wasn't just the fact that her parents could afford it, unlike mine, but it was also because if anyone could get in, it was Molly. She had the personality to pass the interview, the knowledge to pass the entrance exam, and she had the brains to get top grades in her A Levels. I felt guilty saying this, but I, for one, was jealous of her; being around her made me feel inadequate in comparison. As far as I was concerned, going up against Molly, I didn't stand a chance at getting into Oxford, or even Cambridge for that matter.

"So, what was up with you earlier in study room?" I asked.

Molly grinned. She looked at me and then at Louise. "Well, not to toot my own horn, but I met a pretty amazing guy." Louise and I exchanged a look. Molly's last boyfriend didn't exactly go as planned. She rolled her eyes at the two of us and did an annoying hair flick off her shoulder.

"He's not like Kevin, is he?"

"No one could be like Kevin," Louise reminded her.

Kevin didn't believe in boundaries. That isn't the best quality to have when you are meeting parents and friends. Kevin was at the local university and he believed in speaking his mind, like most students I knew. But when he asked Molly's mum when her baby was due, and asked her dad how much money Molly was going to get in his will, he wasn't exactly the boyfriend Molly's parents wanted for her— her mum wasn't pregnant, and her dad didn't discuss the money he had. "His name is Mike. He's a trainee police officer."

"Age?" I asked.

"Twenty-three."

Louise and I were shocked. Molly was the type of girl that preferred older men— Kevin being around twenty last year when she was about seventeen was a surprise to us. Twenty-three was a bit drastic though.

"Don't judge," she told us as she swiped my fork off me to take a chip.

I put my hands up in a surrender motion. It wasn't as if I could judge her. I had never been in a relationship. It wasn't that I didn't try— of course I did. When everyone around you is getting into relationships, you feel like you're pressured to follow the status quo. Sheep. That's all we are as human beings, sheep. So, I tried, like the sheep I am! But no one was interested in me. That was something I unfortunately had to accept.

To me, true romance only existed in novels. Teenagers seemed to want a perfect romance story, but it never worked that way; that's the way the world was for us. Okay, that was how my world worked.

Jane Austen— now she had it right. Hatred and then romance once we pass through our own ignorance, that's romance to me. To be honest, I think I came out of the womb with reading glasses on and a copy of Pride and Prejudice in my hand.

Molly told us all about her new love. I switched off my brain, looking around the common room. The walls were peeling off— at least it got rid of the yucky burgundy colour. But that might have been white that had turned a yellow colour. I wasn't sure which was worse.

"You up for it too, Liv?" Louise asked me. I looked at her. She rolled her eyes when she realised I had been in a daydream the whole time. "Are you up for the party tonight? The annual new semester party at Mark's house."

I wasn't sure how I was meant to answer. I wasn't a huge partygoer. I never drank or did anything that Molly and Louise thought I should do. My face flashed her a polite smile.

"Ehm…sure," I eventually said.

She grinned. "Brilliant! You can be the designated driver." I nodded in agreement, but I knew I would back out of it. Molly and Louise were the partygoers. Unfortunately, I was mostly put as 'designated driver.' It was a job I hated. When it got too late, you had to go and round up every person you were supposed to be driving back home. Then came the fun part of buckling them all in while they kept telling you how much they loved you. When I got back to my own house, my dad always had to come out to help me lift all the black bin bags off the floor and seats of my car. It was almost as if they were babies again.

My parents knew of my struggle with making friends, and while they didn't approve of me going to those wild drinking parties, they allowed me to go to them anyway to try to make friends— as well as to try to keep them. Being an introvert was one of my biggest problems. I just couldn't ever find the words to speak to someone I didn't know. That might sound silly, but it was how I felt. Sometimes, it seemed that my parents' full-time job was actually trying to find friends for me. Molly and Louise continued to debate about what to wear to the party. Dresses, skirts, or jumpsuits. To be honest, I had spent a good few months thinking that a jumpsuit was one of those costumes people wore to jump out of a helicopter for skydiving. That was until Louise turned up to my birthday party last June with one on. I can confirm, it wasn't a skydiving outfit.

"What are you wearing?" Louise asked me.

I looked at the two of them, whose eyes were on me. I felt pressured into speaking. I shrugged.

"Jeans, perhaps?"

"Oh. Right," Molly mumbled.

It didn't take an idiot to work out that I had just flattened the whole conversation. I couldn't have flattened it anymore if I had driven over it in my crappy Polo, which seemed to make a funny noise every time I put it into reverse. Molly and Louise continued to ignore me for the rest of lunchtime.

Saying the right thing at the right time proved to be crucial for making friends. That conversation proved I didn't inherit that quality from my parents. That was probably the reason why I preferred Jane Austen's take on people instead of actual present-day people. A loud cheer came from across the common room, and we all looked to see what it was for. William Hardigan had just walked in.

"All right, Stiffy!" some guy yelled, doing a weird fist pump thing with him. William smiled and waved at everyone.

Rule one to getting friends: have a dirty sounding name. This seemingly had worked for William. It also gave him a nickname. Even though it wasn't the best nickname in the world, he still got one. That was real friendship status. Pretty big steps for the new boy, I must say! The study room incident was probably famous in all the years by now.

"I heard that the first prank of the year is being planned as we speak," Louise informed us.

"What is it?"

Louise smirked. "Setting off the fire alarm. Pretty old school, I know. But they're going to get some deodorant and a lighter."

"I can see where that's going. Basically, a blow torch?" I asked.

"Yeah!" Louise laughed. Molly and I laughed too. It was a classic prank, but it's what our year did best. I guess you could say that we were old school rebels. Well, most of us were anyway.

By the time we were ready to go back to class, the fire alarm went off. All you could smell in the common room was 'Sure Deodorant.' Louise smirked at us as if to say, "I told you so." We all made our way out to the playground to line up in our years in alphabetical order. When I say alphabetical order, I mean all correct in line until you get to M and then we're everywhere.

Our headmistress, Mrs. Turner, allowed the teachers to check every year, but she immediately walked down to us. She knew what our year was like and knew that the fire alarm was set off in our common room. She knew the culprit was in our year.

Everyone was amazed that Mrs. Turner was actually married. Not only was she as rough as a badger's ass, but she gave us all the impression that she wore the trousers she had on right now at the wedding. Well, so does my mum and my grandad, but that's a different story.

"Right, which one of you was it with the handmade blow torch?" she asked. No one answered. "I know fine rightly who it was, so don't try to blame someone else. Not even Stiffy."

"It's William or Willie, Miss," Stiffy spoke up. "How do you know I'm called Stiffy?"

"I know everything, and you'll soon discover that."

It was true. She did know everything. Mrs. Turner walked down the rows until she came to Roger, Steven, and Jack— the three biggest practical jokers of our year. They tried to smile innocently at her, but it didn't work. She knew it was them. They might as well have come out wearing "IT WAS ME" signs in bold lettering. Mrs. Turner had a whistle-blower in our year. It didn't take an idiot to work out that the whistle-blower was Cynthia.

Cynthia was Head Girl, and Cynthia loved Cynthia. There was nothing that she couldn't do. We all voted her for Head Girl because no one else wanted it. She was the one who was willing to get up and campaign for herself in front of the entire year and the whole school staff. I thought it was slightly wrong how the staff got to cast a vote. If they didn't like you, they wouldn't have voted for you in a million years— maybe if you paid them in money, or alcohol, or (in some cases) cigarettes. But Cynthia got the teacher's vote by one simple act—whistle blowing. What teacher didn't love a whistle-blower?

"You three. My office. Now. Let's see if we can expel you this time around," Mrs. Turner said. The three of them walked to the office.

Eventually, after checking the common room wasn't aflame, we were all allowed inside. It was my last class of the day— English.

Cynthia bounced past us, her blonde curls flapping about as she did. She smiled at me.

"I'll see you in English, Olivia," she sang as she walked back into the school.

We were all trying not to laugh at her. She was five foot two and had the cheek to act like she was above us all.

"I see the poisoned dwarf is heeding your presence in English. I bet she can recite Shakespeare and probably adores Jane Austen. She seems like the type," Molly commented. Louise laughed, but I just smiled.

'And I'm not the type to adore Jane Austen? Do I need to act like her to portray my love of literature?' I thought. As usual, I was too chicken to talk back. To live peacefully with my friends, I understood that the best idea was never to reveal your true self. Comments like that proved my theory.

"I better go off to English now. See you tomorrow!" I called. They waved at me as I went into the first school entrance I could find. My idea of a safe haven was to hide at any sign of trouble, anywhere! For me, right at that moment, my safe haven was the school. On normal days, it was my house. When I was fed up with getting nagged at, I took shelter in my bedroom. To me, my bedroom was where I could be me without trying to be happy around other people. Right then, all I wanted to do was to crawl up on my bed with a Jane Austen novel or my laptop and a big bag of Cheese and Onion. Cheese and Onion crisps always make life that one bit better.

Three

It appeared to me that everyone in my family was as glued to their own lives as a teenager on a phone. When I got into the house, no one was speaking to each other. Mum was in the kitchen making dinner. Dad was in the study. My sisters were doing their own things even though they were in the same room as each other.

"I'm home," I called. I didn't expect anyone to answer. My expectations were fulfilled as I was greeted with a silence that seemed to emphasise the whole "middle child gets ignored" theory.

I had two sisters: Ava was twenty, and Harper was ten. Unfortunately, I was placed slap bang in the middle. I was the one with the highest expectations— constantly! It didn't matter what my other two siblings were up to, it was me who had the shoes to fill. If Harper decided to paint the car pink, she would probably get a reward for it.

When I got to my room, I slung my bag on to my bed and checked my laptop. There was a knock at my door and my mum came in. She grinned at me, as if she was happy just because I went to school for six hours straight; I was happy at myself for doing that.

"How was your first day?" she asked.

I rolled my eyes. "Do you even care?"

"Of course I do. Don't be so insolent. Anyway, there'll be plenty of time to talk about all things school at the dinner table. But for now, these came in the post. You really need to decide soon. I'm sure you've been told that already from all of your teachers," Mum told me. She set down university prospectuses on top of my bed. I looked at them and then back at her— it felt like I was in a Wimbledon court.

"Look, Mum—"

"I know, I know. It seems like a lot of pressure right now. But please just think about it?" she asked. She came over to me and kissed the top of my head affectionately. When I didn't reply, she sighed. "Dinner will be ready in an hour."

With that, she left my room, also leaving the dreaded hundreds of glossy pages declaring my future on my duvet. I cautiously picked them up, as if at any moment they were about to come alive and eat me whole. The names gazed up at me.

Durham.

Oxford.

Cambridge.

London.

The top universities. The top universities that I was apparently destined to go to. I didn't want it. But how on earth did you admit such a thing to your parents? It seemed impossible.

My sister Ava was at Cambridge University studying biomedical science. I knew my mum wanted her two eldest to be at the top universities in the United Kingdom. The difference between the two of us was that Ava was naturally smart. She could waltz into an exam and get a B without revising. In order for me to get a B, I would have to revise for hours on end (and probably cry a few times, too). Ava was the star child. She was the success of the family.

Then there was Harper. The ten-year-old prodigy who was about to get into the most private, expensive, and intelligent high school our city had to offer. She loved the piano and loved to play at recitals, or weddings, or anywhere that required her services. In comparison to my sisters, I felt inadequate.

The strange thing was that no one ever told you how difficult it would be when you grew up. You played with Barbie dolls or had your head in a book, and everything seemed perfect. You hardly fought with your friends and everyone got along. But when you got thrown into high school, it was like being left in the jungle and told to make your own way back home. Believe me, saying "Jumanji" wouldn't have worked. I tried that a few times.

My eyes flicked over the grades for all the courses my parents had suggested I do at university. One letter kept appearing over and over again: *A*. Sometimes they even had a star beside it to really emphasise how screwed I was to actually achieve the grades they wanted. I threw the Durham prospectus on the floor alongside the Cambridge one after reading their grades, too.

My parents wanted me to study law, or international law, or even accountancy. They deemed those as "good jobs" that I could actually make a success of myself in. When I didn't take any sciences for A Level, they weren't too happy. The highest grade I got in a science was a C (that was without trying). GSCE science made me cry quite a few times. But my parents didn't care much then, as the main focus was on Ava.

The prospectuses found a home on the floor as I grabbed my phone. The general consensus amongst parents seemed to be that every teenager spent their life on their phone. It only applied to me when I was bored, which was most of the time, in fairness. Life was boring for me one hundred percent of the time. There was no real shame in admitting it.

Cynthia had posted a photo of how excited she was, not only for the first day of school, but also for the gym. If I saw one more video of her doing workouts in said gym, and at that moment, knowing what her body looked like up close and personal, I thought I was going to vomit. I didn't hate her, don't get me wrong. She just had the assumption that everyone loved her. And, surprisingly, I just didn't like her all that much. People had liked and commented about how dedicated she was. I could just hear my mum's voice if I showed her that comment: "It's a pity she's not as committed to her studies."

"Dinner!" Mum called as I logged out of Facebook. There were some voices I didn't recognise as I made my way downstairs. I realised we had guests. One was a woman with long dirty blonde hair. She looked about the same age as my mum. She smiled at me as I walked into the dining room. She was a hefty woman, but seemed jolly. Maybe someone could finally bring laughter back into the house, even if it was only for one night.

"I like your top," she commented gleefully. I looked down at the top I had changed into. It featured a picture of Elvis. Everyone loves a bit of classic rock music, especially Elvis.

Mum looked at me as she put the plates on the table. She sighed, but smiled at the woman.

"This is my daughter Olivia. I apologise for her jeans and choice of top," my mum said to her. I frowned. I didn't see what was wrong with my jeans. Well, they had tons of rips in them, but I was informed they were stylish by Molly. I shrugged and smiled at the woman. "Olivia, this is Sharon. She's my new work colleague."

"Ah! Is this the one you said is pompous?" I asked Mum as I shook hands with Sharon. Mum glared at me behind Sharon's back. "No, it isn't. That's our boss."

I nodded and sat down in my usual seat. I was last to get to the dining room as everyone was already there. I picked up my fork and saw a guy in front of me. I looked at my parents and then Ava. Ava nodded at Sharon to tell me that he came with her. Mum and Dad filled the dining room with mindless chatter. Of course, Ava and Harper got a look in due to how amazing they were. That probably sounded sarcastic, but it wasn't. They truly were amazing at everything I wished I could do.

Sharon looked at me. I could see her out of the corner of my eye. I put a pepper in my mouth as she spoke.

"I hear it was your first day of school. How does it feel knowing that you're in your last year?" Sharon asked me. She clearly felt sorry for me— she was actually speaking to me.

I smiled politely. "Yeah, it was my first day. I guess it's strange, but I'm excited for the start of a new adventure at university next year."

"What university do you plan on going to after the end of your A Levels?"

The dreaded question. I had to hold back a laugh at the fact I had no clue yet. I took a sip of water, but Mum had already answered the question for me with "one of the top ones." Of course that was her answer. I wouldn't expect anything less from my mum.

When dinner had finished, I went to the living room to watch some TV. I was more than aware of an annoying presence on the sofa beside me. There he was…whoever he was.

"Who the hell are you?" I asked him.

He laughed. "You actually want to go to a top university with that mouth?"

I glared at him and then back at the TV. I turned up the volume and tried to ignore his presence beside me.

"I'm Gareth. I'm Sharon's nephew. She's letting me stay with her for a few months while my parents sort things out back up north," he told me, and I noticed his Geordie accent. He talked loud enough so I could hear him above Noel Edmunds presenting *Deal or No Deal*. I didn't even like the show, but it was something to watch.

I nodded. "How wonderful for you."

"Do you even have any friends with that attitude?"

"None of your damn business."

He smirked. "I take that as you like to lose friends."

"I prefer the term 'alienating people.'"

We sat in silence and didn't speak to each other. The TV and laughing from the other sitting room filled in the silence well. When the programme I was watching was over, Harper ran in. Her long brown plaits swung at the side of her face. She pushed her pink-rimmed glasses up on her nose.

"Mum says you're to bring Gareth to the sitting room immediately," Harper announced. I sighed and got up. Gareth followed me. When we walked in, we saw exactly what we were in for— Harper playing the piano.

The thing about my parents was that they loved to show off what their children could do. Most people saw it as a way to show that, at least to them, their children were better than their guests. I chose to say nothing, as was my routine during most of my parents' dinner parties. Harper's piano playing always was the main feature of any party. She could play Mozart blindfolded. Believe me, Ava and I tried it with her before. She didn't miss a note. But when one of your children doesn't have an outspoken talent, what do you do?

"Olivia, would you mind going to the kitchen to make some tea and coffee for us all?" my dad asked. I smiled and nodded before walking to the kitchen.

That's exactly what happens to the talentless child.

I could hear Harper chiming away at that wretched piano all the way from the kitchen. Don't get me wrong, her melodies were beautiful, truly they were. I admired and loved both of my sisters. I just wished I could have a talent like them, or anything that would make someone proud of me.

I felt like I was back in primary school and the teacher decided to do show-and-tell. You know, that tedious event that happened once a week where there was always one child who wanted to bring in their pet? Yeah, that's what it was like. Only I was the one who brought the same toy every week. Or maybe a coloured stone I found. Other children would bring in holiday photos or something more extravagant than a stone. Most items are more extravagant than a stone.

I poured out the tea and coffee as soon as Harper was finished playing. Sharon came in and smiled at me. I smiled back solemnly and put some biscuits on a plate.

"Your sister is *so* talented," Sharon commented. At my nod, she frowned at me. "I'm sure you have a talent, sweetheart. Trust me. Come back and join us in the sitting room. I'll help you carry all that in."

I sighed. "It's fine. You go on in. I'll bring in the tray. But then I have to go...out somewhere."

It was a lie. Of course, it was a lie. It was just like when Miss Harshaw told people she actually liked teenagers— what a lie that was. Sharon nodded and carried the biscuits in for me. I grabbed the tray of glasses and mugs of tea, placing it on the coffee table. Harper came over and hugged me, with me returning the favour.

"Well done, Harp. Your playing was amazing."

Ava smirked as she took a sip of her coffee. "Maybe later we'll blindfold you and get you to try to play one of those musical pieces from Liv's favourite movie."

I laughed. The thing about Ava was that she remembered every detail about each of us. Ava knew my favourite movie was *Titanic*, but she also knew how much Harper adored the musical pieces in the movie. Sometimes, Ava had a tendency to forget how much we knew and cared about her.

Ava was previously in a relationship with a guy who manipulated her badly. He told her who to talk to, never left her alone, told her what to wear and how to wear it. She never voiced her abuse. That was until we all saw that she was a completely different person. She wasn't the Ava we knew. After hours of quizzing, she broke down crying and admitted everything. Dad went to see him and came back with bloody knuckles. We never asked what he did; it was pretty obvious. That was the end of it.

Ava struggled to get back to the person she was. Only in the last few months had she been the person she used to be. But we all knew that Ava would never be herself again. You never can be after suffering something so traumatic.

"I need to go out to see Molly. Something about…Oxford applications," I told my mum. Mum smiled widely— she believed me. She actually believed that I was going to talk with Molly about Oxford entrance. She had no hope of that happening.

"Drive safe and be back by ten," she warned me. I did a salute, which got a snigger from Gareth, who spilt some of his tea down his jet-black stubble. I left as soon as I was able to.

The thing about my family was that I couldn't be myself around them. It was as if I had a different face on with so many different people that I didn't know who I was anymore. I needed time to think. I needed time to breathe. So, in my infinite wisdom, I drove to the library.

The library was a haven for me. I was surrounded by worlds that I could escape into just by opening a cover and reading the first page of a book. It was the magic of reading that got me even vaguely interested in doing English A Level. When I arrived at the library and found my perfect spot, which was in the corner at a desk that only had room for one person to sit, I got out my laptop and phone.

The world of the internet consumed me. It was where people who were just like me, as introverted as you could come across, who could actually come out of their shell. People on the internet listened to each other. Whether you liked it or not, someone would always be keeping an eye on what you were doing.

I was fascinated by it all, but not fascinated enough to study ICT at any level beyond the basics of documenting, PowerPoint presentations, and data sheets. Yet every day when I came home, I religiously checked social media and went on YouTube. In fact, if a teenager told someone that they don't check their phone during school at all, they were probably lying. Somehow adults were not stupid enough to believe it anyway.

My phone buzzed, and I smiled as I checked it. Molly had sent a photo of her new man in the group chat. She was all over him. Out of morbid curiosity, I wanted to meet him. But that wasn't what I had checked my phone for. I checked it to see if there was any word on where people were planning on applying to. It was what consumed my mind.

Everything about school was competitive, at least, that's what my parents had drilled into me from the moment I was old enough to attend.

Sadly, this didn't count as sports for me. Placing first in the egg and spoon race in year three was the highlight of my athletic career (even though I held it on with my thumb for most of the time).

@MollyWilson: Where have you decided to apply for, Liv? I saw you wrote Oxford down. I'm almost sure you could make it.

Almost sure? You're one cheeky bitch, Molly.

@OliviaBernard: Got lots of choices but haven't quite decided yet. Oxford is a possibility.

@LouiseKillen: I'm sure you'll get into Oxford with hard work. Anyway, Molly, give me updates on your new man!

After that, they went back to talking about their love lives, what nail polish they thought was the best, along with the party tonight. Apparently, there was a new mascara out. But none of that mattered to me. I *needed* to get the grades for a good university. All I knew was that I was tired of being the disappointment among my sisters.

I opened up my laptop and looked in my documents for the CV I wrote for my personal statement writer. Much to my enjoyment, my personal statement or reference writer was Mrs. Turner. As I looked at the CV, the grades stood out to me.

GCSE. Ten A Stars. (Yes, science was a struggle, but I got there).

AS Level. Three As and one E. Yeah, Mrs. Turner wanted to try to hide that little oopsie somehow.

If a student like Roger were getting those results, they would be so happy and pleased. I wasn't. I knew I had to keep up those grades. In fact, I had to do one better. I had to get three A Stars this year. Immediately, the pressure of everything began to become a reality to me. No matter where I wanted to go for university, everyone expected me to get those grades. Not just my parents, but also my school. And I realised, so did I. I had Ava and Harper to live up to. I knew I wasn't as intelligent as them. I needed to work hard, and maybe then I'd be in the same league in my parents' eyes.

My phone continued to buzz like mad. I groaned and flipped it over. The screen was illuminating at me. Molly had apparently lost her virginity. Louise had fallen in love with a new brand of moisturising lotion. While I sat in the library wanting to cry because all I wanted was to stop feeling like a failure. Nothing in my life was working out, at least to me anyway. Everyone else in my year were enjoying their final days of high school. All I could think of was fear— how scared I was that my childhood was over when I finally left high school. Suddenly, I didn't want to grow up, even though it was all I had thought about since I could remember. *I can't wait to grow up and live my life like an adult. I can't wait to have my own house and be my own person.* It was all just rubbish. No one really wanted that when it came to it. Now I was afraid more than ever. I wasn't ready to move on.

I wish I could be more interested in moisturiser than my grades.

Four

"You didn't come to the party!" Louise complained. Yes, I'm sure it was a pity that their designated driver failed to turn up despite messaging them to tell them I couldn't prior. They clearly didn't pay much attention to my messages. I smiled, pretending to be sympathetic to their cause.

"I know, I'm sorry. But we had guests last night," I told them. It wasn't exactly a lie. Sharon and Gareth were guests. But I actually spent my Monday night at the library mulling over universities and study plans. Louise shrugged, as if it didn't matter at all. "That's okay. At least we had Molly's boyfriend to take us and pick us up."

"You met him?" I asked, the sting obvious in my voice.

"Oh yeah!" Louise said, with a proud smile on her face. I immediately felt as though I had asked the most stupid question in the universe. "He's lovely. It's such a shame you weren't there to meet him."

Was that supposed to hurt even more? It didn't, really. I shrugged it off and acted like I didn't care. Yet somehow, I still felt like I had missed out on some good events that happened last night. From the looks of it, everyone had been drinking heavily. As a non-drinker, I took that as a sign that people would have done many things that they couldn't remember. If I went, I could have had secrets on every person in the year just because they were drunk and couldn't remember what on earth they did. Unfortunately, I didn't fulfil my role this time.

When I got back to the house the previous night, Gareth and Sharon were leaving, but apparently Gareth was coming over to fix our shower tonight. He was an irritating idiot.

"Oh, Olivia!" Cynthia called as she walked into the form room. Speaking of irritating idiots. "I was just looking for you in common room. We need to have a little chit chat. Come."

I frowned, but followed Cynthia to her desk in form room. Uncharacteristic of her usual butt-kissing self, she sat at the back of the room. She pulled out the chair beside her and tapped it. I felt like a dog. I sat down cautiously. Cynthia pulled out a list of names. I noticed Molly's name was on it along with others. She smiled at me.

"So, Mrs. Turner and I were looking at potential Oxbridge students. Assuming you're applying, would you like to give a talk to the Year Twelves and, of course, give a talk to the parents and pupils on the open evening?"

The way Cynthia asked it made everything seem so real. Everybody I knew expected me to go to Oxford or Cambridge. Besides that fact, I never talked in public or did speeches. The last time I tried to do one, I threw up. I really wish that was a joke. Thankfully, I didn't get any on my clothes, but unthankfully, everything else that came out of me landed on my dad's shoes. Fortunately, however, he and my sisters thought it was funny. The same couldn't be said for how my mom felt.

How did I turn down the nicest girl in school? Well, I did what anyone normal would do in my situation.

"Of course. Not a problem."

Yeah, I agreed to it. I think Mrs. Turner better ask the Buddha to help me for this one.

Cynthia put a hand on her heart and laid her other hand on my shoulder. "You're an angel. I know you're destined for Oxbridge."

"As are ten others on your list," I replied. She just gave me a quick smile, not impressed with what I just said, before scribbling a 'yes' beside my name.

"That will do. Shoo!"

I got up and sat back down beside Louise. Louise didn't speak to me. Was it the whole Oxbridge speech thing that annoyed her? If that were that case, I would have allowed her to take it. While the register was being taken, Louise did her makeup. I tried to talk with her, but got ignored. That's when I caught on. She was still annoyed at me for not being the driver last night. I didn't realise that my whole high school life was to trip after others, especially in my final year. The bell rang to signal I was free to leave the tension-heavy environment of the form room. Cynthia waved at me as I left the class in an unsettling way.

My first class was English. When I walked into the classroom, it was obvious that everyone was basically dead. Their heads were slumped on the desks and water bottles were out everywhere. It must have been a good night. So good, in fact, that I could have gotten drunk off the alcoholic fumes that lingered from all twelve pupils who decided to do English A Level. Thankfully, Cynthia wasn't joining us this morning due to a meeting with Mrs. Turner.

The desk I sat at was right by a window in the back of the classroom. I liked it that way— it was a chance to take a step back from everyone and to observe how the other half live. People began to pass around packets of pills. On a regular day, people would think they were drug dealing. Fortunately, today it was classed as being a good person if you were passing around paracetamol. Hangovers are apparently a pain in the ass, not that I would know.

When our teacher, Mr. Henderson, walked into the classroom, he flung open all of the blinds. Groans went around the classroom as natural light hit hangover city.

"Yeah, yeah. This is the joys of alcohol. Suck it up and get out your books!" Mr. Henderson called. He couldn't be bothered with us when we were hungover. On days like this, I stayed even more out of the way than I normally did.

We all got out our books as Mr. Henderson wrote up a mind map we had to fill in on Jane Eyre. Ah, the Brontë Sisters. Who didn't love a piece of classical literature on a Tuesday morning? Apparently, Jay didn't.

Jay was the equivalent to the school drunk. No matter where he went, he was wasted by the end of it. We all blamed the issues he had at home on his dependence on alcohol. He had a dad who hardly saw him. His mum didn't want him after giving birth to him. I guess he was lonely. No matter what any of us did, it didn't help him get off the drink. Even Mr. Henderson tried to help. Nothing worked.

I watched as Mr. Henderson picked up the empty bin at the front of the classroom. I was confused until I spotted Jay running to the front. He made a horrible noise before puking into it.

"I'm sorry to ask this of you, but Olivia, would you take Jay to the nurse? From this smell, it seems he can't hold down vodka," Mr. Henderson said. He was an expert on alcohol smells. I nodded and pulled on my disgusting burgundy blazer. Jay grabbed the bin in his hands, hugging it like a child would hug a teddy bear. I opened the classroom door and walked him down the corridors to the nurse's office.

Is it me, or did I get the short end of the stick in this game called life? You always seemed to be the most trustworthy student when you were labelled as the introvert. You were their personal security guard. If something went wrong, they called on you to take anyone and their mother to their necessary destination. Yeah, I think most people would agree I got screwed over big time. Sometimes I wished I was extroverted and puked in bins in class. Actually, maybe puking in a public place where everyone is watching you isn't the best scenario in the world.

"So, how was the party?" I asked Jay with his head still in the bin. Jay hurled in response. It was *that* good then. I rolled my eyes and knocked on the door of the nurse's office. She opened it and smiled at me.

"Ah, Olivia. Thanks for bringing him here. You're a good girl," Nurse Erin told me.

I smiled. "No problem."

Wasn't telling someone they were a good boy or a good girl something a primary school teacher would say? Did I look five years old? Sometimes I was afraid to ask that, especially when I had my hair done in ponytails. I ignored the comment and simply went back to class. After all, grades were my life now. Everything else didn't matter.

Five

Gossiping was a hidden talent everyone had in my year. When one person did something wrong, stupid, or plain evil, *everyone* knew about it. You couldn't escape the all-consuming gossip disease. If there were a major in gossiping, Lola would be first to get a degree in it. Lola was the biggest gossipmonger about. She knew the ins and outs of every single person in our year— even the teachers!

Before school let out for summer holidays, Lola informed us that Hannah Brooks (a girl who hardly spoke to anyone) had lost her virginity. Somehow, losing your virginity was some sort of a reward, as that so-called "achievement" got Hannah into the popular squad with Lola. That wasn't the only highlight of our end of term; our history teacher, Mrs. Kilwood, was having an affair with the pastoral care teacher, Mr. Hanvey.

It came to me as no surprise when Lola said that she had compiled some quote unquote *rumours* about me. I rolled my eyes. We were outside, walking toward our cars.

"What is it?" I asked.

Lola smirked at me. She buffed one of her perfectly manicured nails with her finger before flicking her long black hair over her shoulder. "Lucy Felix is back in town. And she's applying for Oxford, I hear."

I felt like everything had frozen. I couldn't move. Everyone knew about the Lucy Thing that happened last year, and this just proved it. My mouth let out a shaky breath as I closed my back-passenger door after putting my school bag in my car. Lola was still standing there. She was smirking at me. She was clearly waiting for a reaction more than she was waiting for a reply from me. I wanted to punch her in her perfectly painted pink lips. I wanted to pull her hair and tell her that she knew damn well what she was doing to me. But I couldn't. I wouldn't. I learnt never to give in to Lola.

"That's great news," I eventually replied.

Lola nodded. "I thought so too. I hope you have a safe drive home."

With that, she walked off to her Audi. Like, who would give their teenager an Audi as their first car? Yes, clearly Lola's parents.

Lola's mum didn't work, and she looked like a Barbie doll. Barbara Miller was a blonde, tanned, skinny, perfectly made-up woman. She had three boob-jobs and counting! Lola's father, Harold Miller, did all the work. He owned three businesses and was apparently working on setting up the fourth one— just like his wife's boobs.

I wasn't jealous of Lola, or Molly, for having rich parents. I was happy with my parents. They had time for me. Molly and Lola's parents didn't. That made me feel sorry for them. My parents would sit down with me and help me with my homework. They would read to me when I was upset or couldn't get to sleep. From what I knew of Molly and Lola's parents, they never did anything like that for them growing up.

I got into my car and drove home. Lola's words kept circling in my head. I thought I had put the Lucy Thing to bed last year. It was over— for me, anyway. No one in my year would forget about the Lucy Thing. It was the hardest hitting event to impact our school. The new pupils all learnt of it as soon as they entered first year. No one wanted the same thing to happen again, and maybe that was the reason for informing every year. Either that, or my year was more addicted to gossip than I thought.

Mum was home when I got in, but she wasn't going to be the only one home for long. When I went into the kitchen, Mum was baking. Tonight was her night at the Ladies Book Club that women in our town decided to run. As per tradition, Mum always baked for them. The only good thing about it was that she brought Harper, Ava, and I all the leftovers the other moms didn't eat.

"Hey, Mum," I said when I walked into the kitchen. She came over and hugged me.

"How was school?" she asked. I told her it was okay and informed her about all of the hangovers I had to nurse today. She tutted and mumbled about "teenagers these days" before pulling out some cookies from the oven. "I made some earlier and put them into the tin over there. Help yourself, sweetheart."

I smiled and opened up the tin and began nibbling on a cookie. Mum transferred the cookies just out of the oven onto a cooling rack. "You'll never guess what I heard today," Mum gushed. Okay, okay, my mum liked to gossip, too. But she never really told me much unless it was *really* juicy. "Lucy Felix is back in town!"

I stopped eating. Everyone knew. Mum must have remembered about how bad I was last year. She sighed. "I'm sorry. I didn't think before I opened my mouth," she mumbled.

I smiled. "It's okay, Mum. What book did you have to read for tonight's book club?" I was desperate to divert the subject.

Reading was one thing Mum and I had in common. When I was growing up, I would always read to my mum or she would read to me. She was the one who gave me a copy of *Pride and Prejudice*. Since then, I never looked back on books. It was the reason I found myself wanting to sit at home rather than go out to parties and drink. Mum informed me that her book was *Jane Eyre* by Charlotte Brontë. It was a book I adored, even though constantly studying it was tiresome. I loved the fact that Mum read, because it meant that we shared something. It was something that I could talk to her about and discuss. That meant a lot to me.

"Mum! I'm home!" Ava called out. Ava did a placement in the local hospital while she did her bachelor's degree. She walked in and hugged us both. "How was school, Liv?"

"The usual. Lola thinking she's the greatest. Hangovers galore. And Molly lost her virginity yesterday," I answered. I was open with the things that went on around me to my family. The one thing I wasn't open about was myself. If someone in my family said they truly knew me, they were probably referring to the face I put on in front of them. Ava groaned. "School is so clique-y. You're lucky you've found your crowd."

Mum nodded. "I agree, Ava."

I found it funny how Ava and everyone else in my family actually thought that Molly and Louise were my crowd. I didn't feel a connection to them. They had a connection between themselves. But I was nothing like them. I didn't desire to be like them, either.

I smiled politely, not wanting to tell them the truth. I knew they would have thought I was going back to how I was last year if I had. I mumbled something about essays and revisions and went up to my room.

The time passed slowly as I checked my Twitter, Facebook, and even Tumblr. No one had messaged. I didn't expect them to. Who would message me, anyway? I was alone in the world. I was happy about that… to an extent. I don't think anyone could be truly happy being alone. I just got used to it.

My phone buzzed, and a sense of hope came over me. I wondered who wanted me to meet up with them or who wanted me to help them with homework. When people get a text from the phone company when they've waited all day for someone important to text, they get annoyed. That was basically how I felt when I looked at who bothered to text me: Dad.

Dad: When I'm home and your mum is at book club we need to have a talk kiddo x

I groaned. I was almost certain that I wasn't the only person who hated when parents said they needed to talk to you. For me, that was a sign I had done something wrong. Whatever it was, it was something that Dad had discovered, but Mum hadn't. Dad really didn't sound too happy about it.

After dinner, Dad appeared at home just as Mum was about to hurry out the door. I heard them quickly chatting from my room. As soon as the door was closed, I heard Dad's footsteps coming up the stairs. I knew they were Dad's footsteps as they were slow, dragging his feet up the steps. No matter if you got on with your family or not, you could always tell who was coming up the stairs by their footsteps. There was a knock on my door, and Dad poked his head around. I smiled at him from my bed. I had my laptop on my lap as I was mindlessly looking through Facebook. I closed my laptop screen to meet his eye.

"What have I done?" I asked him. *Boom*. Right in there with the question.

Dad smiled and walked over to the bin I had in my room. He said nothing, but when he lifted up the bin, I knew what the issue was. The university prospectuses that Mum had given me hung out of it. I smiled innocently at him, but he wasn't stupid. "What's going on, Liv? You can talk to me."

Parents always said that. Since last year and the Lucy Thing, my family kept a closer eye on me. It was obviously Dad's turn to check my room to see if I was okay without asking for my consent. Next, I guessed they would probably attempt to read my diary. I didn't even own a diary, but that's not the point.

"Nothing. I'm fine. I just need space to think about all of this university malarkey," I told Dad, waving my hand dismissively. It wasn't exactly a lie. I felt like my head was going to explode with all of the Oxbridge talk. I didn't want the pressure to get to me. Mocks were coming up in a few months and I had my applications to work on.

Dad nodded, but I knew he didn't believe me. My parents didn't force answers out of me anymore. Not after last year. They learnt that sometimes, people need a private life, even if they may be your children. That clearly didn't stop them from invading my privacy rifling through my room, though.

"Your mum just wants the best for you. I know you understand that," Dad told me. I nodded. "Her parents didn't push her or encourage her to achieve all that she could have. That's why she's so intent on bringing out the best in you all and giving each of you a chance in life that she never had."

I nodded to tell him I understood. He kissed my head before leaving the room. I wanted to make Mum proud— Dad, too. It's all I ever wanted. My achievements in school made them proud. So, I always tried as hard as I could to get my grades as high as possible. The more I thought about making everyone proud, the more I knew I needed to make my choices for university.

I walked over to the bin and pulled out the prospectuses. I looked through Oxford's first and marked courses I could do with my grades and subjects. Mum and Dad would discuss it all later with me. Oxford had been my dream and my mum's dream for me since as long as I could remember. They always tell you to never give up on your dreams. I couldn't give up on Oxford now, not when Mum wanted it so badly for me.

An hour later, I was busy working on a personal statement draft. All around the room, crumpled up scraps of paper lay on the carpet. Nothing sounded good enough for Oxford standards. I gazed at what I had written so far and read it over.

"The world of literature is one to be admired and one to be explored. It has always been my dream to study English Literature since..." I trailed off and groaned. I pulled the page from the notebook and scrunched it up. It landed on the floor beside the other ones. "Balls."

I heard a snigger and looked up. Gareth. Just when I thought that my night could not have gotten any worse. I glared at him. "Yes?" I asked.

"I need to come in your room. I have to lift part of your carpet. The pipes for the bathroom go under your floor," Gareth replied, as if it was the most obvious thing in the world. I rolled my eyes.

"Fine. I'll lift the rubbish," I replied.

Thankfully enough, I was an uncharacteristically tidy teenager. I didn't have any clothes lying about or old pieces of pizza left to fester in the box. I liked to keep my space neat. Gareth helped me pick up the pieces of paper and throw them into the bin.

Dad came in to help him move the furniture around in order to lift the carpet. I called Dad over before he left, once the carpet was lifted up.

"I think I have my five choices and the course I'm going for," I told him.

He grinned and read over my list of university choices. I had to narrow it down a bit more, but I knew which ones to remove from the list.

"That's brilliant! We'll discuss it later with your mum," he assured me before leaving the room. I put the notebook down on my bed and flipped open my laptop screen. Out of the corner of my eye I could see Gareth looking at me.

"What?"

Gareth shrugged and continued to work at the pipes as if I hadn't said a word to him. I didn't know what he was thinking, but it was times like this I wish I could read minds.

I began to do some homework at my desk, which thankfully hadn't been moved at all. My history essay was on the American Revolution; the topic itself fascinated me exponentially. It really helped capture my imagination. It showed me that everyone had motives for doing different things— even if it was starting a war. You could never second guess your opponent, or even your ally.

"If you don't want to go, why don't you just admit it rather than pleasing them?" Gareth questioned quietly. I stopped scribbling down my essay answer and swivelled around in my chair to look at him. He looked up and sighed. "I can tell you don't want to go. So, find out what you *actually* want to do and go for it. Don't waste the next few years of your life trying to impress others or living their dreams. You're not your parents."

Before I could protest to what he said, he walked out. I wanted to call him all the names under the sun, but I couldn't. Something about what he said was true. I knew I was living in the shadow of my sisters, but also the life my mum wanted. But I presumed it was the life I was meant to have. I hadn't known anything different in life.

"I hate you, Gareth," I mumbled under my breath. I only hated him because he was right. I couldn't admit it to his face, but he could tell exactly what I was thinking and feeling.

*

When Mum came home, Gareth left the house. He had refused payment for fixing our shower. Thankfully, he had also put my bedroom and carpet back the way it was. I couldn't hate him for that

We hadn't spoken since he said what I should be doing with my life. And I knew he was right. But how could I let my mum down like that?

I went downstairs to see how my mum was. It was late, and Harper was already in bed. Ava had gone out for the night with some friends from work. I walked into the living room where my parents were.

"Hey Mum! I've picked out my choices; I'm sure you'll be glad to hear. I'll have to run through them next week with my personal statement writer. Want to hear them?" I asked her. A sense of pride washed over me. I knew Mum would be so happy to hear them.

Or so I thought.

"Honey, I'm speaking with your father. Would you mind a minute? There's a book one of the ladies wanted you to have. Look it over," she replied, fobbing me off with a few flicks of her hand.

I frowned. "But Mum, I have my choices. I need to run through them with you as soon as possible."

"I said I was busy, Olivia!" Mum snapped.

When people ask me what the most hurtful thing is in the world, I never tell them the truth. I always said it was when Mum yelled at me. But the truth was, the most hurtful thing is when someone you love leaves your life without warning and you never got to say goodbye to them— it didn't even have to be death that took them away.

I swiped the book off the coffee table and stormed upstairs. Mum was always too busy for me. I sometimes imagined what would have happened if Harper tried to talk to Mum instead of me. That's when I realised that she would actually reply to her and take interest. I was a disappointment.

The comfort of my bed calmed me down. I picked the book up that Mum had brought home. It was a poetry book. I fell asleep reading it, feeling the words come alive as I read them. The feelings expressed were my feelings. The poems were me. At the time, that was all I needed to feel wanted. I needed someone to understand what I was going through.

Six

From studying history, I learned an important lesson; never underestimate my opponent regardless of the situation. I understood why this was so important when I arrived at school. Molly was in the common room at break time working on her speech for the open evening. When she saw me, she waved me over.

"Hey," I greeted.

She grinned at me. "I just had my meeting with Mrs. Turner, our reference writer, and she told me I would be excellent for the universities I picked."

"What ones did you pick?"

"The top five in the U.K., of course! She told me I was sure to get in *without a problem*," Molly informed me, putting emphasis on the "without a problem" part. I could have bit back, but that would just give her satisfaction.

Instead, I simply smiled and replied with, "I'm sure of it. Good luck. I have my interview with her after lunch."

Molly just nodded. We both looked up as Louise came out of the lady's restroom. Her school shirt was unbuttoned down to the point where the lace of her bra cup was showing. Her tie was undone and lying loosely around her neck. She had done the dirty deed. I'm surprised that Lola didn't want to recruit her now.

Louise's father was a Pastor in the local church. He was kind and caring. No matter who you were or where you came from, he took you in and treated you like family; that's what I had always found any time I was over there, anyway. Her mother was just as nice— what else could you expect from a primary school teacher? She taught Year One at the local primary school. If either of her parents saw her now, they would be disappointed in her. They had morals, but Louise wanted to be herself, too. This was her way of being herself. When I saw her grinning, I guessed it made her happy. Louise fixed herself as she sat down. We both looked at her as she sat in between the two of us. She smirked.

"He's good at it," she said. Yeah, she had just lost her virginity. It couldn't be any clearer unless she wrote it on her forehead.

"Who?" Molly and I asked simultaneously. That was when Stiffy walked out of the girls' bathroom and into the common room. He looked just as dishevelled, and he carried his blazer under his arm. We looked back at Louise who nodded at us. Stiffy walked over to us and sat down beside Louise. Molly and I watched with our mouths hanging open as the two of them began to make out on the sofa. When they finally finished, Stiffy pecked her lips before getting up to go and see his friends.

"You did it with Stiffy? You lost your virginity to Stiffy?" I asked.

When Louise glared at me, I knew that my tone sounded a bit more judgmental than I had planned.

Louise scoffed. "Don't you dare judge me, Liv. At least I've got the courage to lose my virginity to someone who cares about me. You can't even get anyone."

"Lou, isn't that a bit harsh? It's not Liv's fault that she isn't..." Molly trailed off. I knew what she was going to say. It wasn't my fault that I wasn't attractive. It wasn't my fault that I wasn't skinny.

"That...she...isn't what boys look for."

"She shouldn't judge me. Stiffy and I have been going steady for a week. Liv, you haven't even had a boyfriend, let alone been kissed."

I wanted Louise to shut up. Everything she said was true. I couldn't deny it. But did that make me not normal? I stood up and grabbed my bag. I refused to turn back and look at their faces.

I didn't cry often. As a teenager, spots and blackheads were more common than tears. But something about Louise's comments made my eyes just gush out uncontrollably. I had no boyfriend, stable virginity, average grades, no makeup, and no parties— I was nothing like them. I could understand why I was so alone in the world. Perhaps I just hadn't met 'my people' yet.

With my blurred eyes, I walked to the main bathroom. Locking the stall door behind me, I plunked myself down on the seat and continued to cry. Everything began to fall into place at that moment. The world had showed me where I stood in the ranking of things. To me, my life was a mess.

I blotted away the tears with a piece of toilet roll and took my phone out of my blazer pocket. I needed confirmation that I wasn't normal. To me, there was no better place to look than to the haven for all teenagers— Facebook.

Molly's profile. 1278 friends.

Louise's profile. 1270 friends.

My profile. 200 friends.

Yeah, I was a loser. But the more I thought about it, the more I realised I had to be okay with this eventually. I couldn't let it get to me.

When I looked at the door of the stall, I remembered what had happened in the bathrooms last year. While I was sitting there worried about not fitting in, worse things had happened. Things I should have fixed. Things I should have put right. Things I should have stopped. I didn't.

After lunch, I found myself in Mrs. Turner's office. I had never been to the Head's Office in my life. The prospect scared me slightly. When you get to high school, one of the places you will never go is the Head's Office (unless you make a blow torch from deodorant and a lighter). I could feel my heart racing as I waited for her to come into the room. I had no idea why I was nervous.

Mrs. Turner came in with a groan and sat down across from me at the desk. I smiled at her, but she didn't smile back. The day Mrs. Turner smiled at a pupil out of politeness, and not sarcasm, would be when hell froze over.

"Right. I'm doing all of the Oxbridge applications. By your grades, I assume you're attending?" she questioned. She looked up at me over her glasses. I nodded and smiled at her. No smile. She grunted and looked back down at my student file. "Very good. I'm glad to hear it. At least some of you won't embarrass your year. Do you have your five choices picked?"

I nodded and got my university application folder out of my bag. Since I realised the work I needed to put in and all the research I needed to carry out, I knew that I needed to somehow organise my life. I opened the folder and took out the notepad page with my five choices on it.

"I've picked Oxford, London, Edinburgh, Cardiff, and Durham," I told her. She jotted them down.

"To study?"

"Ehm, English Literature."

She nodded and noted it down. Mrs. Turner asked me for the grades for them. When I told her, she took off her glasses and sighed. From having a dad who wore glasses, I knew that when someone did that exact action it meant that something was wrong.

"Those grades are high. I have no doubt you'll be able to achieve them. But to be safe, I'd advise you pick a lower university as a back-up plan," she explained. I nodded.

While she rambled on, I could just imagine going home to tell my mum I had to pick a university that was lower down on the grand scale of universities in Britain. Now I was even more scared than I had been.

Once Mrs. Turner got all of the information she needed from me, she was happy to let me go. "Are you still happy to do the speech at the Open Night tonight?"

I frowned and nodded. "Of course."

"Molly told me you wouldn't be up for it. She said you would be too nervous," Mrs. Turner informed me.

I couldn't believe it. Did Molly seriously think I wouldn't go through with it? Like I said before, never underestimate a strong opponent.

"Bitch," I mumbled under my breath.

Mrs. Turner squinted at me. "What did you just say?"

I knew I had to come up with something fast. "Betcha she never thought I would go through with it."

"Obviously not. But I'm glad you are. I'll speak to you later."

I nodded and quickly left the office. Boy, was that a close one. I couldn't get over Molly's attempts to sabotage me. It sounded childish when I put it like that. She hadn't changed at all after last year. I thought she would have learnt. The rest of us had. At least, I had. Tonight, I was going to show her exactly what I was capable of.

Seven

The assembly hall was flooded with parents of potential and current pupils. My parents sat at the back of the hall with Harper. I could see them from the gap in the curtain at the side of the stage. Everyone was so busy bustling about that they couldn't hear the commotion going on behind the curtain.

"Everyone, get ready. No one even think of doing anything wrong!" Mrs. Turner hissed at us all. She was like a snake who could see and hear *everything*. We all nodded, and she walked on stage. Mrs. Turner was greeted with a loud round of applause before beginning to speak.

Molly stood beside me. She was going to be the first one to speak. Of course, I was second, as always. I saw Molly brushing pieces of her hair away from her face. She didn't look at me at all.

"Good luck. Don't barf this time," she spat at me, before going on stage when Mrs. Turner called her name. I rolled my eyes and looked down at the piece of paper I held in my hand.

My speech was rehearsed and perfectly presented, but I never did it off the top of my head. Without any flashcards or pages, I'd be lost. Looking around backstage in the dim light, I could see that all the potential Oxbridge students speaking tonight had flashcards or sheets of paper; even Molly was reading hers off a sheet of paper, too. I wasn't alone for once. I looked back down at my page and rehearsed my speech in my head.

My parents had run through the speech enough times with me that I could recite it in my sleep. I knew when to pause, when to smile, and even when to gently clear my throat. I woke up every morning being able to recite it word for word in my head— even if it was just a toilet wake up at an unholy hour of the morning. My parents would be proud of me for a change, and I could finally match up to Ava and Harper. After all, that's what I wanted to do— I wanted to be on the same level as my sisters in my parents' eyes. I put my page into my blazer pocket when Mrs. Turner called my name. My hands shook in fear, or maybe nerves, I wasn't quite sure which.

I walked on stage and smiled at everyone. Mum was nodding at me from the back of the hall. She knew if I read off the sheet, I would be fine. I stood at the podium and pulled out the page. It fell on the floor. A small snigger from Molly made me realise I had already messed up before I even began.

Taking a deep breath, I looked at the hundreds of parents and children who had come to hear about the school. They were all expecting an inspiring speech from me. A speech that was now lying on the floor in a mess. I couldn't do anything about it. My mum was glaring at me from the back of the room. I knew what she was thinking, 'there's my daughter, the laughingstock of the school. She's just messed up this whole speech'. I wasn't good at making up speeches on the spot. But it was my only option now because I couldn't even remember my speech. It was as though everything I had prepared up until this moment was now wasted. I was going to let everyone down unless I acted as fast as possible.

I glanced down at the page on the floor and then at the audience again. "Isn't it funny how we always rely on something to help us out when we're nervous?"

A murmur went around the audience. I had no idea what I was doing. I only agreed to do this stupid thing because at least then Mrs. Turner might write me a nice reference for my universities.

"I'm the type of person who relies on my own intelligence to get places in life. I don't trust the opinions of others. But at school, I discovered a whole new world of people who were willing to help me. I began to rely on my teachers and, of course, Mrs. Turner," I told everyone. It was a pile of balls. I knew it. Mrs. Turner knew it. Even my parents knew it. But I had to say it just to capture people's attention.

"Through trusting and relying on my teachers to help me, I knew I could get the grades I needed to go to Oxford. Now, I'm applying for it. I look forward to the whole process. Thank you," I said. I got a loud applause, and I picked up my page.

I lied to Mrs Turner that I was going to apply for Oxford in the meeting. I didn't want to go there anymore. But I needed to keep people happy until I put down my choices myself. I needed to work out exactly what I wanted. If that meant lying to people, then it meant lying to people. Perhaps this was me slowly starting to learn to seek my own dream rather than being told what to aim for in life.

Mrs. Turner took over at the podium as I sat down beside Molly. When the parents were dismissed to tour around the school, Molly turned to me.

"Nice speech. But I'll get into Oxford before you," Molly spat.

I looked at her. "Haven't you learnt anything from last year?"

Molly glared at me, as if I shouldn't have even brought it up. She knew I meant the Lucy Thing. Molly walked off, her shoes clacking as she went. I sighed and got up.

My parents were waiting for me with Harper. I walked off the stage and fought my way to the back of the hall to see them.

"Well done, sweetie!" Mum called to me. I smiled and gave her a hug when I got to her.

"You did us proud, kiddo," Dad told me. I thanked him and agreed to take them around the school.

Many people thought it was strange that my parents sent their children to three different schools. I found it strange, too. They wanted each of us to experience school without being compared to our siblings. Instead, my parents thought it would be healthier to compete with our peers. While no one compared me to Ava at the school, my parents still insisted upon doing it at home.

The first stop we made was to the English room. Mr. Henderson smiled over at my parents. He came over and introduced himself. I made myself busy and looked around the work that was on display. Year Seven pupils were writing poetry while they were studying it. I smiled at their poems. It brought my mind back to the book Mum had given me from a woman at the book club. I hadn't read it since the night Mum and I got in a fight, but I had loved the way the words spoke to me in a greater way than words in a novel could. I still remembered the lines that had stuck out to me that night:

> *The hurt, the bad times,*
> *they must fuel your fire.*
> *The fire in your soul is stoked*
> *with every painful moment.*

As I picked up one of the poems to read, someone else picked it up too. I looked up and swore.

"Hey! You're meant to be representing your school!" It was Gareth, being as annoying as ever.

I rolled my eyes. "As if you care."

"I don't, actually."

"What are you doing here, Gareth? Stalking me?"

He laughed. "You wish. No, I'm here to see the school for a friend. They were busy tonight and couldn't make it. I genuinely didn't know you went to this school."

I nodded and handed him the poem to read. He placed it down and followed me as I walked to the other side of the room to look at some of the work from my year. Gareth stood beside me and picked up one of my pieces.

"You're smart. You got a B!" he complimented me.

I just smiled. "I could have got an A."

He frowned at me and placed the paper down. "You do realise that getting a B is amazing, don't you?"

I shrugged. Mr. Henderson brought my parents and sister over to see my work. Harper spotted Gareth immediately and began to talk to him.

Unfortunately, at my parent's insistence, I now had to bring Gareth with me on my tour of the school. I wanted to dump him off at the gym and let him try out all the exercises, which would result in him losing us, but my dad insisted I had to be nice.

They all wanted to see the science block. This wing of the school looked like it had been built in 1910 because the architecture was plain with a boring red brick exterior. When I got there, everyone had a look around. I saw Gareth texting on his phone and went over to him.

"Thought you were meant to be looking around for a friend?" I asked, hoping that pointing it out would irritate him enough to leave.

Gareth smirked at me. "I am. I was texting them with an update, actually."

I stuck my tongue out at him and walked towards my parents. I heard him laughing behind me.

"Oh, that's real mature!" he called. I couldn't help but smile. Something was making me happier. I couldn't put my finger on it just yet.

While my parents, Gareth, and Harper looked around the chemistry lab, someone tapped my shoulder. I turned around and saw it was Molly.

"Can we talk?" she asked. I nodded and quickly ran over to my parents to tell them I would be back in a few minutes.

Molly and I walked in silence down to the common room. It was still open, as many of us sixth formers left our bags there. We sat down on one of the sofas. Molly didn't look at me. It was at that moment I thought maybe I had been nasty to Molly or I had said something wrong. I like to call that part of my brain "the overthinker." Even when people did me wrong, I thought that I had done the wrong thing instead of them.

Molly put her phone in her blazer pocket and turned on the sofa to look at me. She smiled at me, almost sympathetically.

"I'm truly sorry for how I've been treating you," Molly told me. "It's this damn competitiveness of getting into university. You're technically my opponent for a place, even if we're friends. The way I've been treating was totally uncalled for. Last year, I was awful. I don't want to remember who I was or what I did. I know I didn't act alone, but I take full responsibility. Maybe this weekend we could go out somewhere?

"Sure," I replied with a smile. I never went out on the weekends. To me, weekends were for eating crap and binge watching *The Simpsons*. But I guess I could do with a change.

Molly hugged me, and we both left. I went back to the science building.

Gareth was standing outside. When he spotted me, he took his car keys out of his pocket. I frowned, and he laughed.

"I'm taking you home. Your family went on. Harper was feeling tired," he explained. I just nodded, not bothering to argue because I was tired, too.

Gareth's car was a red Audi. I was jealous. Everyone knew an Audi was one of my favourite cars. I didn't like the Audi TT, but any other type was beautiful to me. Gareth saw my face as I took in the red Audi in the school car park. He chuckled and opened my door for me. I raised an eyebrow at him. "Opening my door? I feel honoured." He laughed. "Get in, you."

I got in and Gareth closed the door behind me. He ran around to the other side of the car and hopped in.

The journey back to the house was pretty much silent. I wanted to know what exactly he was doing there, since I didn't believe a word he said. When he went around a roundabout and onto the main road, I decided to ask him.

"Why were you there?" I asked.

"I told you why."

"I don't believe you."

He laughed and quickly glanced at me. "I'm telling the truth, believe it or not. A friend of mine wanted to see the school, but she couldn't go tonight. So, I offered to go in her place. Before you ask, she couldn't go because she needed someone to babysit her little girl."

I nodded. I would have to believe him. Who would lie about having a friend who had a baby? Gareth seemed too genuine to lie about something like that.

When we got back to my house, we hadn't talked much. Gareth talked about his friend's baby, and as he pulled up at the house, he took out his phone and showed me a picture of her. She was adorable. She wasn't even one yet.

Gareth walked me to the door and I opened it, inviting him in. Dad came out to the hallway to meet us both.

"I better go upstairs. I'll see you soon," I told him. He nodded at me and smiled.

"See you soon, Liv."

My dad talked to Gareth as I walked up the stairs. He tried to talk to him in a whisper, but I heard everything. Dad was saying about me. I didn't know why.

"Liv…she probably pushed you away quite a bit, but she doesn't mean to. It's how she copes with new people after what happened last year," he whispered.

"What happened last year?"

That was when I walked into my room and closed the door. I didn't want to hear about the events of last year. I played them through enough times in my head. Sometimes I wished I could erase the memories…and the guilt.

*

The next morning, I was glad to be off. I had a long weekend, but that meant I had to ferry Harper around while Mum, Dad, and Ava were at work. Luckily, Mum had taken her to school that morning. I walked downstairs in my pyjamas and hoodie. My hair was a mess and I wasn't looking to impress.

I walked to the kitchen and got myself cereal. The doorbell rang as soon as I started pouring the milk. Halting my breakfast preparations and subsequently opening the door, I wasn't amazed to find Gareth standing there with a grin on his face, which made me groan.

"Nice PJs," he told me. I folded my arms over my chest to cover myself up, even though I wasn't revealing anything.

"Why are you here?" I asked.

He lifted the toolbox he held in his hand. "There was a problem with your shower this morning, so I told your parents I would come over immediately. Can I come in?"

"I suppose so."

He smirked as I let him into the house. I closed the door behind him and made my way into the kitchen. Gareth walked upstairs to start working.

Molly had messaged me several times throughout the night to see how I was and to apologise. I didn't really know how to react to Molly's sudden change of personality, and I didn't know how long it would last.

The previous night, I woke up in a hot sweat after a nightmare. It had to do with the Lucy Thing. I told my mum about it all that morning. She said it was normal, but if it got bad again to tell her, so she could get me some help. The more I thought about the way I was after the Lucy Thing, the more I wondered how Molly and Louise were. Did they even react like me? Or did it not affect them one bit?

Reviewing the last message that I received, I decided to reply simply.

@OliviaBernard: Molly, don't apologise. Let's just move on from here. I'll talk soon. I have a guest over.

The thing that my parents *always* criticised me for was forgiving people far too quickly. If someone did something to me, after being angry for a few hours, the next day I would forgive them. I don't know why I

59

did it. I just thought that if it was me in the wrong and I apologised, I would want to be forgiven. Naivety. That's what my parents called it.

I sighed and put my phone down before finishing up my cereal. Gareth came downstairs in his dirty jeans and an old grey top. He had a spanner in his hand and wiped his forehead with his arm. I looked at him as I washed my bowl and spoon.

"Yeah?" I asked.

He squinted at me. I knew what he was thinking: something had changed. Well, I had— for the minute. "You're being nice to me."

I rolled my eyes. "Is that what you seriously came downstairs to tell ask me?"

"Ah! There's that stubborn personality," he replied. I dried my bowl and waited on him to tell me what he wanted. "I just came downstairs to tell you that I'm going to turn off the water."

"Sure. No problem."

He smiled and walked back upstairs. I put my bowl and spoon away before going upstairs to get dressed in my parents' room, since Gareth was working on the pipes under my floor.

As I got myself ready, I looked in the mirror in my parents' room. I pulled out the bobble that was holding my curly, plum hair up in a bun. I remembered when I first asked my mum if I could dye my hair. It was after everything that happened last year. She agreed, because she thought it would help me. I fell in love with my hair as soon as it was dyed. It was the first thing about me that I loved. I got my ears pierced the same day, and a week later, I asked Ava to take me to get a nose piercing. Mum and Dad shouted for a few minutes when I came back from that. Ava enjoyed that a little too much, but then again, so did I. Something about risking people's judgment gave me a thrill. But I only seemed to have that thrill around my parents. If I did something that would make people at school judge me, I would never, *ever* do it.

I heard a laugh come from behind me as I pulled my hair into a bun. I looked in the mirror and saw Gareth.

"You're not admiring yourself, are you?" he asked. I rolled my eyes.

"Surprisingly, I'm not. I'm tying my hair up."

"I wish I could do that," he replied sarcastically. I turned around and smirked at him.

"I wish you would shave your beard."

"You call that a comeback? It'll just grow back anyways."

I smiled slightly. Something about his comments made me smile. They were just a playful tease and didn't put any pressure on me or even make fun of me in the harsh way that I was used to from people in school. He made me smile. But I wasn't letting him know that. I had to keep my guard up.

"What's wrong?" I asked him while adjusting the straps on my black vest top.

"I think it's fixed. But could you check all the taps downstairs for me? I've checked them all up here," he requested. I nodded and put my pyjamas in my room before going downstairs.

I did what Gareth asked and informed him that all the taps were working and were at the right temperatures. He came downstairs. Mum had left some payment for me to offer him, but he refused.

"I don't want payment," he said. "Your mum is my aunt's friend. I can't expect payment. It's a favour."

I sighed. "Will you let me make you a cup of tea or coffee, then?"

"I'll let you make me a coffee."

"Go on into the living room and make yourself comfortable."

You see, this was a thing that many people who met me couldn't understand. I actually could be polite and nice to people when I got to know them. If I didn't know you, I pushed you away until you eventually gave up trying to talk to me. I always joked that alienation was my middle name.

I made Gareth a milky coffee and got myself a glass of water before going into the living room. Gareth took the mug from me and I sat down beside him on the sofa.

"Not a coffee drinker?" he asked as he took a sip.

I shook my head. "Nope. I don't take tea or coffee. Hot chocolate or water for me."

Gareth smiled and nodded. "That's actually far healthier. I can't live without my caffeine, though."

"That's why you were up so early to come to the house then?"

Gareth frowned and showed me his phone lock screen. Most people would notice the time and that, in fact, it was after twelve p.m. Not me. I noticed the little girl who was on his lock screen.

He spotted me looking from him to the phone and back again. He put the phone in his pocket and sipped at his coffee. I was confused. Was he a father? Gareth didn't look like he was a father, but then again, what did a father even look like? It was the same girl he showed me last night on his phone, his friend's daughter.

"I'm a dad, before you ask," he mumbled, as if he knew what I was thinking.

"What age is she?"

Gareth smiled at the fact I wasn't judging him. "She's about seven months old."

I nodded. "Name?"

"Poppy."

I thought that was a wonderful name. I didn't want to judge him. I had been judged enough in my life. No one deserved to be judged.

Gareth began to talk to me all about his little girl. He wasn't with the mother anymore, but they were friends for the sake of Poppy.

"Who's the mother?" I asked. Curiosity got the better of me. I wanted to know. I *needed* to know who she was.

Gareth sighed, but smiled at me. "She doesn't really want many people knowing she's a mother. I can understand that. I have no intention of being in a relationship with her again and she doesn't with me. But we are close. She has bigger dreams than being with me."

I could tell that Gareth's passion in life was to provide for Poppy. All he wanted was for her to have the best life possible. In fact, that was the reason he was down in the South of England with Sharon. His parents didn't want him anymore. Poppy's mother lived down in the South, too. He wanted to be close to her.

I supposed that Gareth wasn't as much of an idiot as I had thought. He was actually caring, especially for his little girl.

"Since you now know something about me, tell me about you," he demanded as he downed the rest of his cup of coffee.

I laughed nervously. What on earth did he want to know about me?

"Ehm... I... My favourite movie is *Titanic*, I have a newfound love for poetry, and I have depression," I admitted.

It felt like a weight had been lifted off my shoulders. I have depression. It was strange to announce it to someone other than my family. Gareth nodded. I was waiting for him to judge me like everyone did when I told them I had depression. It was as though you were now this strange object placed in the room that they didn't want to go near. Maybe that was just my experience of it.

I also had anger issues, but I never talked about them. My parents knew I didn't want people knowing about them. I got angry at the slightest thing. Perhaps it was because of how low I felt, or how much I had been forgotten about when I was growing up. I think the real reason was because it was easier to get angry with the outside world than to get angry with myself. Although, I always got angry with myself when something I did wasn't right. Depression and anger for me went hand in hand.

"You do know *Titanic* is historically inaccurate. They wanted to base it more on the romance than getting the facts straight," Gareth announced. He hadn't judged me. It was like he didn't even care if I had depression or not. I liked that.

"You're historically inaccurate."

"That makes no sense."

"You make no sense."

That was when we grinned at each other. He nodded at me.

"Touché, Liv. Touché. But did you cry at Jack's death?"

I laughed. "No, I didn't."

"Really? Everyone does! You cried at everyone else's, though?"

I shook my head. I smiled shyly at the ground, suddenly becoming more and more aware of my oddities. My abnormalities from humanity were seeping through.

"I cried at all of the officers' deaths. And when Lightoller clung on to the boat helplessly, just trying to stay alive," I informed him.

He smiled at me. "I hate it when girls cry at Jack's death."

Eight

I don't know what I had expected from my final year of high school, but it wasn't this. We all stood in our form classes while Mrs. Turner patrolled the lines. She was more than angry— infuriated.

"The toilets in the common room are a disgrace!" she spat. No one seemed to care. Then again, who would care about the toilets? There were other ones all over the school to use if we were really stuck.

She stood at the front of the hall again, watching us. She was waiting for one of us to breathe the wrong way in order to be able to accuse someone of the toilet issues.

"The toilets were blocked!" Mrs. Turner yelled.

"Someone did a big sh—"

"Quiet!"

The person who spoke out immediately shut up. Mrs. Turner took out a bag from a plastic box she had. We were all confused. The plumber was standing at the front, too, with a plunger in his hand. When I caught wind of who was standing before me, my face immediately became bleached with paleness. It was Gareth. He was going to have to be the one to pull out used condoms from the toilet. To anyone looking in, it must have been comical. To the rest of my year it was, too, but they

65

couldn't laugh. I didn't know what to do except avoid eye contact with him entirely.

"Used condoms. This is the amount of them. There must be about twenty here. You're all as bad as rabbits," she commented. We would have begun to snicker, but Mrs. Turner's red face, flaring nostrils, and darting eyes told us otherwise. We chose to remain silent. "Now, I'm not one to listen to gossip, but word gets around. I know which of you lot wouldn't have sex and which of you would. Gossip is wonderful— especially in situations like this. I'm going to go around the rows and ask the people to leave who I know are not responsible."

Everyone secretly hoped that the gossip hadn't caught up to them. The ones who hadn't ever had sex were safe. The ones who weren't da- ting anyone in the school or had previously dated anyone in the school were also safe. I knew I was in the clear. Molly and Louise…not so much.

Mrs. Turner got to our row and stopped at me. She nodded at me to tell me to leave. Molly and Louise looked at me, but I kept my eyes forward.

After patrolling the lines, she walked back to the front and stared us all down.

"Those who I have indicated may leave now," she announced.

That was our cue. I felt a kind of awkwardness you only experi- ence when you're the only person travelling on a bus. It's just you and the bus driver. Cars that drive past you or that pull up beside you at traffic lights, their drivers just stare. Even though you should feel like a princess because you are basically being chauffeured around, you don't. Right then, I didn't feel like a princess, even though I was getting off without a punishment for something I didn't do— Mrs. Turner knew from ru- mours and gossip that I hadn't even had a boyfriend, so it would be impossible for me to shove used condoms down the toilets. I felt every-one's judgmental eyes staring at me.

The eyes I felt more than anyone's on the back of my head were Molly and Louise's. They hadn't changed. I didn't know if anything would ever make them change.

I soon found out how true that was when I got to the common room during my free period. Molly and Louise glared at me when I walked inside. It was as if I had reversed into their car and never apolo-gised for it.

"Hey," I greeted. No one responded. I wasn't even sure if I ex-pected them to respond to me.

"You do realise that we're in detention for a full month after school now, don't you?" Louise spat at me.

I frowned. "I'm sorry to hear that, but—"

"No, no. You don't understand. If you were like Molly and I, you would be in detention too," Louise informed me. I didn't know what to reply. Louise laughed. "You're as pathetic as Lucy."

Neither Molly nor I believed that those words had just escaped Louise's lips. No one had brought up Lucy since last year. Molly looked at Louise.

"That's a bit harsh," Molly whispered.

Louise looked at us and scoffed. "Harsh? Molly, your boyfriend isn't even at school. You weren't responsible for the condoms. Everyone here knows that Little Miss Perfect is a virgin. That's why she got off with it!"

I didn't make a response to what Louise was saying. It wasn't worth the aggravation. I didn't think it mattered whether you were a vir-gin or not. It was how people viewed you that gave you your reputation, not because they knew everything about your private life.

She just rolled her eyes at me when I didn't reply. "You and Lucy always stuck up for each other. Lucy was a pathetic virgin, too. Sometimes, I wonder why you still stay with us when you don't even fit in." I'd had enough. It felt like I didn't have control of my body. My hand reached up and collided with Louise's cheek. My nails scraped along her face, leaving bloody red streaks. I was sure that her foundation was probably under my nails, but that didn't matter.

Louise screamed at me, her breathing becoming more aggressive as she launched herself towards me, sending us both tumbling to the floor. People had gathered around us at this point as we both fought on the hard, wooden floor. Molly ran to get someone to help as we refused to stop. Louise tried to pull at my blazer. I pulled at her perfectly-straightened, badly-dyed blonde hair.

Suddenly, I was lifted off Louise and she was pulled away from me. Her legs continued to try to kick me. Mr. Henderson dragged me out of the common room. I was well aware that I looked like a mess, but all that I could think about was Lucy. Now I knew how she felt. I didn't resist as Mr. Henderson pulled me by the arm towards the nurse's room to get cleaned up.

When the nurse fixed the cuts from Louise's nails on my face, she went to wash her hands. Mr. Henderson looked at me.

"You've never fought with anyone in all of the time you've been here. I'm going to have to ring your parents," he informed me. I shrugged. Tears fell from my face. Mr. Henderson sighed. "I personally think it's better to be alone than to have people pretending to be your friend. Louise and Molly truly seem like fake friends to me."

"It's hard to admit you should be alone. I don't connect with anyone. I have no one," I whimpered. Tears couldn't stop falling down my cheeks, stinging the cuts that were on them.

Mr. Henderson nodded. "I know. I'm sure Nurse Erin here will agree with me; you need to be you. Don't be afraid of what others think of you."

Nurse Erin nodded and smiled at me. Mr. Henderson used the phone in the nurse's room and rang my parents to come and collect me immediately.

Mum didn't speak to me for hours. I didn't blame her, to be honest. My actions were out of character to how I behaved in school. Even Dad was surprised at me. I sat in my room and heard them arguing downstairs over me.

The sound from my earphones didn't block it out. I pressed pause on my iPod and shoved it all into my bag. I grabbed my laptop, too.

When I got downstairs, Mum glared at me.

"I told you to get up the stairs and stay there until dinner!" Mum warned me.

I ignored her and grabbed my car keys. I pulled on my jacket.

"You're not going anywhere," she told me. I ignored her again and walked to the door.

Mum stood by the door. I didn't speak to her. Dad came out to us and took Mum into his arms.

"Go on, Liv. You need to be home for dinner at six," Dad said with a smile. I nodded.

"Thank you," I replied to him.

Mum didn't look at me as she spoke. "I can't believe you're my daughter sometimes. You're nothing like how I raised you. You've disappointed me."

"I always do," I told her before walking out of the house. It was true. I had always been a disappointment to her. I was fed up acting how Mum wanted me to.

Being me, I drove straight to the library. I wanted to be alone. When I got there, I walked inside and went to my usual table out of the way of everyone. I took out my laptop and had an urge to get down my feelings. The last time I held them in, things didn't turn out well. That was when my depression began.

I opened up my blog page and furiously typed out exactly what came to mind. These were my feelings, and I wasn't allowing them to be read or witnessed by anyone else. No one followed me, so no one would ever see what I typed.

I'm always a disappointment to everyone I meet. It's as if I can't do anything right. My family doesn't understand me, and they don't take time to understand me, either. It is like I have to go through life by myself because not one person gets me. I guess I'll always be alone in the world. I don't feel like I belong anywhere. That's not just a usual teenage whine, but a plea for help. A plea that someone would take time to understand me. A plea that just for once, someone would treat me how I deserve to be treated. I'm not a selfish person and I try to be kind to everyone I meet. Yet why does no one treat me like that? Why can't we all just love each other how we want to be loved? It's not that difficult. But humanity can never change if we don't change how we love others.

Humanity depends on us, and the moment we become selfish, humanity's nature changes to that, too. We need to love everyone and make

70

```
them feel like they belong somewhere in this
world. We should be taking time to understand
every single person that we meet. We shouldn't
be expecting them to love us more than we love
them. Humans shouldn't be selfish. Humanity
should be selfless and loving. At the minute, I
don't feel like it's that way. We've lost our
humanity among our selfish desires and selfish
nature.
```

When I finished typing, I felt a weight lifted off my shoulders. People standing at the bookshelf near me were discussing their internet friends. It's not like I was eavesdropping or anything; their conversation just happened to be in close vicinity from where I was sitting.

"So, you know my friend from Twitter, Hannah right?" the girl said. "She told me how her parents are always nagging on and on at her about the littlest things: how she dresses, the makeup she wears and even her grades. Like, I can relate so much."

"Uh huh, I can get that. Sometimes it feels like the internet is there for us more than our families are."

That was when it clicked. Maybe this mini rant of mine could actually help people. I doubted it, but I risked it. Social media was the first thing I thought of to get my words out there. Everyone I knew had a blog page. I had a personal one. But these words were too personal to me; I didn't want to be associated with them. I needed to take a step away from them.

I decided to create another Tumblr page for myself. When I opened the blog page, I realised that I couldn't create one without thinking of a name. My online alias. I didn't know what to call her just yet. It was a mystery to me.

I slammed the laptop screen shut and sighed. Nothing was working out for me. I wanted the world to swallow me whole. I felt like crying my eyes out. You know those bad days where it felt like your life was falling apart at the seams? Yeah, today was one of those days.

I gave up and packed up my laptop. I decided to stop for a hot chocolate at the library café before driving home. As I waited for it to be made, a familiar presence approached.

"Hey, Liv," someone said. I turned around and saw Gareth. He noticed the marks on my cheeks. "Ouch. Looks like you've been in a cat fight."

"Literally," I mumbled as my order number was called. When I grabbed my cup off the barista, I tried to walk out but Gareth called me again. I turned to face him. "Yeah?"

"Stay for a few minutes. I need to do the plumbing on a house nearby, but wanted to get a coffee first," he suggested. "Unless you've got somewhere to be."

I smiled slightly. "Nope, nowhere."

Nowhere important, anyway, I thought to myself.

Gareth waited on his coffee as I took a seat at a table by the window. I watched people walking past the library on their way to wherever their life was taking them today. They all had histories I couldn't see. I wondered how many of them hated their lives just as much as I did.

Gareth sat down in front of me at the table. "What happened to your face?"

"It's a long story." I shrugged.

He frowned. I could tell from his expression that he knew I didn't want to talk about it, so I decided to change the subject. I swallowed back the tears and tried to put on a smile.

"I'm going to be handing in my university choices soon."

"And you've decided on them all?" he questioned.

I shook my head. "They want me to pick a university that I'm 100 percent likely to get into. I just don't know where."

"Well, what do you like to do?"

I admitted my new love for poetry and blogging, even showing him the mini-rant I just wrote out in the library. He read it. And re-read it. Then read it again before looking up at me. He grinned widely.

"This is amazing. I can tell, while it is a short piece of material, you have so much emotion put into it. I'm sorry you feel alone, though," he commented. I shrugged at his last comment.

"I'm used to being alone at this point in my life," I admitted to him.

He smiled sadly at me. "Why don't you study creative writing? Bangor in Wales has it. Go for it!"

"My parents wouldn't approve of a course like that. They don't even really approve of me wanting to study English Literature at university. But as long as it's Oxford, they're not overly fussed."

"My parents didn't approve of me not wanting to go to university. I did a course in plumbing. Now I'm earning money every day and I'm happy."

I nodded. He began to tell me all about North Wales.

"In North Wales, there's this amazing place by the sea. It's unforgettable. Lewis Carroll apparently got some of his inspiration for *Alice in Wonderland* there. To mark his memory and the inspiration he took from there, statues are placed all around the town. There's a Mad Hatter statue

73

just by the sea. You need to go! Bangor University isn't far from there. In fact, they must be having an open day there soon."

I hadn't ever been, but the more he told me, the more I desired to go. Gareth took out his phone and googled Bangor University's open day.

"Yep, I was right. It's in two weeks' time. You should definitely go."

I was a bit taken back by how excited Gareth was at the prospect of me going to Wales. "While I do want to go, and I'm so thankful that you found that information for me, my parents would never take me. To them, it's not a top university like Oxford and Cambridge so I shouldn't be looking at it. But it seems more for me. Those top universities aren't for me."

When I told him that, he smirked. "I'll take you, then," he offered.

I laughed. "Try telling my parents that."

"I will. You just watch me."

I thought he was crazy. Everyone who knew my family knew you couldn't try to persuade my parents with anything, and you most certainly couldn't try to bargain with them. Granted, Dad usually broke quicker than Mum did. But Gareth doesn't know what he's getting himself into!

He began to talk about my blog post again. He seemed to understand everything I was trying to convey in the few lines I had written: loneliness, hurt, and desperation.

"Post it online," he told me.

I smiled. "I tried to, but I don't want it associated with me."

"Then think of a new name."

I scoffed. "I tried to do that. But I couldn't think of anything."

"Come up with something that means a lot to you."

How was I supposed to do that? What means a lot to me? It was a question I just couldn't answer. I told him the obvious things: family, friends, life, summer, and my favourite foods. Then it came to me.

"Hope. After last year, that was what got me through. Hope." He nodded and took a pen out of his pocket, scribbling something down on a napkin that he had got with his coffee before handing it to me.

"Don't look at it until you get home," he instructed. I nodded and put the folded napkin in my bag. "What happened last year?"

I felt like my world had stopped. Every time someone brought up the topic of last year, I felt uncomfortable, like I would be judged. I *hated* telling people about it all.

"My dad told you," I reminded him.

He took a sip of his coffee and shook his head. "He told me something happened at school and that you got depression from it. He didn't tell me exactly what. If you don't want to tell me, it's honestly fine. I'm not going to pressure you."

I looked up at him, and he smiled at me reassuringly. I knew that he was well aware of what happened. I knew Dad too well. Yet, I felt like I could tell him myself. I hadn't talked to anyone about it since last year. Since it all kicked off, I'd preferred the company of silence in my bedroom than the company of others.

But right then in that coffee shop, I decided that enough was enough. I decided to tell him *exactly* what happened last year.

Nine

I didn't exactly know how to start about my past. The thing you needed to understand about me was that I constantly replayed everything that went wrong in my life. At night, I liked to think of how things could have gone and make up conversations I'd probably never have with people I'm too scared to talk to.

"Well, there used to be four of us in our friend group; of course, there was Molly, Louise, and me. But there was also Lucy. Lucy and I were especially close. I never really had a connection to Molly and Louise compared to Lucy. Hell, I still don't have that connection with them."

He nodded away. "So, what ended up happening?" he asked.

I sighed. "Lucy got a boyfriend, and everything seemed great. She was so happy. We were all happy for her, too. But something changed one day. She had been talking with Molly and Louise. When she got back from talking with them, she was upset. I kept asking Lucy what was wrong, but she didn't want to talk about it. About three weeks later, I went to the bathroom during class. When I got to there, I saw Molly and Louise shouting and yelling at Lucy. They must have thought no one was there. They slapped Lucy. She looked to me for help, and I didn't help her. Maybe it was because I knew she didn't confide in me? I'm not sure why. She probably related more to Louise and Molly— I was inexperienced in everything possible. I still am, mostly. That shouldn't have stopped me. I shouldn't have been so annoyed that she didn't talk to me first. I get it, I sometimes wasn't around. But we were so close. The next day, we found out not only that she left school, but that she left town, too."

Gareth couldn't believe it. I knew what he was thinking, it's what everyone thought: *why were you such a coward?* I asked myself that every day since it all happened. I thought of Lucy applying for universities with us all now. She was so smart— smarter than Molly and I put together.

"I felt so guilty," I explained. "For weeks, I blamed myself. It was the one time that Molly, Louise, and I didn't speak at all for ages. The guilt got far too much for me and I sunk deep into depression. I put myself into Lucy's shoes. I would have wanted someone to help me. But I didn't help her. Molly and Louise didn't seem to feel guilty, at least not on the surface. I know I still hang around with them, against people's better advice. But it's easier said than done to just walk away from them when you have no one else." I explained all of that to Gareth before packing up all my stuff.

He looked up at me, confused. "Are you leaving?"

I nodded. "Believe me, it's better if I do. You probably don't want to be around someone like me."

He stood up with me. "If you leave, then I should too."

I smiled slightly. I just nodded and grabbed my bag. Gareth followed closely behind me, not speaking. I was so sure that he hated me. Or so my head told me, anyway. That was probably because I hated myself after what happened. I always had and probably always would. I thought everyone would have hated me, too.

Gareth walked me to my car. His plumbing van was parked nearby. He smiled at me.

"Maybe Lucy has forgiven you," he suggested.

I sighed. "I haven't seen her since it all happened."

"Make a point of going to see her," he told me. I knew he was right. He hugged me. No one had ever hugged me when I felt like crying my heart out. No one had ever sat down and listened to me when I needed it the most. There's an old but true saying that you never know what you have until it's gone. But that wasn't for me this time. I never knew what I needed until I had it in front of me. I didn't want to let it go.

I took a shaky breath and hugged Gareth back. The warmth of his body made me feel comforted, a feeling that was somewhat strange to me. Being in his arms felt like home, and somehow, that meant everything to me. I swallowed hard, trying to keep in the tears. I didn't want this moment to end. It wasn't often that people comforted me. Too often, we forget that other people need comforted— we're a self-centred society. I'm even guilty of it, too.

"I'll see you later," he told me. I nodded and reluctantly pulled away from the hug. I got into my car as Gareth walked away.

Pulling down the sun visor, I saw how watered up my eyes were. I was afraid to blink, because if I did, all my tears would cascade like a waterfall down my cheeks. But it was useless. I blinked mindlessly and felt the heart-breaking waterfall flow. Mascara flowed down with every tear, making sure to mark black lines down both of my cheeks.

Lucy's helpless face kept appearing in my mind. I should have helped her. But I didn't. When people asked me what my biggest regret was, I told them the usual ones of not following my dreams or not spending enough time with family. My biggest regret not standing up for Lucy. I was a coward. I would never get that back. That will be a regret that I'll remember forever. All I wanted to do was make it up to Lucy, just like how she deserved. If I messaged her like Gareth suggested, I hoped she would let me repair what happened between us. It was the least I could do.

When I eventually calmed down, allowing myself to cry out the anger and frustration at myself, I started up the car. I was going home to get an early night. My dad had texted saying that him and Mum had to go out to Harper's parent-teacher interviews. I would be home alone. I didn't mind being home alone— I loved it. It was a chance to be independent, but also a time to be alone with my thoughts. Many people didn't like that. They thought that being home alone meant to have a house party or go out drinking. But what was so wrong with spending some alone time with yourself and learning more about who you are? We never spend enough time alone with ourselves. Perhaps if we did, we wouldn't take people for granted. We would appreciate their company and their friendship. But in today's society, we can't seem to be alone with ourselves. We crave other people and their attention. That's why no one practices enough self-love anymore.

The house was dark when I got there. I opened the door and got inside. Mum left me a note telling me dinner was in the oven, but it wasn't her usual note with an "I love you" at the end of it. She was still mad at me. I was too tired to care.

After grabbing my dinner, pasta bake and garlic potatoes, I turned on the TV and put in *Titanic*. It was a timeless love story that always made me a tiny bit happier when I was feeling down.

I watched the movie closely as I ate. Every time I rewatched this movie, each scene always revealed something I hadn't noticed before. This time, I realized how desperate everyone was to find the person they loved before the ship went down. While I had initially noticed it before, I hadn't seen the frantic looks on their faces or the anguish in their screams. Life was too short to hold grudges— something I was trying to learn. My life sounded pathetic sometimes. While I didn't love my life, I was used to it. I'd become somewhat content with it despite all the storms I've been through.

I turned the movie off early, and after getting a quick shower, I put on my pyjamas and shoved my hair in a bun. Out of the corner of my eye, I saw the folded napkin Gareth had given to me before. Grabbing it, I sat back at my desk and opened it, reading to myself aloud as I was drying myself off.

"You said hope was important to you. When I think of hope, I think of blue skies. So, here's your pen name—Blu Skyes. You have got to be unique!"

Ten

Gareth's pen name was perfect. Blue skies…Blu Skyes…I was now a whole different person. I was living two lives. It felt strange. I went on to the blog and adjusted everything accordingly. I saved the page and uploaded the blog post.

The Facebook app buzzed on my phone. I opened it up and saw a friend request from Gareth. I bit my lip as I grinned. I accepted it. A message came through immediately. Opening it, I laughed. He sent me a picture of a blue sky and grass.

@GarethJohnson: I hope you like the pen name

@OliviaBernard: I do. Here's my page. Guard it. I'll come for you if it gets out

@GarethJohnson: I will guard it well. Night Liv

@OliviaBernard: Night night

Suddenly, I felt like things were going well. I knew I had to do one thing: meet Lucy. I searched her up on Facebook. As soon as I saw her face in her profile picture, I hit the add button. I hoped she would accept. I needed to see her. When she left, I constantly blamed myself for it. I should have done more for Lucy, but I didn't. That guilt played on my mind more than I care to admit. I looked through Lucy's photos and saw how happy she looked now she was away from all the trouble. There were only pictures of her.

Looking through her friend's list, I noticed she didn't have Louise or Molly on it. She only had two friends, her mum and dad. When she left school, she decided to delete her Facebook. Lucy must have only added her family to her new one. I still hoped she would accept my friend request; all I wanted was forgiveness. If I knew she had forgiven me, maybe I could begin to forgive myself.

I closed down my laptop and climbed into bed. I couldn't get over how private Lucy's Facebook was. She never posted anything or accepted anyone. Louise and Molly must have hurt her badly if she felt she couldn't be personal on her personal social media. No one had a private life anymore. Maybe that's what shocked me so much about Lucy's profile.

As I began to drift off to sleep, my phone buzzed twice. In the darkness, I looked at my notifications. I was now wide awake.

@LucyFelix accepted your friend request

@LucyFelix: Hey Liv. Do you want to meet?

In the illumination from my phone I watched as my fingers typed two simple words: "of course."

*

Weird. That was one of the many words people used to describe me, but that was the word I would use to describe school the next day. I went into form class and sat at the back of the room. Louise looked at me, but I wouldn't look at her.

I wondered what Louise would think if I told her I was meeting Lucy for dinner tonight. Lucy and I had been talking on Facebook all morning. She hadn't changed at all, just like Molly and Louise.

Lucy didn't tell me where she was. She just told me she needed to be away from town for a while and was staying with her dad in the meantime. Something about that didn't ring true at all, but I didn't argue. I was just happy she wanted to meet me, too.

After the register was taken, the bell rang. I grabbed my bag and walked out. I could hear Louise calling after me, but I ignored her. Mr. Henderson was right; I needed to be alone, because it was better than spending time with people who faked being my friend. My first class was in study room.

I didn't know who I would sit beside now. Molly and I were in the same study room periods. Now I was by myself. I guessed, in some sense, I was used to being alone. Molly and Louise rarely included me since Lucy left. It was as if I left with her, too.

I got to study room and sat down beside John. How do I describe John? I probably would say that John wasn't a man, but a machine, considering how much time he spent studying. But most people didn't see him that way. They saw him as…well…a pompous ass. People thought that Lola and Molly's parents were rich, but believe me, they came nowhere close to John's family's prosperity.

We were all waiting patiently for the day John put the title "Lord" in front of his name. That's how pompous he was. He called women "birds" and spoke as though he had a silver spoon shoved up his ass. Despite this, John actually did have friends. I know, I couldn't believe it either.

John was applying for Cambridge. He would fit right in. I was pretty sure that Oxford would want me to be a bit more proper. I wasn't the type to try to speak with a silver spoon or to pout at every person who looked at me like Lola did.

"Applying for Cambridge, are we?" John questioned.

I smiled at him sarcastically. "I'm not sure yet."

"Hmm, yes, I can see why. Good luck, anyway. I'm sure you'll go where you want to," he replied.

I just tried to smile. I was still thinking about it. I had researched the university that Gareth had suggested. Their creative writing course looked amazing and so did the city that the university was situated in. But my parents would never allow me to go even if I begged them. The university wasn't in the top ten. That's all my parents seemed to care about.

Miss Harshaw came in and everyone was silent. I began to write a Spanish essay about my aspirations for the future. I looked at the previous draft I had done. All I put down was university. That wasn't my dream. I wanted to find my own definition of "home." I wanted to be me. I hadn't felt like I achieved anything yet.

My phone buzzed. It was a message from Gareth, and I happily grinned at it.

@GarethJohnson: Bangor University open day is the same week as Cardiff open day. I can get you there, if you still wanna see the uni?

@OliviaBernard: Of course, I wanna see it! But you'll never persuade my parents

I sent the reply and put my phone back into my blazer pocket. I looked at my Spanish essay and decided I was going to detail exactly what my dreams and aspirations were: to find my own home and to be who I wanted to be in life.

By the end of first period, I was beginning to get nervous over the thought of meeting Lucy tonight. What if she wanted to have a go at me for what I did, or rather didn't do? My stomach had butterflies and I felt sick. The only thing I had had to eat that morning was toast, so I knew it was nerves. I just wanted it over and done with.

When the bell rang, I got up along with others to go to the next class. Molly stood up, too, and walked out. I was thankful then that she didn't wait for me, but once I got outside the hall, there she was.

"Can we talk?" Molly asked. I don't know what came over me, but I didn't want to be near her.

"What's the point? You haven't changed! I'd rather be alone than be friends with fake people," I told her.

I walked off from her and went to English. I couldn't handle her anymore. I was listening to the advice I'd been given. People never changed. They never would. People may act differently with you, but that doesn't mean they've changed. Underneath, they're still the same people and always will be. I just hoped that Lucy didn't think the same about me.

It was strange. By lunch time, I had gotten used to being on my own. When you sit on your own, you can see all of the cliques in the common room. I tried not to think of the famous scene in *Mean Girls*, but it was difficult not to.

I sat by the window in the common room. Molly and Louise were whispering and looking over at me. Both Louise and I still had the cuts on our cheeks. Everyone knew about the fight. They knew that's why I was staying away from them that day. I had heard several people mention Lucy. Since Lucy left town, she was more popular than ever in our year. I knew she would find it comical. She was always like that.

I checked my Facebook messages to see if Lucy had cancelled the meeting, but she hadn't. To have her back would be amazing. I miss her more than I thought I did.

The common room went from a loud roar to a whisper as Mr. Henderson came in. He looked over at me and nodded his head to tell me he needed to speak to me outside. An idiot could have worked out what he wanted me for. My parents wanted him to check on me to make sure I wasn't causing any more trouble, even though the trouble I was in wasn't my fault in the slightest. I followed him to his classroom upstairs.

Once we got inside, he closed the door and asked me to take a seat. I sat there and began to wring my hands together. It was the one thing I always did when I was nervous. For job interviews or university interviews, Dad always told me to sit on my hands.

"Don't worry, you're not in trouble," Mr. Henderson assured me. I just nodded. "I wanted to see how you were doing."

"I did what you suggested."

He smiled and nodded, as if I had just passed the ultimate psychological test. To be honest, it felt like I had. "Good, good. How do you feel?"

"A lot better."

I gave the answers he wanted to hear, and he even made notes on everything I said. I knew when I left the room that he would take out his phone, call my parents, and update them on the lack of a cat fight I had. When he dismissed me, I went straight to my car. That was the thing I loved about sixth form: when you were free for the rest of the day, the school allowed you to go home.

My parents would be pleased to hear of my fight-free day, but they had no idea about me meeting Lucy yet. I didn't exactly know how to tell my mum. I wasn't sure what she would think about it all. She would probably think that I would spiral again if Lucy accompanied me at dinner. But I knew that I wouldn't. I just needed to see her to know all was forgiven.

When I got home, I thought things were going to go from bad to horrendous. I walked inside and heard chatting in the living room. Gareth sat there with my parents. He smirked at me. Oh, hell no. He was telling them about the open day. I wanted to tell him to shove off right there and then until my mum spoke to me.

"Gareth tells me that he offered to take you to Cardiff's open day and your Oxford interview. That's amazing, sweetie. I'm so glad you two are getting along," Mum said. I looked at him and wanted to squeal with excitement. The sneaky ass had pulled it off. I couldn't conceal my happiness.

"Y-Yeah," I said, biting back a grin. "I'm excited to go with him. I was grateful that he offered."

"Oh, I'm sure you were," she said to me. She looked at Gareth and began to chat with him and Dad. I took that opportunity to sneak upstairs.

When I got to my room, I grabbed my pillow and screamed into it with excitement. I stamped my feet and gripped the pillow. I wasn't able to conceal a grin any longer. While I was having my little moment, I felt something hit my head. I pulled the pillow away from my face and looked around to see a cushion from my bed had hit me.

Gareth stood at my doorway with an inane grin on his face. His facial expression was what I was feeling inside.

"Hey!" I complained to him for hitting me with a cushion.

Gareth chuckled and picked up the cushion off the floor. He threw it on the bed beside the pillow.

"I told you I would persuade them somehow," he reminded me. He was right. "I sat down with them and explained that perhaps I should take you to Oxford for your interview. They were a bit jumpy about it at first. They wanted to take you themselves— as any parents would. But I told them that you'd prefer it if perhaps there was someone there to calm your nerves, that them being there was putting too much pressure on you and you might mess up the entire interview. That certainly persuaded them."

But it was all a lie. Of course, it was a lie. The only way around it was to lie to my parents. I felt a bit guilty for it.

I smiled. "Thank you."

"You're very welcome. I'll book everything."

"How much do I owe you?"

Gareth laughed, as if I had just said the funniest thing. I frowned. He smiled at me and shook his head. "I don't want any money. I'm doing this so you can have freedom to do something you want for a change."

"But you shouldn't be doing that. If I need to go for my dreams, then you need to let me at least pay a small amount. Why are you constantly wanting to pay for me?"

"Because you need to see people care for you. Sometimes, you fail to see that."

I shook my head. "That's something you don't understand— I know you care for me. Let me care for you, too."

He sighed and agreed for me to pay half. I thanked him. He nodded and walked closer to me before hugging me. I smiled slightly and found myself embracing him back. I wasn't the hugging type, but it felt like the least I could do, seeing as Gareth was taking me away for a few days.

"You enjoy your night with your friend Lucy," he told me. I frowned. "How did you know about that?"

"Your text telling me, silly," he explained. I nodded as a warm glow appeared on my cheeks from embarrassment.

Gareth asked me about my blog page. I proudly opened up my laptop and showed him the stats for the blog page. I had twenty followers. It wasn't much, but it was a lot for me. It was twenty more than I thought it would be.

Gareth beamed at me. "That's amazing. Keep writing and publishing on it. Your followers will go up."

"I hope so."

"I better go now and let you get ready. I'll see you soon. Message me and let me know how it goes."

I nodded. "Sure thing. See ya."

"See ya," he replied, before proceeding to hug me again. I hugged him back before he left the room.

I could still feel that I had a huge grin plastered on my face from being told I could actually go to a university I wanted to see. It was a gift of freedom, which I gladly accepted.

*

As I sat in the restaurant waiting for Lucy, I began to feel my hands shaking. My palms were sweaty, and I tried to discreetly rub them on my black jeans. Even though I was wearing a pink vest top, I still felt like the room was 100 degrees.

The waiter came over with some water for me. That was when Lucy walked in. I barely recognised her. She always had long, blonde, curly hair. It was untamed but beautiful, as it still was. She was wearing a tight, pink, knee-length dress— people who knew Lucy knew it was her signature style. But Lucy was now wearing black rimmed glasses and flat shoes; Lucy never wore flat shoes when I knew her. She adored heels because she was a bit shorter than the rest of us, having different colours and styles for every occasion. When we would go out to parties, no matter what she was wearing, she would always wear heels— no one could convince her otherwise. Even her physical appearance had changed. Despite the makeup she was wearing, I could see how tired she was. Her figure was fuller. Regardless of all of this, she was smiling; it was the happiest I had ever seen her. Maybe going away was good for her.

I stood up from my seat to greet her. She grinned at me and gave me a hug.

"Oh, my goodness. You've no idea how glad I am to see you after this last year. It's been mad," Lucy replied.

I nodded. "It really has."

We sat down, and after Lucy looked over the menu, she ordered her meal. I had ordered before she came. Lucy checked her phone quickly before placing it face down on the table. She smiled at me.

"I hear you're applying for Oxford," Lucy said.

I nodded, knowing if I told Lucy I wasn't applying that she would tell her mum. I couldn't risk my parents finding out. "I am. I'm hoping to get in. But I hear you're applying, too. Are you at school?"

Lucy took a sip of her water and shook her head. "I'm not, actually. I have a job, but I'm studying at home. A test centre has agreed to let me take my exams there," Lucy told me.

I nodded and smiled. Lucy was still as smart as ever. It took everything in me not to ask why she left the school. I desperately wanted to know if she had forgiven me, but I didn't have the balls to ask her that, either.

Lucy made small chitchat with me about returning to town. She was happy to be back, but a lot of painful memories had returned. That

92

was the part that hit me deeply. I knew I could have stopped those painful memories, but I did nothing.

I took a deep breath. "I'm sorry for not helping you that day."

Our food came, and Lucy kept just looking down at her roast dinner. She picked up a fork and didn't speak to me. My heart broke. She finally looked up at me.

"I can't say I blame you. If it was the other way around, I would have run the opposite way, too," she said with a smile. I felt tears fall from my eyes. Lucy looked heartbroken at my reaction. "Don't cry. I forgive you. I always have, because I would have done the same thing. To be honest, when I pulled out of school, I was terrified they might have started on you."

I laughed slightly and ate a piece of lasagna. "Well, as you can see from the cuts on my face, Louise had a good go."

Lucy looked at my face and was speechless. She opened her mouth a few times but closed it again. Nothing came out.

"I would hug you, but I know how much we both love our food," Lucy joked. I laughed and nodded. She clearly remembered our movie and junk food nights together. Lucy and I were always inseparable. Everyone knew it. I knew that my mum had remained good friends with her mum, even after the incident. I became jealous of that because I wished Lucy had still kept in contact with me. She was the only one who actually seemed to care about me when I was at school. Mum never spoke much about Lucy. She probably thought that if she talked to me about her that my depression would sink me. All I wanted was a bit of normal.

"You know, I used to think that Lola, Louise, and Molly could act out the three girls in *Mean Girls*," Lucy told me. I laughed. We both had a laugh while we ate our dinner. Lucy was still as bubbly as she had ever been. I had found out one piece of information I had been dying to know, if she had forgiven me or not, but now I needed to know why she left.

When we finished our meals, we went to pay. Mum had told me to pay for Lucy's meal, so I did. She seemed very grateful. We walked to our cars in the car park at the side of the restaurant.

"Why did you leave?" I asked her.

Lucy sighed and shrugged. "A lot of reasons. You know, I made a mistake, and I thought that Molly and Louise would understand what I was going through and support me. They both had boyfriends…"

And I didn't, I thought to myself. I could see her point. I couldn't exactly help out with boy problems when I hadn't ever been in a relationship.

"They didn't help me. They judged me. They bullied me. I don't regret leaving. It was the best thing I did for myself. For my family. I wish I had done it sooner. I do regret not telling you, though. You probably would have understood better than those two would have," Lucy mumbled.

"Are you still with your boyfriend?"

Lucy shook her head. "I'm not. But we still talk, which isn't so bad. Anyway, I better go on now. Mum will be wondering where I am." She hugged me tightly. I smiled and hugged her back. "We need to meet up again. I'll give you a message when I'm free."

"Definitely!" I agreed. "I look forward to it."

Lucy got in her car and drove off. I walked further down the car park and got into my car. I smiled to myself. Things were actually going well for once. I didn't need to have Molly and Louise as friends for things to go well. I had Lucy again. I even had Gareth as a friend— though that sounds strange now, considering I originally called him an irritating idiot.

I realised then that maybe I was better off being alone at school than being with people who didn't want me at all. Lucy taught me that. When I saw how happy she was being away from everything, I knew that happiness was what I wanted. I wasn't giving up until I got it.

Eleven

"At this time in two weeks, you will be sitting for your mock exams," Mrs. Turner announced. A grumble went around the hall as our year listened to her. "Yes, yes, I know, you all hate exams. But be thankful that you're taking them before Christmas and not after the holidays."

Of course we didn't object to that. We were all grateful to have them before Christmas this time around. During our GCSE year, she tried to arrange it so we had exams just after Christmas. Unsurprisingly, most of our year signed a petition not to participate in the exams. With the prospect of a student riot on her hands, she changed it. The staff decided to postpone our fun day as a punishment for the petition. We always had a fun day before big exams— it was a school tradition. In retaliation, we went wild the day before our GCSEs throughout the corridors and in classrooms. I envisioned the police or some security officers having to come to sort us out, but none of that happened, sadly. It clearly still haunted Mrs Turner to this day with the change in exams yet again.

"I just want to say good luck. While these exams may not be worth much to you, we still expect you all to put in 100 percent effort," Mrs. Turner reiterated.

We all mumbled in agreement before she let us go. It was Friday, and I was leaving for Wales with Gareth on Monday. My parents had rung the school and told them I wouldn't be in for a week because I was going to see universities. No one really minded, thankfully!

I hadn't told anyone about my meeting with Lucy— well, no one in the school knew. Gareth and my parents knew about it. Gareth asked me how it went when I got home, but by the time he messaged, I was already fast asleep in bed. He had a call-out job to do or he would have messaged sooner.

Molly and Louise hadn't spoken to me much at all. For once, I didn't mind. Lucy and I had met up once more since we went for dinner. We just went for a walk around the local park to catch up. I still hadn't found out the real reason that she left, but I didn't want to force her to tell me, either. I didn't want to lose the one friend who had just come back into my life. The last thing I wanted was to do something that would upset her.

My first class of the day was Spanish. It went by slowly as we conjugated verbs and recited them off to Señora Stone. The only good thing about the class was that I had gotten my essay back with an A on it. It wasn't an A Star like Mum would want, but it was good enough for me.

"Only second to John," she told me. I just smiled and thanked her. I didn't mind being second in the year to the biggest study machine that Willow High had ever seen! It was quite frankly an honour and a privilege that I willingly accepted.

Not only did I feel less pressure on me now, but I also felt happier by surrounding myself with people who actually wanted to be with me. I hadn't been that happy in a long, long time. I quite liked it.

When I got to the common room at lunch time, Molly and Louise didn't look at me. I walked over to where I usually sat and left my bag. I heated up my curry chip in the microwave and sat down to eat it. Molly and Louise kept looking over, as if they were expecting me to go sit with them. I didn't.

I took out my phone and flicked mindlessly through my Facebook newsfeed. It fascinated me how people could spend hours just scrolling through their newsfeed and think it's only been five minutes, but I was taken out of my Facebook trance when Ava texted me.

Ava: Tonight is a special dinner. I'm bringing my boyfriend over to meet you all.

Please be nice and be home early!

Olivia: I'm always nice. I'll be home as soon as possible. Don't worry.

I smiled to myself. Ava had been so happy for the last few days, and now I knew why— she had gotten herself a boyfriend. Ava's secretive nature was back, but for a good reason. She wanted to keep her new man to herself in case things didn't work out. It must have been getting serious between the two of them, because Ava hadn't ever brought a boyfriend home to meet us. Ava was a very outgoing person, but she kept a lot of things private. As I ate my lunch, I began to wonder what exactly her boyfriend was like— was he younger or older than her? Was he handsome or was he not?

When I finished my curry, Mr. Henderson walked into the room with Mrs. Turner. I put my lunchbox with the curry chip and the fork in my bag. Mrs. Turner motioned for me to leave. What did I do this time?

We walked to the office. No one spoke to me, and I began to think of the worst. I tried to think of anything I had done wrong, but I couldn't think of anything. I sat down on the chair in front of Mrs. Turner's desk. She sat down and pulled her cardigan over her big bosom. I was amazed it even pulled around that far, but I didn't say anything of the sort to her. I just smiled innocently.

"We just wanted to check up and see how things were going, friend-wise and university-wise," Mrs. Turner informed me. As Mr. Henderson had dealt with the issue of me and Louise, Mrs. Turner wanted him there, too.

I smiled. "Everything is great. Everything is really great, actually." I surprised myself with that comment. It didn't sound like me, and from the look Mrs. Turner and Mr. Henderson shared, it surprised them, too.

"Are you sure?" Mr. Henderson asked. When he frowned at me, the laugh lines at his eyes creased slightly. I nodded and smiled.

"I've picked my five universities. I'm happy by myself. There's nothing else to say," I told them both.

Despite their surprise, I still couldn't stop smiling. Things were going right for once. For the minute, anyway. If I got away with sneaking off to Bangor University on Monday, then nothing would stop me going for real if I liked it.

Mr. Henderson shrugged. "I don't think there's anything left to say, then. Mrs. Turner?"

Mrs. Turner shook her head, too. "Nothing at all. You're free to go."

I stood up and walked out. Mr. Henderson followed behind me and smiled. The laugh lines around his eyes and mouth were both as clear as day. He scratched his jet-black hair.

"You're a tough cookie to crack, Olivia. But I hope I managed to, so you could see it's okay to be alone," he commented.

I nodded. "You did, Sir. Thank you."

"You're welcome."

He walked upstairs to his classroom, and I made my way back to the common room before my last class of the day. I took out my phone. I needed to blog.

I opened up the blog page and began to type out my thoughts. The amazing thing about blogging was that you could be yourself without anyone knowing who you were, yet somehow, someone out there seemed to know *exactly* what you were on about. You were free to express yourself however you wanted to.

Happiness, I've discovered, has to be found within yourself, not through others. I didn't truly know that until now. I've learnt to appreciate the tiny, fleeting moments of happiness along my own journey. This is the beginning of the biggest change in my life— university and moving away from high school. What's happened here won't follow me forever. This is the start of a new hope for me…

What I didn't know was that this blog would be a timeline of the journey I was about to face.

*

When I got into the house, Mum ran to me. She had her apron on. and her hair was everywhere even though it was tied up in a ponytail. "I'm glad you're home," she said.

I smiled. "Me, too. Is everything okay?"

I followed her to the kitchen. She was busy preparing dinner for tonight. Ava was due to arrive with her boyfriend.

"Everything is fine. Ava told me she messaged you about tonight. Harper is upstairs doing homework and getting ready. Your dad will be home soon from work. You go on upstairs and get ready, too. Do your work!" Mum blurted out. I was amazed she could get so many words out in one breath.

It was obvious that Mum knew it must be getting serious between Ava and her boyfriend. She was frantic and panicking. She didn't want anything to go wrong. Despite Mum and I having so many differences regarding my future, Mum always wanted to make us happy. She didn't want us to suffer heartbreak or agony. Mum wanted to make the dinner the best she could, so that Ava's boyfriend would feel welcomed into our home. I loved that about Mum.

I began to get started on some work before hopping into the shower. I wanted to look presentable, too. In spite of everyone's worries and expectations, I was going to be on my best behaviour and put my sarcastic humour to bed for one night. After I dried my hair, I put on a hot pink skater dress.

As I was tidying myself up, Harper burst into the room. She was wearing a pure white dress that looked more expensive than it actually was. She grinned at me. Harper clearly loved the dress a lot. She twirled around in it, holding up the front while it was unzipped.

"Can you zip up my dress?" Harper asked. I nodded and zipped it up for her. She grinned at me. "You look pretty, Liv."

"Aww," I replied, hugging my little sister. "You do too, munchkin."

"Can you do my plait for me?"

We went to Harper's room and I brushed her hair to the back of her head. I began to do a French plait for her. It was Harper's signature hairstyle. From the day her hair was long enough, she always wore a plait. It suited her well. I often attempted a plait in my own tresses, but that frizzy plum hair of mine just didn't want to sit still. When I finished, she pulled her hair over her shoulder.

"Thank you," she said.

I smiled. "No problem, Harp."

The doorbell rang as I went to my room for my white open-toed high heels. I pulled them on as Harper ran in. "Ava's here!"

Just then, Mum called up the stairs to tell us to come down. Harper and I checked over our appearances in my mirror before going down the stairs. Harper ran ahead of me, while I was afraid to rush down the stairs in case, one: I fell in my heels, and two: my dress flew up and my knickers would be on full display for everyone.

I walked into the living room and inwardly groaned. This was my mum's doing, every single part of it. There were fresh flowers on the coffee table, the living room looked squeaky clean, and every couch cushion was neatly placed in a way where it looked like no one had even sat in it before. Dad had just gotten home, and he hadn't even had time to take off the nametag on his shirt. Gareth sat beside him.

"I invited Gareth tonight, Liv," Mum said. "I thought we should thank him for taking you to Wales next week." I smiled at her and nodded. I couldn't argue with it now.

Ava grinned at me. I knew why— I had actually made an effort for a change. She coughed to get all of our attention as I sat down beside Gareth.

"Everyone, I would like you all to meet Michael, my boyfriend," Ava announced. We all looked at the man who sat beside Ava. They held hands. We all introduced ourselves to Michael.

"It's nice to meet you all," Michael said. Dad asked him to tell us all a bit about what he does. "I'm an accountant. I have a good job which allows me to have my own house. I'm very thankful for that."

Michael had brown hair and ocean blue eyes. His brown stubble was clearly something that irritated him, or else he was just nervous, because he kept scratching at it. His face was well-defined. He looked slightly older than Ava's usual type. The way that Mum and Dad looked at him, I knew that they thought the same.

"You've very successful for your age," Dad stated. "What age are you?"

"I'm thirty-three," he announced. Mum almost choked on the glass of wine she had. Dad had the same reaction. Neither Harper, Gareth, nor I cared much. Ava seemed to be in love with him, and he seemed to be in love with Ava, too.

"I think that's a good age to be. A lot of…life experience, I guess you could say," I commented. "I know when I'm asked in interviews what the most important life lesson I've learned is, I just sometimes wish I was a bit older to truly be able to answer it. Maturity is key to most situations in life."

Ava smiled at me standing up for them. He was thirteen years older than her, but he seemed to have his head screwed on properly, and he really wanted to give Ava everything she desired. She looked down at their hands. Their fingers were entwined, and she played with the ring he had on his hand. It wasn't a wedding ring, just a casual ring. But from how Ava was playing with it, paying close attention to it, I knew she had bought it for him.

"D-Dinner will be out in a few minutes. Darling, would you help me?" Mum stuttered to Dad. The two of them made a beeline for the door. Harper grinned at them and began to quiz Michael about his love for music.

I looked at Gareth and then looked down at the glass of water I held in my hand. Mum and Dad called us for dinner in the dining room. Ava, Michael, and Harper walked on ahead. Gareth smiled at me.

"That was a very nice thing you did for your sister," he said. I smiled. "She would do the same for me."

We made our way into the dining room. The last two available seats were beside each other at my Dad's end of the table. He smiled at us. We all began to eat.

Dad kept asking Michael about his job. It seemed that he was warming up to Michael. Mum, however, was a completely different kettle of fish. She kept looking up at Ava and Michael, probably making sure Michael had his hands on the table and not Ava's thigh.

Gareth struck up a conversation with Michael. It was the end of the meal and all I had left was water to sip on.

"How did you and Ava meet, then?" Gareth questioned.

"Starbucks," Michael answered.

Ava laughed. "He loves coffee and so do I. At least we had one thing in common before we met," She giggled.

Michael looked at me and then at Gareth. "So, are you and Olivia dating?" He asked.

I choked on my water.

"Oh, hell no!" Gareth and I both said.

Ava smirked. "I think you just offended the two of them," She joked with Michael. I suddenly found myself too shy to look at Gareth. I didn't think we acted like we were dating.

Later that night, after Mum, Dad, and Harper went up to bed, Michael, Ava, Gareth, and I decided to have a movie night together. Ava put on a romantic film, but she was attached to Michael's lips for most of it. Halfway through the film, the couple fell asleep. I laid down on the sofa and curled my feet under me so that I didn't touch Gareth, who was sitting on the other side.

He looked at me and smiled. "You can put your legs across my lap, if you want. I don't mind."

I moved them over his lap and laid them down. I smiled slightly and tried to keep my eyes open for as long as I could. The night dragged after dinner, especially with Mum quizzing Michael as though he was a convict and she a prison officer. Michael didn't seem to take notice. The most annoying part for my mum was that Michael passed with flying colours at every question. Dad had even asked him to go fishing with him next week. Michael had agreed. Ava couldn't have been happier with how the night went.

The next thing I knew, I was being carried up the stairs to my room. In my half-asleep state, I assumed it was Dad, although there was no way he could have lifted me up. He didn't have the strength to lift me anymore. I opened my eyes slightly and saw Gareth looking down at me. He smiled slightly and laid me in my bed. He pulled the duvet over me and closed my curtains.

"I'm heading home now," Gareth whispered to me. "Michael and Ava are fast asleep in the living room. You get a good night's sleep. You'll need it next week."

I managed to nod. "Okay. Message me... when you get home."

"I will. Night, Liv."

"Night night..." I trailed off. I closed my eyes again.

But I didn't forget what happened before I fell asleep. Gareth leant on my bed and kissed my forehead. I could feel myself smiling. It was probably just the tiredness making me smile. It couldn't have been Gareth. He smiled against my forehead.

"Sleep well."

He left straight after, closing my door gently before walking down the stairs. I managed to stay awake until his car pulled away from the house. I was exhausted from the dinner, yet despite it, I still had a laugh to myself.

"Just wait until you see those two in the living room in the morning, Mum," I mumbled with a slight giggle, before I dropped completely off to sleep.

Twelve

Today was finally the day I'd leave for Wales with Gareth. The idiot had gotten us airplane tickets for a flight scheduled for seven in the morning, meaning I had to get up at four while frantically trying and failing to get myself together. I could have killed him for it, but I was too excited at the prospect of freedom to care. No one likes Mondays, but when I got up this morning, my insides felt like fireworks were going off and every nerve in my body was on overdrive.

When I got dressed, I made sure that everything was packed up before heading downstairs. Dad had gotten up early to see me off. He was downstairs making breakfast for me— a full fry-up! I left my suitcase and travel bag at the front door before going into the kitchen. Dad smiled at me.

"You excited?" he asked me.

I grinned and nodded. "Yeah, I am! How's Mum?"

Dad shrugged. Mum and Ava weren't on speaking terms at all. It had all kicked off when Mum walked downstairs, saw Michael and Ava under a blanket in the living room, and started a whole ruckus that woke up *everyone*.

Mum, being Mum, had presumed they'd had sex. When she saw both of them were still fully dressed, she tried to apologise. A blind man could see they hadn't moved since Gareth had carried me upstairs. Michael's arm was still around Ava, holding her close to him for warmth and comfort, and Michael's other hand was in the bowl of Salt and Vinegar crisps we had been eating last night. Ava hadn't forgiven Mum, leaving with Michael shortly after. She had stayed at Michael's house all weekend, only coming home last night.

Dad and I remained pretty silent, not wanting to wake up Mum, Ava, or Harper. I had messaged Gareth to tell him to knock on the door rather than ring the doorbell. When I finished my breakfast, I went upstairs to brush my teeth. I heard Gareth knocking on the door and Dad opening it. I quickly checked over my appearance before going downstairs. Dad was putting my suitcase into Gareth's car. Gareth smirked at me and then at the suitcase. I knew what he was thinking— why did I need a large suitcase to go for a week? As I was packing, I just seemed to need everything: straightener, hairdryer, shoes, trainers, clothes, makeup. It made sense to me.

"Did you really need that much stuff for a few days?" Gareth whispered.

I nodded. "Most definitely. Shouldn't we get going?"

"Of course."

We walked out to the car and Dad closed the car boot. He hugged me tightly.

"Now, you be good. Ring us when you get to Cardiff," he told me.

For a second, I was confused. I almost blew our cover. But I knew that I could only talk about going to Bangor University with Gareth, so mentioning it in front of Dad was almost a critical mistake. Instead, I nodded.

Dad kissed my cheek and stood in the doorway while Gareth and I drove off. I watched him close the door behind him. Gareth smiled at me.

He turned on the radio. "You can change that to whatever channel you want to. I just like the sound of the radio as I'm driving. I hardly pay attention to the lyrics."

I didn't adjust it. I stayed quiet and thought of our true destination. I didn't know if Bangor was truly what I wanted. Gareth could tell there was something wrong with me. He kept looking over and asking me if I was okay at every red light we stopped at. I just told him yes and blamed it on my tiredness. But I wasn't actually tired at all; I was too wound up to be tired.

When we got to the airport, Gareth took my suitcase out. His suitcase was half the size of mine. I put my other bag over my shoulder and dragged my suitcase. Gareth took the suitcase off me.

"I'll wheel that," he said. I nodded and smiled slightly.

I hated flying, yet I loved it at the same time. The thought of being up in the clouds inspired me and almost made me wish I could stay up there forever. But I hated the take-off and landing aspects of the flight. I didn't want Gareth to laugh at me for it. I planned to write some blog posts about my trip to Wales while we were in the air so that I didn't think about the landing that was to come. My readership had grown on the blog. I was surprised that an autobiographical blogger like myself would get a growing readership. From the comments, I was starting to understand why: people were relating to my life more than what I expected.

We checked in our suitcases and then got our boarding passes. After security, we sat down together at a McDonald's. Gareth was shocked when I ordered a chicken nugget meal.

"You just ate breakfast an hour and a half ago," Gareth told me.

I grinned and shrugged. "I'm still hungry. McDonald's is the way to a woman's heart, you know."

Gareth laughed, and I allowed him to share my meal with me. We made mindless chit-chat. Every time I tried to ask what we were going to do for the few days and where we were staying, Gareth changed the subject as quickly as I brought it up. I didn't know what he was hiding, but something told me it wasn't anything bad— at least I hoped not.

"Gate Eleven is now open for the flight to Cardiff. Please be ready with your passport and boarding passes. Thank you," the voice from the ceiling called. Gareth took the empty McDonald's packaging and put it in the bin. He grabbed his backpack and I grabbed my bag before we attempted to make our way to Gate Eleven.

When we got onto the plane, I stuffed my bag under the seat in front of me and strapped myself in. Gareth did the same and smiled at me.

"I'll tell you a little secret. I hate take-off," Gareth whispered.

I smiled. "Me, too."

After the passengers all sat down and the flight crew went through the safety procedures, the plane began moving down the runway. I looked down at the arm rest beside me. Gareth's knuckles were turning white as he gripped the plastic as hard as he could. Looking out the window, it was obvious the plane was speeding up. I loved the window seat, but at take-off and landing, I hated it with a passion. I put my head back onto the headrest of the seat and breathed heavily. Gareth and I quickly turned our heads to look at each other before turning them back to look dead ahead.

I found myself moving my hand from my thigh to Gareth's hand. I squeezed it. He gripped my hand and I gripped his. In that moment, we were experiencing the same fear and the same comfort as the plane rose higher and higher into the air.

When we levelled off, we loosened our grip on each other's hands until the seatbelt sign dinged. Gareth and I let go and merely smiled at each other. I reached down and grabbed my laptop out of my bag. I pulled down the tray and placed the laptop on top.

Gareth took out a book and began to read it. I had no idea he liked to read. To be honest, I hadn't really gotten to know him.

I smiled at him and nudged him. "You like reading?"

"Oh, yes," Gareth replied. He folded the book over and used his index finger as a bookmark. "I love reading. I read to my little girl all the time when I have her. Mystery novels are my favourite."

"Why mystery books?" I asked, curling my nose up. I hated mysteries! But I was trying not to judge him for his taste in books. I wouldn't want him to judge me for my taste, or anything for that matter.

Gareth laughed. "Because they show you that sometimes life isn't all that it seems. The person you suspect the least always surprises you in the end."

"Fair enough. Seems plausible."

"It is," he said. He opened the book again and I turned back to my laptop. I opened a word document. "I'll get you to read a mystery book, Olivia."

"I'd like to see you try."

Both of us smirked at each other before going back to what we had planned to do for the half-hour flight. We were absorbed into our own worlds as the plane floated amongst the clouds. As I wrote out the start of my blog post, I gazed out the window. A beautiful sheet of blue and white was below us.

It felt like I was beginning a new life. Nothing in my past seemed to bother me anymore. Not this week, anyway. I knew that, with my depression, I would still have down days. But that didn't matter to me at that moment, because I had a chance to see a place that I had never laid eyes on before.

Gareth nudged me. I looked at him. "Do you want anything to eat or drink? The lady is coming around with the trolley now."

"I'll have a hot chocolate," I told him. I reached down for my bag, but he stopped me.

"I'm paying."

Before I could protest, he ordered a coffee for himself and a hot chocolate for me. He paid them and handed me the travel cup. I thanked him. After placing it in the cup spot on the tray, I continued to type. I stopped and looked at Gareth.

"Can we not go to Bangor University?" I asked.

He looked at me and nodded. "We don't have to. What changed your mind?"

I shrugged. I knew Gareth wasn't my parents, and I knew he didn't exactly force me to go to Bangor University's open day either, but I didn't want him to be disappointed in me. Family pride was always something my parents thought about. For goodness' sake, the only reason they allowed me to take a full week off school to go to Wales was because they thought Gareth was taking me to Cardiff University. Gareth didn't push me any further when he realised that I didn't want to talk about it. He just smiled and assured me we would do something else instead. I thanked him and sipped at my hot chocolate.

When we were ready to land, we tidied up where we were sitting, putting the trays back up and putting whatever we were doing back into our bags. Gareth wasn't tense when the plane began to smoothly decline for landing. I, on the other hand, was crapping myself. I swallowed hard and closed my eyes. I didn't want to see. While my eyes were closed, I could feel the decline. A whimper escaped my mouth, but I still didn't dare to open my eyes.

I felt Gareth take a hold of my hand. His breath was on my ear.

"Don't worry. Grip my hand," Gareth whispered. I nodded and squeezed my shut eyes even tighter. I gripped his hand and felt him clasping mine in return. It was a small act of comfort, but it was exactly what I needed at that moment.

After we landed and got our suitcases, Gareth led me towards the exit. He was pulling both of our suitcases again. I offered to take his backpack, which he declined until I kept asking him so much that he wanted me to shut up and handed it to me. I grinned as I pulled it over my other shoulder. He shook his head, but smiled at me; I could be annoying, but somehow, I didn't think Gareth minded how annoying I was.

We got into a taxi at the front of the airport. The driver helped Gareth place our suitcases into the boot of the taxi.

"Where to?" he asked in a thick Welsh accent.

"Train station, please," Gareth said.

The driver nodded and began to drive off. He looked in his rearview mirror at us when he left the airport area. "You from Geordie land?"

Gareth laughed and nodded. "I am, indeed."

Eventually Gareth and the taxi driver began to get into conversation all about Newcastle. The taxi driver had apparently visited it many times because his daughter moved there. He loved it. I hadn't been to Newcastle. I hadn't visited London, either. I'd never been away by myself from home before. I guess that was one of the reasons I wanted to erase everything that was planned out for me. But I knew no one would understand my wishes if I voiced them. I wanted to see the world and discover what lay ahead of me, and I wanted to do it by myself and for myself. It was a dream of mine, but one that no one else would approve of.

When we arrived at the train station, Gareth paid the taxi driver, including a reasonable tip. I looked at Gareth as we walked into the train station.

"What? He likes where I'm from," Gareth defended. I smiled and laughed slightly.

"You're so easily pleased."

"Maybe, but sometimes that's how you get the most out of life."

I didn't reply as I noticed our train had just arrived. Gareth handed me the ticket he had booked online, and we made our way to the platform. I helped Gareth to carry my suitcase down the stairs as I was 99.9 percent sure it wasn't easy to carry, especially downstairs.

"Platform nine. Train to Bangor will be leaving in ten minutes. That again, platform nine. Train to Bangor will be leaving in ten minutes," the voice through the speaker announced. We pushed our way through bustling crowds and got to platform nine. I pulled my suitcase onto the train despite Gareth attempting to grab it off me several times.

We found a cosy seat in the middle of the carriage. Gareth placed our suitcases on the racks provided and sat down opposite me at the table. Both of us sat so close to the window that we might as well have been hugging it. I looked across at Gareth. His eyes were starting to close as his head leant against the windowpane. I smiled and looked out of the window. The city whizzed past us.

I found a new sense of freedom. It was something I had longed for since I had started sixth form. Other people had dropped out after GCSEs, and were starting jobs, and moving out, and all sorts! Part of me desired to have that life experience, too. But I knew that if I dropped out, my parents would be disappointed. I knew deep down I'd be disappointed in myself, too. I liked learning. No, I loved learning. My grades mattered to me. Sometimes, when I think back to that time, I realise that's what got me through the Lucy Thing— my dedication to school and getting good grades.

The train journey took four and a half hours. I had gotten most of my first full-length blog post written, which I planned to post online before I went to sleep tonight. For some reason, the views and followers on my blog had gone up and up! I was so pleased about it. But I didn't understand how it was getting out into the world when I never told anyone about it except Gareth. When the train stopped, I had packed away my laptop, but Gareth was still fast asleep. I kicked him under the table.

"Ow!" he complained, opening his eyes right away. I grinned at him.

"We're here, sleepyhead," I told him. He groaned and stretched. When the doors opened, Gareth got up and brought down our suitcases— though he waited until everyone had gotten out of our carriage before bringing down my monster of a suitcase. We got out of the train and, immediately, I saw a difference between the two train stations we had now been in.

The Bangor station wasn't as grand as Cardiff, but that was what I loved about it. The train station seemed homelier and less out to impress than the one we had come from. It was nowhere near as busy as the other station, either. Some groups of people busied themselves, but

117

there was no pushing or a constant "excuse me" because you were walking too slowly for the businessman who was late for work.

We walked through the station and got a taxi. Gareth told me he had booked it before studying the insides of his eyelids for a solid three hours, which I teased him about relentlessly. He swore he would get me back for all of the teasing, but I didn't believe him.

By the time we reached Bangor, it was one p.m. I was so hungry! My stomach announced that to Gareth as we took the seven-minute taxi journey to Bangor town centre. He smirked at me as we pulled up at the cathedral.

"We'll go and get something to eat first, I think," he told me as we carted our suitcases up the small hill of a street.

"I think that would be wise."

Gareth nodded. "Indeed. Your stomach might call all of the *Wales* that are currently swimming around the United Kingdom."

"Ass," I mumbled with a smile. Gareth laughed.

We walked down past a street full of shops. I instantly looked in all of the windows. There were shops whose windows were filled with books, others that were filled with clothes for all genders, and even shops that were aimed for kids with toys outside in buckets. I was fascinated, because I hadn't seen so many shops on one street before. It was as though the street was never-ending.

Both Gareth and I looked out for places to eat. We wanted to look at all of the different ones available to us before picking. As we continued our walk down the high street, I spotted a red café. It had a chalkboard easel outside advertising homemade pizzas. I stopped, and Gareth stopped with me.

I grinned at him. "Pretty please?"

He laughed and nodded. We walked inside. I dragged my own suitcase, as I knew it would be impossible for Gareth to fit through the door dragging both of them behind him. A waitress showed us to our table and handed us two menus. We sat under a sunroof, which shaded the place.

I gazed at the menu and observed some of my favourite foods— lasagna, pizza, and even homemade ice cream. I felt like I had died and gone straight to heaven.

"This food sounds divine," I moaned. Gareth agreed with me.

"I'm paying. You take your pick," he told me.

I was shocked. I knew I couldn't order too much, especially if Gareth was paying for it all. I was going to offer some money, anyway. In the end, I had picked a pizza with red and green peppers on it. Gareth hadn't gone quite so exotic and settled for a pepperoni pizza.

When the waitress took our orders, we got a glass of Coke and a glass of water. Gareth was on his phone again, but didn't spend long as he looked up to me.

"My little girl is causing havoc, apparently," Gareth told me. I smiled. "She's been crawling into the washing machine and her mother caught her trying to crawl behind the sofa, too."

I couldn't help but laugh. Dad always told me I had a habit of running and hiding in different places.

"I used to do that," I informed him.

He nodded as he took a sip of his Coke. "I did it, too. I bet you that's where she's got it from, but I daren't tell her mother. She'll think I'm teaching her bad habits already."

We both laughed. I quieted down as my thoughts overwhelmed me. Part of me still felt as bad as I did last year. I was constantly tired, I didn't want to eat much, and I was so quiet that people would think I

119

never talked. I don't know what triggered it. Sometimes, I just felt as depressed and down as I did last year after the Lucy Thing. I didn't want to tell anyone. I didn't think they would understand. Yeah, I was doing better than I had been, but that doesn't mean I still didn't have the feelings that I did. It sucked.

Gareth noticed my sudden quietness, but two huge plates carrying our pizzas came out, interrupting anything he was about to say. When the plates were set in front of us, there was hardly enough room for our glasses at the small circular table.

"You can't complain about the size of the portions," Gareth joked.

"I know! This is crazy. I'm not going to be able to eat all of this," I told him.

Gareth smirked and took a slice of my pizza. He began to eat it.

"Hey!" I complained.

Gareth laughed. "You did say you couldn't eat it all," he reminded me as he talked with his mouth full.

I pouted, but ended up grinning. I just couldn't stay mad at Gareth.

The pizza was delicious. It was my favourite pizza I'd ever had, and I'd eaten many, *many* pizzas in my lifetime. When I finished eating, I couldn't help but think of what people at school must be saying about me. They probably thought I had left like Lucy did. I wondered whether they would whisper about the "Olivia Thing." What I found true about high school was that people started rumours even if they knew they weren't true. It was a chance to get popular, a chance to be someone that everyone wanted to be with. I knew that was how Lola got to the top— or maybe that was just rumours, too.

Gareth went to pay our bill. I had offered him the money for my pizza, but he refused to take it and acted like I wasn't begging him every ten seconds. He walked back over to our table and pulled the handle up on his suitcase. He swung his backpack over his shoulder.

"Ready to go?" he asked me. I nodded. "We have about twenty minutes until a taxi gets here to take us back to the train station."

I frowned. "Back to the train station? Aren't we stopping here?"

"Nope. But I hope you'll like where you're staying," he informed me. I smiled slightly. I hadn't ever been on a holiday where someone treated me so nicely. In fact, our family hadn't been on a holiday in ten years. Harper didn't like going away from home. She was a home-bird, and we had to accept that. I missed holidays, but I was thankful I had this small holiday.

I began to wonder what the place we were staying in was like. Bangor was a gorgeous little town. I wouldn't have minded staying there, but that wasn't what Gareth had planned. After today, I trusted his plan completely.

As we walked down the high street, I spotted a bookstore. I stood outside it like a lost puppy, and even gave Gareth puppy dog eyes. "Can we?" I asked sweetly.

"You called me an ass earlier," he reminded me.

I shrugged. "I meant a nice ass."

Gareth shook his head, but he was smiling. He nodded at me. I grinned and dragged my suitcase into it. The bookstore was the one place I could feel at home in. I loved the whole concept of having a thousand worlds around you in the pages of a book. It captured my imagination. I walked around the store and got to the Young Adult section. Gareth was following behind me as I looked through all of the books.

While I was looking, a book was flung in my face. I looked at it, and then I looked at Gareth. It was an Agatha Christie book. Curious, I read the back of it.

"I'll buy it for you," he said.

"No way. I'll buy this. But in exchange, you buy a Jane Austen novel," I retorted.

Gareth smirked and showed me what was in his other hand. It was a copy of *Pride and Prejudice*. I grinned and immediately got out my purse. I didn't need another book, but I wanted to read this book for Gareth. Mysteries had never captured me before, but now that Gareth had offered me this book, I felt I should read it.

"*And Then There Were None* is my favourite mystery," he said. "I won't spoil it for you."

"Good. I won't spoil *Pride and Prejudice* for you, either."

I began to do the self-checkout when Gareth leant into me.

"I already know how it ends."

"Shush," I replied with a smile. Gareth chuckled and used the self-checkout beside me.

When we were finished, I asked Gareth if he wanted to go to any shops. He told me he didn't, as it wasn't a trip for him. I felt guilty, despite him telling me not to. Our taxi arrived and took us back to the train station.

For the whole train ride, I asked him where we were going. Gareth refused to tell me anything. He claimed that it would ruin the surprise of it all. That only made me even more curious as to where we were going. Something told me I would like it.

I had fallen asleep on the train. Suddenly, the early start had caught up to me, and as the sun began to get warmer, I felt sleepier. I woke to Gareth gently shaking me awake. I opened my eyes slightly. He smiled.

"We'll be arriving in ten minutes," he told me. I yawned and nodded. I wanted to close my eyes again, but knew I couldn't. "You see how I didn't wake you up aggressively like you did?"

Llandudno train station was cosy and not very busy. The red bricked walls gave a Hogwarts feel to the whole train station. The glass doors made it look a lot bigger than it was, but gave an open and welcoming feel to the station and the town itself. Gareth got a cup of coffee before we left the station.

When we got outside, my mouth fell open. The town was beautiful. You could immediately tell that it was a seaside town. The buildings were white, and the sky was pure blue with not a cloud in the sky to spoil the look of the town. I spotted grass that was as green as a fern leaf in summer. The heat hit us as we walked further from the train station. Tourists were going about with ice creams and food from the chip shop. I looked at him.

"Llandudno?" I asked.

Gareth was desperately trying not to laugh at me. "It's pronounced 'Clandudno.' Not Land-dud-no."

"I'm not Welsh!"

"Clearly," he laughed. I pushed him playfully. "You like the place so far?" I nodded. He beamed at me. "Well, Liv, you haven't seen the best part, yet."

I frowned, but followed him across the road. The train station was only a five-minute walk away from where we were staying. I looked around the city as we got back onto the pavement. It was like I had stepped into a Victorian city. I truly felt like I was in heaven. A bookstore didn't even come close to what this place felt like— and we all know how highly I rate any bookstore!

We walked down the street, which wasn't littered with cars like you would expect. Gareth knew his way, so I knew this place held something in his heart. That's why he brought me here. He knew it would capture me. It already had.

Despite the short walk, I was struggling with my suitcase. Gareth noticed and took it from me. When we spotted some benches, I immediately walked over to go sit down on them. Gareth laughed.

"Not a chance. Come on, you," he told me. I groaned, but followed him along the footpath around North West Gardens. We crossed two pedestrian crossings and spotted a Starbucks.

"Need a top up of coffee?" I asked Gareth hopefully.

Gareth stopped and looked at me. "Do you really hate walking this much?"

I nodded. He rolled his eyes, but I noticed the small smile on his face. "We're literally on the last street now. Just calm down and we'll take it slow."

Somehow, taking it slow seemed to feel like forever. When we got to the bottom of the street, my eyes blew wide open. I almost felt like crying. Gareth looked at me, yet I couldn't look at him. He had planned this. He had planned this whole beautiful trip. I unconsciously put a hand over my mouth, taking a deep breath. My warm breath hit my hand and seemed to slip through my fingers. The view! In front, past the promenade, I could see the ocean. The blue sky met the sapphire sea in an unforgettable kiss. The sun glittered on the ocean like a secret diamond waiting to be discovered. The green hills around the town made it look even more beautiful than it already was.

"We're in this hotel," he told me. I nodded and helped him to take my case up the small flight of steps.

When we walked in through the doors, the grandeur of the hotel hit us immediately. Gareth got our room keys while I looked around. The stairs were exactly like the ones in *Titanic*. They were posh, antique, and magical. The small sitting area had a warm feel to it; the cream sofas were complimented by the lit fire behind them. I couldn't have imagined this hotel if I tried. It was beautiful.

"Ready?" Gareth asked me. I nodded and took my suitcase off him. We walked down the corridor and called the lift down. I still wasn't able to speak. The whole beauty of the town had just consumed me.

The room was just as stunning as the rest of the hotel was. Two beds sat on the left wall, there was a dressing table on the right wall, and by three huge windows was a small desk with two chairs. The TV was on a table beside the bathroom, next to the dressing table. I ran over to the bed closest to the window.

"I call this bed!" I told him.

He laughed. "Fine! But at night, you'll get cold first."

I realised he was right and groaned. Gareth couldn't wipe the smirk off his face.

After we got unpacked, Gareth went to grab a shower. He took his washbag into the bathroom and locked the door. I grabbed my laptop and sat at the table by the windows.

"Wow," I mumbled as I gazed out of the windows. We were looking out at the sea. Every morning when we woke up and opened the curtains, the sea would greet us. It made me giddy with excitement. I hadn't ever woken up to the sea. It was a dream of mine to have a house near the beach and to open the curtains to gaze at the wonders of the town I lived in. Now I could, if just for a few days.

The shower began to run. I knew that after Gareth finished, I would be getting a shower to prepare for dinner. I opened up my suitcase and got everything out and ready to go. I laid it on my bed before going back to the desk at the window. I smiled as I gazed out at the sea.

This, to me, was the perfect place to let my imagination flow. This was heaven. Inspiration didn't cease. I opened up my blog, and instead of typing out more of my previous post, I knew then I needed to write a new one. This moment was too good not to miss. Other people live their lives through the lens of a camera, but I lived my life through my words:

At some point in our lives, we arrive at a destination that we eventually call home. I am home now. I've only just arrived in this heaven, and already I know it's my new home. All my life, I've waited to find the one place where my heart feels free— where I feel free. I know now that this place is it. If any of you wish to travel or see a certain city, do it now! Tomorrow isn't promised to us, but to witness beautiful towns and cities is a treasure out there for us to take. Don't wait. Hop on that plane and explore the wonders of this world; the wonders of your heart…

I smiled and posted it. My viewings had gone up even more. I couldn't believe it. Suddenly, I realised that this was my dream job— being a writer. Growing up, we all thought we would be a doctor, or a teacher, or even a judge. As you grow up, you realise your true calling in life. At that moment, I had found it.

I was so busy daydreaming that I hadn't heard the shower stop. Gareth came out of the bathroom fully dressed in a shirt and a pair of clean jeans.

126

"Bathroom's all yours," he told me. I nodded and shut down my laptop before going for a shower.

I was nervous for the dinner. I hadn't eaten in such a fancy place before. Was there a rule for what to wear? How were you supposed to wear your hair? And how did you have to order? Social etiquette was not my forte. I decided on a pair of black jeans and a simple, white, fancy top with lace. I even decided to wear a pair of heels, too. My hair was thrown up into a bun on top of my head. I smiled at myself in the mirror, almost feeling accomplished that I had managed a hairstyle that didn't consist of a ponytail or leaving my hair down in some shape or form.

When I left the bathroom, Gareth burst out laughing. I frowned. I didn't understand what was so funny.

"Yes?" I asked abruptly.

Gareth walked over to me and ruffled my damp hair like a five-year-old kid, messing it up after me fixing it for dinner. He was laughing like mad. I looked in the mirror at the dressing table to see that I now had hair sticking out everywhere from my bun. I pulled it out of the scrunchie and glared at him.

"You little scrote!"

Gareth stood between the two beds, not being able to contain his laughter. He was bent over in two. I ran for him in anger, and he grabbed my hands to stop me trying to playfully hit him.

"And here I was, thinking you didn't start that cat fight at school. You're feisty; I'm telling ya!" Gareth commented.

"And you're a pain in my ass."

When I tried to kick him, he grabbed my arms and threw me on to the bed. We were both laughing like mad. Gareth was using his leg to prevent me from lifting mine. He grabbed my hands and put them above my head. When I looked at him, our faces were inches from each other.

127

I could feel his warm, minty breath on my face. We were breathing slightly heavy from fooling around.

"You have time to fix your hair. But it looked perfect down. When you put it in a bun, you look like a weird munchkin," he told me with a slight laugh. I laughed at his munchkin comment. My eyes darted everywhere except his face.

Finally, when I looked at him, he was already looking at me. Our breaths, for a moment, lingered together. They danced together in the small space between our faces. Neither of us moved. Neither of us said anything.

That was, until I looked away. "I better go and fix my hair, then."

He nodded and released me from his grasp. He stood up fully, and I grabbed his hand for him to pull me up. I went back into the bathroom to fix my hair. It was now fully down, and I grabbed a few bobby pins to hold some strands back from my face. When I gazed into the mirror, I saw that my cheeks had a warm flush on them. I didn't know if it was from the fact that I had just taken a hot shower, or whether it was because of Gareth.

It was from the shower. It just had to be. At least, that's what I kept telling myself.

Thirteen

Dinner. One of the best words in life. A full three-course dinner awaited us at the hotel. The dining room was extremely fancy. It had tables covered in white cloth, the walls were pure white, and the carpet was a gorgeous red colour that made you worry that you were going to get it dirty just by standing on it. Everything screamed grandeur. We were ushered to a table near the middle of the room.

The dinner at the hotel consisted of tomato soup as the starter—well, it was my starter, anyway. Gareth went a bit exotic with the beginning of his dinner plan by ordering a shrimp cocktail. As we ate our appetizers, we talked about things that were utterly meaningless, from the weather to the beautiful town we were in. It felt a bit awkward after we fooled around in the hotel room, but neither of us commented on it.

"At least we're getting decent weather for being here," I commented.

Gareth nodded. "Yeah that's true. But it's a beautiful town whether in sunshine or rain. I hope you like here. It's one of my favourite places on earth."

"I really do. Thank you for bringing me here."

Gareth smiled at me. "Now that I know you a little better, tell me something I don't know about you."

I laughed. "You know everything."

"Lies!" He replied. "You can never know everything about a person. It's just impossible. Now spill it!"

I thought as I finished off my soup. I wiped my mouth with my napkin and smiled. "All right, I have something."

"What?"

"Every day I wish that people would like me."

The atmosphere at the table fell flat. I seemed to be in the habit of causing that way too much. The waitress came and took our dishes before going to the kitchen to get our main course of roast dinner.

Gareth looked at me and tilted his head to the side. I asked him what he was doing. He smiled. "Why do you desire to be in a world where every person likes you? You're in a world where your family likes you, your friend Lucy likes you, and I like you. Isn't that enough?"

"You don't understand," I mumbled. How could he understand? Maybe it was just my own thoughts making up this whole idea of wanting people to like me. I didn't quite know.

"Then help me to understand," he almost begged. We were given our main course, and I poured some gravy over my roast dinner.

"In school, I'm a nobody. Barely anyone acknowledges me, I'm not well liked as it is, and at home, I'm the middle child. Do you know how bad that is?" I asked. Gareth opened his mouth to reply, but I was in a ranting mood; I didn't want him to open his mouth until I was finished. "I feel like Mum cares more about Harper and Ava. It's almost like I'm the disappointment of the whole family. Dad and I try to please everyone, but you can't just do that at all. Life doesn't work like that. You can't just please everyone."

"Your dad really looks out for you."

I shrugged. "I know he does."

"I'm an only child. Do you know how bad that is?" Gareth questioned, using my own words against me. He didn't wait for my reply, either. "I don't tell anyone my story. To me it doesn't matter. But my parents basically didn't even want me. I was an inconvenience to them. I ruined their rich lifestyle."

"Oh yeah, you ruin mine, too," I joked to lighten the mood. Gareth and I smiled at each other.

He shook his head but continued on, "The worst thing is that when I told them about Poppy, they didn't want to know. Like, she's their granddaughter. If Poppy is my only child, then she won't be treated like I was. She'll have the world, because I'm going to work my butt off to give her it."

"You really love your daughter, don't you?"

Gareth laughed. "Of course, I do. She's adorable. Why, just last night she said 'dada' to me. That just…meant a lot to me. I know that people will say I made a mistake, and Poppy was a mistake, but I know for a fact that she wasn't. She might not have been planned, but she's my little fallen angel."

That's when I realised something: no matter how much your children annoy you, or if the two of you bicker and fight to no end, you'll still love them.

We finished off dessert with sticky toffee pudding. When we finished the meal, we went upstairs to the room again; Gareth suggested that we go for a walk. I just couldn't turn Gareth down after all he had done for me the past few months, so we grabbed our coats and went back downstairs.

Before we went back out, Gareth stopped to grab some leaflets of things to do. I wasn't the best at making decisions, so I let him choose. Decision-making just wasn't my thing; I'm the kind of person who would change an outfit at least three times before going out. But he also paid for half of the trip, so he should at least get a say in all the activities we did on it. We walked across the road from the hotel to the seafront. The promenade was lit up with streetlights, yet you still couldn't see much around you. I didn't mind that.

The only noise between the two of us was the sound of the sea lapping up on the shoreline. I looked out towards it, but was met with darkness. Yet I knew there was something beautiful in the darkness. It was a long walk to wherever Gareth was leading me. It was a bit chilly, too.

I shivered, and Gareth looked at me.

"We're going to have to run to keep you warm," he told me. I gazed over at him.

"Don't you dare."

"Come on!"

I groaned as Gareth began to run down the promenade. No one else was there except us two. I liked it that way. Gareth kept calling me. In the dim light, I could see he was running backwards. I rolled my eyes, but couldn't hold back a smile. I began to run after him. He ran even faster on purpose.

"Hey! Hold on! I'm not wearing a sports bra!" I practically screamed down the promenade. Gareth stopped and was killing himself laughing. I finally caught up to him. He nodded at the benches under the streetlights. An old couple were sitting there. They looked horrified at my confession. "Oopsie."

Gareth grabbed my hand and ran on. I laughed and had to run with him. I stopped Gareth when I was breathless. I put my hands on my thighs and hunched my back over.

"I-Is that sand?" I breathed out.

Gareth squinted his eyes in the darkness. He nodded. "It is, indeed."

"We're so going to the beach," I told him with a grin. Gareth laughed.

"Deal. Now, come on. I want to show you something," he replied. He took my hand and pulled me further down the promenade again.

Gareth walked me down a side path. I saw little buildings around us. The place was lit with yellow lights. He smiled at me.

"The best is yet to come," he promised. I just nodded and let him take me gently by the hand. We walked past closed stalls and shops on our left, but I didn't care. I looked out to my right, knowing the sea was out there. Gareth didn't speak. He didn't need to.

Eventually, my feet began to clack on wood. We were on the pier. I looked and saw that the whole way down the pier was lit with lampposts. It was magical. A lit-up runway was waiting for us to walk down. These piers only ever existed in movies or books to me— but now it was here in front of me. I smiled at Gareth, who was already grinning at me, as if to tell me he understood the wonder and amazement I was feeling.

No one could possibly understand this feeling unless you were there.

The sea breeze flowed through my hair as we walked down to the end of the pier. When we finally reached it, a white building which held the arcade on the pier stood in the middle, filling most of the end of the pier. Gareth walked me around to the back of it and pulled me gently into his arms.

"What do you think?" he asked me.

I was unable to think as his body heat warmed me up in the freezing night. "It's beautiful. It's amazing."

He agreed. He took my right hand in his and wrapped an arm around me. He began to dance with me until the yellow lights became our spotlight. I couldn't stop laughing. Gareth stopped dancing because of how much I was laughing.

"What's so funny?" he asked.

"There's no music and you know damn well that you can't dance."

Gareth smiled. "Sometimes you have to roll with the punches. The orchestra couldn't make it."

Of course, he was being sarcastic. We both smiled at each other. The pier was completely empty, just for us. Gareth spun me around and attempted his best two-step. I knew he was looking at me, but for some reason I couldn't look up at him. I looked out at the darkness that surrounded the pier.

Gareth twirled us around and around the Victorian building. I smiled at him, eventually. He smiled back down at me.

"Why didn't you want to go to the university today?" Gareth asked.

I sighed. "In truth, I wanted to see what the town had to offer before deciding on the university. I'm positive that the university is great, but if the town hasn't got life and character, then it will be a boring time. University…it is my dream, but blogging gives me an outlet. And even travelling has made me feel like I'm home, despite the uncertainty of where I'll end up. I'm just still a bit uncertain about what to do."

Gareth nodded, telling me that he understood my dilemma. We kept swaying, but the moves seemed so natural now that it didn't feel like we were dancing. He leant his head down. Our cheeks met. I knew Gareth was smiling by the way his cheek all of a sudden pushed into mine. Somehow, that caused me to grin like an idiot, too. The rain slowly began to pour down, but we didn't move.

I turned my head to look at him. Our noses rested against each other; our lips were so close. The rain raced down. We didn't care. I laughed and so did Gareth.

"I'm going to look like a drowned rat," I laughed.

Gareth chuckled. "I'd go for a drowned alpaca."

"Why?"

"They're cuter."

We both smiled at each other. Gareth's lips gently grazed mine. I smiled as I felt his lips fully. He kissed me. That was it. That was when I discovered that, despite Gareth being an annoying idiot, I liked him. I truly liked him.

When we got back to the hotel, we were both drenched. We hadn't spoken since the kiss. But luckily, we had stopped for pizza. Gareth placed the pizza boxes on his bed. I bought the pizzas for us, but he swore it would be the *one of the only things that I paid for on this trip.*

I went to the bathroom and got changed into my pyjamas. My hair was still wet from the pier, so I wrapped it up in a scrunchie. When I walked out, Gareth was moving the TV to the dressing table.

"Are we allowed?" I asked.

Gareth shrugged. "Who cares? We're doing it now. Plus, I did spot the *Titanic* DVD in your suitcase."

I blushed, as if he had just discovered a hidden secret about me. As a little kid, I brought the movie everywhere our family travelled on vacation. The urge to pack it again had seized me, and I couldn't help myself. Gareth took out the disc and put it into the DVD player. We sat on our separate beds and ate pizza while the movie began. I glanced over at Gareth, who was now wearing his pyjama bottoms and a short-sleeved pyjama top. His eyes met mine and smiled. I looked back at the screen immediately. I couldn't believe I was still shy around Gareth.

I began to drop off to sleep during the film. But I woke to Gareth moving the pizza box from my bed and putting it into the bin. He smiled at me.

"I didn't mean to wake you," he told me.

"It's okay. I'm not tired."

He scoffed and ignored my comment. As Gareth was about to go back to his bed again, I took his hand.

"What did that kiss mean?" I asked. He looked at me confused. "Like, what's happening with us?"

"Whatever you want to happen," he replied.

I smiled up at him. "Will you stay with me tonight, then?"

He nodded. We both got under the duvet of my bed. *Titanic* continued to play in the background. They had just hit the iceberg. While disaster was forming on the TV, my disastrous life seemed to finally have some hope.

Gareth pulled me close to him. I laid my head on his chest as we watched the rest of the movie. I didn't reach the end. The next thing I knew, I had fallen into the darkness of a sweet sleep with Gareth's arms around me.

Fourteen

Across the table at breakfast, Gareth handed me a leaflet. I ate the last remaining piece of my fry and looked at it. I felt nauseous. I was *not* doing it. Never. Never. Never!

I shook my head and handed him back the leaflet. "No thanks."

"It's only a mile walk," he argued.

"That's not my point. I can see that frigging thing from our window! I'm not doing it. Don't you dare even suggest it," I warned him.

We glanced around us to see that the hotel guests near us were looking at us like we were an old married couple. Gareth smirked and showed them the leaflet. They just nodded and pretended we weren't there for the duration of breakfast.

"The Great Orme. You serious?" I asked.

"I actually am. It's an hour and a half walk. It's our last day here. We are going to go for a walk, an afternoon on the beach, and an ice cream lunch."

I sighed. "I did agree to that last night, didn't I?"

"I'm afraid so, Liv."

I began to fake cry. Gareth chucked a tomato from his fry at me, and it splatted on my head. I pulled a face.

"Ew."

"Serves you right."

Gareth had a triumphant grin on his face. He had won. I was going to have to walk an up-hill trail. Why did I agree to this three-day trip again?

I stood in front of the mirror before I went to leave. Gareth was changing in the bathroom. No way did I intended to go out looking like this. I had on a pair of tan shorts, a black vest top, and a red plaid shirt opened on top. That didn't sound too bad. Believe me, I was happy enough with that. But then I looked down at my feet— I had workmen's socks on and hiking boots. I looked ridiculous. At least I could be proud of myself for shaving my legs in advance. I even put my plum hair into plaits for the occasion. Gareth came out of the bathroom and burst out laughing.

I pouted. "Don't laugh. I know, I know. I look like John Hammond from *Jurassic Park*."

"Just a bit. But don't worry. Bring your coat in case it's cold on the top of the Orme."

I pulled my hair out of the two plaits before grabbing my coat and bag. Gareth took one more comical look at my appearance before walking out of the room with me.

Gareth and Little Miss *Jurassic Park* marched up the Orme. If I was writing a novel, that would have been my beginning. Only, I would also have to add that was where I died. I wasn't melodramatic—I just exaggerated everything to my liking. No harm in that, right?

People gave me funny looks as we began to walk. Gareth liked to act as if he was various animals that I was taking for a walk— until I pushed him playfully. He laughed and pretended to bend over in pain. I tried not to laugh.

"Serves you right," I said, quoting his own words. He gave me the finger as he knelt on the ground. By now, it seemed like something was going on between Gareth and I. To tell you the truth, I had no idea what.

We had kissed and fallen asleep to *Titanic* last night. But when we woke up, nothing had changed. People always acted differently when they got together with someone, like it was this big climatic moment in their life. I know Lucy did. She once told me that she had felt like a different person when she was with her boyfriend. But if Gareth and I were together now, I felt no different than before. I didn't act any differently, either. I was still just me.

I was beginning to struggle. I stopped and took a sip of water. Gareth finally joined me. He glared at me.

"You know, if you weren't so pretty, I would be raging with you right now," Gareth informed me.

I fastened the lid on my water bottle and threw it into my bag. "I'm not pretty," I mumbled. I didn't think I had said it that loud. Passers-by didn't hear, but Gareth did.

"Why do you say that?"

I rolled my eyes. "For goodness' sake, Gareth, look at me. I have the dress sense of a five-year-old."

"Who clearly loves *Jurassic Park*."

I stopped and furrowed my eyebrows at him before walking on. "I'm not skinny. I'm a size fourteen. Do you know how many girls I know that are that dress size?" I asked. I didn't wait for a response. "None. None whatsoever. I'm like the little fat friend that people try to ignore because they're not pretty and they're not skinny. They probably have a personality issue, too."

"I don't agree with any of that. Not even the personality part. I'd say you're more of an anger issue chick," he responded. He was smiling at me. I looked into his brown eyes and found myself smiling back. He didn't care about my weight or the fact that my bra bunched up at the sides. Well, he didn't know about the bra bit.

"You really like me that much?" I asked. He nodded. "When people tell me that they actually like me, eventually, they break me into tiny pieces."

"I won't."

I gave him the benefit of the doubt. He grinned at me and took my hand. Our fingers interlocked. A squeeze of his hand ensured me that I could trust him. I knew that we were together and that was all I needed to know.

The whole way up the trail, Gareth assured me that it would be worth it. It was easy to see he had walked it before. I wouldn't dream of doing this for pleasure. But when we got to the top, I knew why he was so insistent.

"Wow," was all that came from my lips as I stood looking over Llandudno.

"It's amazing," Gareth commented. Even though he had been here before, he said the sight never failed to amaze him. I could see why. Anyone could see why. It was only something you could understand if you were actually up there.

I could see everything. The sandy beaches, the dreamy blue sea, the pier, and even our hotel. Beautiful. It was just beautiful. I hadn't seen anything like this before. It was as if I were standing on top of the world. I could see everything for miles around. We sat on the grass in awe at the sight that was laid before us. Everything seemed different when you looked at it from above. It was as if you had been looking at the world in 2D vision, and only when you were up high could you see the 3D world you lived in. It gave me a whole new perspective on the place I was looking at. I didn't want to leave. It felt like I had been in a cage and now I was finally released while I was up here. I breathed in the fresh air and smiled. I knew I would be back at school in two days. I knew things would be worse. But, for now, this was what I had. This was what I wanted.

Gareth squeezed my hand. I looked at him. He leant in and kissed my lips gently. I smiled and kissed him back. I didn't want this moment to end.

"Let's go back down when you're ready," he told me. I nodded and laid my head on his shoulder. He wrapped an arm around me and held me close. As long as I was here, I was okay. And as long as I was with Gareth, I knew nothing could go wrong. It was the bright day I knew would eventually come out against the darkness of my life. The walk down from the Orme wasn't as bad as the walk up. We talked all about what we were going to do for Christmas. Christmas may have been almost a month away, but I couldn't think of that just yet. I had universities to apply for. I had mocks to do, too. My mind seemed everywhere except the immediate future.

When we got to the beach, it was crowded with families and couples, both young and old, spending a day with their significant others under the blazing sun. We sat down on the sand near the sea. I took off my socks and boots to feel the ocean going under my feet.

I smiled and looked at Gareth to find him already looking at me. I could tell he was planning something. He had that mischievous sparkle in his eyes.

"What?" I asked.

He smiled. "Want to go into the water?"

"No!" I said, as if it was obvious. "I didn't bring a swimsuit."

"Did you bring clean underwear?"

"Yes... why?"

Gareth stood up and took off his jeans and top. He stood proudly in his black boxers. I looked around, but no one cared. They all thought they were his swimming shorts. I shook my head. I was self-conscious enough without stripping into my underwear in front of a crowd of complete strangers.

"We don't have towels," I told him.

He bent down and opened his backpack. It was stuffed with clean towels. He smirked at me.

"I-I can't do this. My body..."

Gareth sighed. "We don't know these people. The odds of them ever seeing us again are slim to none. Besides, look at my mini-beer belly." He shook his stomach to show me he had a tiny bit of fat on his stomach.

Well, I couldn't let him run into the water by himself in his underwear. So, I quickly followed suit. I stripped down to my black bra and pants. I wrapped my hands around my stomach, hiding the very obvious awkward bits and blobs. Gareth took my hand.

"These people don't know you. Come with me and try to relax," he assured me. I nodded. He took both of my hands and pecked my lips before we went into the water. I screamed in shock from the cold as a wave flew over us. Gareth laughed at me. "Drowned alpaca, again?"

"I can't help it if I resemble a cute creature when I'm drenched. I'm just missing the fringe," I pouted. He smiled and pulled me close to him.

"I hope this place gives you a new beginning."

I nodded and wrapped my arms around him. "It has. Until something comes along and messes it all up again."

"That won't happen."

But it would. I wasn't trying to be pessimistic, but in my experience, nothing ever worked out how I wanted it. That's why I just wanted to stay in this moment for as long as I could. I wanted to be under the blazing sun of Llandudno. I wanted to be in Gareth's arms. I never wanted to leave.

Part of me wondered if Gareth would be the same with me when we got back home. The thing I learnt about people was that their attitude towards you could change so quickly once they were around others.

We got out of the water and got dressed again after drying off. We sat down on the sand and Gareth beamed at me.

"So, what universities are you applying for?" Gareth questioned. He shook his wet hair.

"Oxford, to keep my parents happy. Bangor, too. I'm not quite sure about the others yet," I admitted.

"Why do you want to go so far away from home?"

"It's a new start. A whole new place to discover. Soak up the culture from it," I told him. I gazed up at the blue sky and smiled. "It's a chance to begin again. Live out the American Dream at home."

"Why not make your own dream?" he asked. I looked down at my feet as I curled my toes into the sand. He was right. But who would even let me live out my dream? It was somewhat pathetic probably. People wouldn't understand me.

"I'm not sure I know what my dream is."

Gareth laughed slightly and looked at me. "Oh, please. You do. You have your head screwed on right. You know what your dream is."

I smiled slightly. Gareth was too positive sometimes. "I guess." I thought for a few minutes before speaking again "I want to be the best version of myself I can be. I love blogging, but I still want to go to university."

"To get away from life at home?"

We both smiled at each other, knowing my answer. I wanted to just start over. Gareth seemed to be the only one who understood how I felt. Moving away from home, setting up my own little life and becoming the best version of myself— that was my dream.

"You know me too well," I stated.

Gareth hugged me. "I really do. But come on, we better get going before it gets cold."

Eventually, we finally got back to the hotel for the night. We were going to relax before our early morning flight back home. Gareth began to run a bath in the bathroom. I flicked through my blog. Gareth came out of the bathroom and put his hands gently on my shoulders. He kissed the top of my head.

"You okay?" he asked.

I smiled. "I am. My blog is going so well. I don't understand it at all."

Gareth smirked. "Well, I am a plumber. When I spot a self-help book or some life quotes around the house, I tell them about this amazing blogger I just came across. They check you out and your views and following go up."

I couldn't believe he had done that for me. I got up and hugged him. "Thank you so much."

I kissed him passionately. Eventually, he was pulled away to check on the water. The last thing we needed was a flood in the hotel room. My laptop screen turned to black when I switched it off. My heart felt at peace. I felt at peace for a change.

Later that night, we laid in our beds. The TV blared in the background, but we were both stuck in the books we wanted the other to read. I had to admit, I was reading Agatha Christie intensely. Every guess I made about whodunit was proved wrong in the next part.

"Screw it," I mumbled and threw the book on the bed. Gareth looked over at me.

"Guess wrong again?"

I glared at him. He smirked at me. He put *Pride and Prejudice* down on the bed. Gareth came over and sat down beside me. He hugged me.

I pouted up at him. "I'm always wrong about people."

He smiled. "You won't always be like that. You'll guess who it is at the next chapter. I promise," he told me. I nodded. "I do have to ask, has being away for a few days helped you?"

I couldn't form into words how much it had helped me. Writing was my calling in life. I knew what I wanted to do with the rest of my life now. But my parents wouldn't like it. Maybe I was being too hasty.

"It has. I'm applying for university. If I get in, then I'll make more of a solid decision from there. But I want to see the world. I don't want to be stuck in my town forever. It's not for me. There's so much out there I want to see."

"I'll support you. Even if your family won't."

I didn't believe it. Not one single word of it.

Fifteen

"There's something strange about your half American, half English accent. I can't quite put my finger on it," I told Mr. Henderson as I ate lunch with him.

My face appearing at his door with my lunchbox was probably the last thing he wanted. To be honest, it was the last thing I wanted, too. But then again, here we were— living out our worst nightmares together. What a great group work activity!

I took out my buttered bread and opened the packet of crisps I had. I noticed Mr. Henderson watching me carefully.

"Cheese and onion?" he asked.

I looked up at him and put the crisps into the bread. Yes, a crisp sandwich was my lunch. I didn't have time to make myself a good meal. Most girls in my year were eating salad. Prom was in January and, of course, they had to have the "perfect" body for it— despite eating it all back over Christmas. Those girls would eat their weight in Pigs in Blankets and Quality Streets, but never tell their friends for fear of being judged. You know what I would say to that? Being judged is crap, but what's even crappier is not being who you are.

"Do you have an issue with my eating choices?" I asked back.

He shrugged and put down the red pen he was using to mark papers with. "Nope. But I do have an issue with your attitude sometimes."

"Well, when you've been as screwed over as I've been in life, it sort of comes as a given. 'I didn't choose the attitude, the attitude chose me' kinda thing," I explained through a mouthful of my crisp sandwich.

Mr. Henderson looked at me and stifled a laugh. "Rumour has it you have a boyfriend. Do you use the same bad attitude around him?"

I nodded. "I guess you could say that. Like, I used to think he was an ass…I think I used the term ass, maybe I didn't. My mind isn't overly good at remembering terms I use for people. You know, all that seems to be stuffed up there sometimes is books. I could recite the first line of Jane Austen's *Pride and Prejudice* to you, but I couldn't tell you Gareth's phone number cause, one, I'm not that weird, and two, I'm not obsessed with people."

"Obsessed with people?"

"Yeah. People seem to be obsessed with other people. You look at Lola and it's 'oh, I want to be like Lola,' but then you look at that big butt celebrity woman and they want to be like her, too. Lola isn't curvy. That woman is. How can you be like both? My generation has gone mad. Mad with emojis on top— because nothing is complete without an emoji," I replied. I looked down at my sandwich. "Haha… smiley face. Little poop guy."

Mr. Henderson laughed and took out a big-ass chicken panini. He took a bite of it and shook his head at me. I frowned.

"You're not going to start that whole 'no one understands me' crap, are you?" he asked me. "You know, no generation is good or bad. Your generation is just as good and bad as the others. When I was growing up, we had the exact same problems, only we didn't advertise it on computers. But you can bet that if we had computers and phones, we would have been posting it everywhere, just like you lot."

I was. Oh, believe me, I was certain no one understood me. But I shook my head. I had gotten better at lying. It was scary how good I had gotten. Ava even complimented me on it. She knew I had gone to Llandudno. I felt close to Ava. I didn't care if she knew, because there was no way she would tell our parents. Ava was so secretive. Sometimes that was bad, especially during that time when she was being manipulated by her boyfriend. She didn't tell any of us, and that just made the abuse worse. Thankfully, she at least talks to me now about things bothering her.

"I wasn't," I lied. "But do you ever notice how this generation seems to have nothing in common with each other until they go online and find this whole group of people who are fans of the simplest things? I even found a fandom for playdoh! Like, if they just talked to each other, they would actually find they have a lot in common with each other."
Mr. Henderson just nodded along and ate his sandwich. I didn't speak again. He put down his sandwich and looked at me. "They are talking to each other. People your age just talk to people over social media, instead of face-to-face. I guess that they do it because it's sometimes easier to express your feelings when the person you're telling them to isn't looking you in the eyes. You don't feel rejection as harshly through a screen than you do in person."

"We all have something in common, though. If we talked more face-to-face, maybe we'd see that."

"If you believe that, then why aren't you in the common room with the other students?"

He had a good point. Well-presented, too. I gave him a look and he knew exactly what I meant— the Lucy Thing. It's amazing how one

149

event can completely damage the person you've been for seven years. He didn't ask me anymore. Everyone knew I was to blame for the Lucy Thing. I should have been there for her more than I was. I should have stopped it. Molly and Louise never let the guilt get to them or the judgmental looks they got every time they walked into the common room affect them; I did. No one ever knew what caused Lucy to leave except for the fact that Molly and Louise had bullied her to extremes. Maybe there was more than that, but those two weren't saying.

I began to pack up my lunch. I asked him again about his accent even though I wasn't interested, wanting to divert the conversation away from myself. Apparently, he met his wife in America, as he went to university there. He lived in the States for a while before coming back over to England with his wife and starting a family.

While he talked, I nodded along to let him know I was listening. He smiled at me as the bell rang.

"Can I ask you one quick question, Olivia?" he asked.

"Yes, Mark, you can," I replied. He laughed and shook his head at my lack of respect in calling him by his first name— he knew it was only a joke, though.

"Does your boyfriend know about your two problems?"

I told him that Gareth did. It was a lie, again, but Mr. Henderson seemed to believe it. To give me some brownie points, Gareth was aware of my depression. But a huge problem of mine was anger. I had aggression problems.

My parents hadn't picked up on it. I half-knew, but Mr. Henderson was the one who noticed it as soon as he began to teach me. It was two years ago, when he told us to hand write an essay. I was getting so frustrated over it and began to crumple the edges of the paper— later attempting to flatten them out. But the key giveaway was when I got so frustrated, I dug my pencil into the back of the last page of my essay and scribbled hard. I tried to rub it out, but it didn't work.

When I handed in the essay, I was called to his classroom at lunchtime. He asked me about it, and when he did that, I broke down crying. Anger was something I had struggled with for ages. It's probably where my bad attitude came from. Throughout my life, my older and younger sister always got all the attention. Mr. Henderson supposed that anger could have built up from that lack of attention, but I wasn't sure. I guessed it was because I strived for perfection constantly— my theory being if I actually did something good and perfect, then my parents might finally see me.

I hadn't told Gareth about it. Unless I was fired up, it wasn't that often that I directed those anger issues towards others. Dad hadn't told him either, but that was okay. When Mr. Henderson talked to my parents about it, Dad sat me down and discussed it with me. He knew I didn't like people knowing. My depression was something I couldn't hide easily. I knew that my quietness made people think that I was better than them. But it wasn't me being pompous, it was just sadness. Anger was easier to hide.

"Good, I'm glad he knows and supports you. If he doesn't support you, then screw him," he replied with a smile. I smiled back and thanked him before leaving the room. Maybe I should have told him, but I decided not to.

When I got to my next class, Molly was there. I ignored her, but knew I had to sit down beside her. People act so differently when you disappear after trouble happens. Sometimes I wondered what would happen if Lucy had come back. I didn't blame her for not doing it. If I had a choice, then I would have stayed in Llandudno with Gareth and never returned home— not for anything and not for anyone. I wanted to start over with a new life somewhere where no one knew me except Gareth.

"Hey," she said to me. I just smiled.

"Hi."

Molly sighed. "I was so worried that you weren't coming back. I'm glad. Rumour has it that you have a boyfriend now."

I rolled my eyes. It's amazing how one little rumour can go around faster than an STD on a call girl. Lucy told me never to let people into your private life. She made that mistake, and I trusted her advice.

"If you believe rumours," I simply replied. Molly nodded. She gave up trying with me after that. I could be a bitch at times, but only when I was fed up with how people treated me— I personally saw nothing wrong with that. Everyone else seemed to.

*

It was apparent to me that everyone in my family was filled with their own self-importance. I supposed I probably was, too, but you can't see how others perceive you. That's one of the worst things about life. I sat at the kitchen table and watched my parents and two sisters ignore each other. It was quite interesting to watch.

Mum was sitting at the breakfast bar reading her book for her book club and dad was working on his business accounts. Harper was sitting with Mum at the breakfast bar doing her homework. Ava was sitting beside me, texting Michael— in between which she was glaring at Mum. Things hadn't got any better.

I went onto Facebook and quickly messaged Ava, as silence seemed to be the comfortable environment of the kitchen.

@OliviaBernard: Stop giving Mum death stares— even Harper has outgrown that!

@AvaBernard: When you grow out of it I will, ha!

@OliviaBernard: Touché! I'm going to my room. Wanna come chat?

@AvaBernard: Hell yeah!

It was pretty easy for Ava and I to make an excuse for going upstairs. It wasn't that we didn't enjoy family company; it was just that, at that moment, Ava understood my perspective on being on the outside for once.

As we sat on my bed and stared up at the ceiling, I laid my head on Ava's shoulder.

"So, you and Gareth, then?" Ava asked. I looked at her. She was smirking up at the ceiling. "It's just a guess. I mean, he seems to be constantly tagging you in stupid memes and clickbaity posts on Facebook."

"Geez," I mumbled. "Is that how you can tell if a guy likes you now?" Ava nodded. "Pretty much."

I wanted to ask Ava about what Mr. Henderson talked to me about. It had been bugging me since he brought it up earlier. "Do you think I should tell Gareth about my anger issues?"

Ava didn't reply for a while. She was thinking. I could tell because when she thought about things, she ground her teeth together. I could feel her bottom jaw gently hitting the top of my head every now and then.

"Does he know about your depression?" Ava asked. I nodded. "If you don't feel comfortable telling him just yet, then don't. We all hide things at the start of our relationships, but that doesn't necessarily mean you should keep them in forever. We should be honest, because unfortunately, it's human nature to not tell the truth in times of strife. That's why children are so good at lying— we're all born that way until we learn the ways of the world and realise we can't go through life lying."

153

"Well, some lawyers make a good living that way," I told her. Ava and I laughed. I smiled at her. "You sound like you're an expert on keeping things hidden." She knew exactly what I meant by that. "You haven't told Michael, have you?"

Ava shook her head. I cuddled into her and wrapped my arms around her. On the surface, I acted like an annoyed, self-hating type of person who didn't get on well with my family; deep down, my heart broke for every single one of them. The thing about your family is that you know them better than anyone.

Before my depression, Ava struggled with emotional abuse. The man she was dating made her feel absolutely worthless. Every time she wanted to dump him, he made her feel as though she wouldn't find anyone else. That resulted in her suffering out the relationship for fear of being alone. When things were over, she hadn't trusted another guy until Michael. That was probably the reason why Mum was so overprotective of her. Ava knew that, too. She was a smart girl.

"How do you even begin to tell someone you were emotionally abused and manipulated in your last relationship?" Ava mumbled.

I sighed. "I can't begin to imagine what you went through or how you're coping with a new relationship, but if Michael loves you, he'll help you. In fact, if he's anything like the guy I think he is, he'll probably offer to go and sort him out, too."

"You don't need to tell Gareth about your anger. If it doesn't affect your relationship, then don't. Not yet, anyway. Leave it for another week. But mine...it's affecting my relationship right now. Every time Michael comes near me, I wonder whether he's playing silly mind games like James did. Every night, I wonder whether tonight he'll tell me he's going to shag some other girl because I won't put out for him," Ava admitted. I looked at her.

"You need to tell Michael. I know it will be difficult, but if this is how you feel, you need to do it," I told her firmly.

She nodded. "Yeah, I know. He's an amazing boyfriend, though. Every night that I go over to his house, he makes me homemade dinner. Everything is made from scratch. He's such a good cook. No matter what is wrong with me, Michael always tries to solve it with me. He'll sit me down and talk to me if I'm down. Or, he'll even lie with me until my stomach pain subsides. He's just perfect, Liv. I love him so much. I'm so happy."

We sat up, and she hugged me tightly. Ava and I bickered mindlessly as we grew up— even into our teen years. But once Ava needed someone, anyone, I came onto the scene. When I needed someone, Ava was there, too. It's amazing how these past few troubled years actually brought us closer together.

Ava left to go and meet Michael at his house. Our parents knew where she was going, though Mum didn't exactly approve. She couldn't do anything to stop Ava. I laid back on my bed and stared at the ceiling. My phone was lying on my stomach as it buzzed. I grabbed it and looked at it.

@GarethJohnson: You need to upload your post about Wales! Feeling slightly offended here ;)

@OliviaBernard: Calm your tits! I'll write it tonight and upload it tomorrow haha!

Gareth sent me a smiley face in return. I smiled and felt guilty for not telling him the truth about myself. As I began to type out my post about Wales, I felt a twisting feeling in my heart and gut. I had to tell him.

@OliviaBernard: Gareth?

@GarethJohnson: Yeah?

@OliviaBernard: Thanks again for Wales

I chickened out. I expected nothing less from me.

Sixteen

"Before you all go on study leave next week for your mocks, which I'm not sure you've revised for," Mr. Henderson began. At least he was being brutally honest. "I've printed off something new for you to digest. I know nothing like this will be on your exam, but I'm interested to see what you all make of it."

He handed around pages which were printed off a website. The sheets came around to me last, and I handed Mr. Henderson back the spare pages. I looked down and thought my stomach was going to fall out of my butt. I felt sick. I knew I had gone pale without even looking in the mirror.

This page had two of my blog posts on it. I had written these. Mr. Henderson was making people in my A Level English class read my work. I wanted to vomit, but swallowed it down.

"This is a blogger called Blu Skyes. Very catchy name. My wife told me about her. If you didn't know, my wife studied English at UC Berkeley. When she showed me these two posts, I fell in love with the writing and formatting. It's so raw and original and pure— that's something hard to find with bloggers. A lot of people online make the posts

157

all about them. While this blogger does do that sometimes, she also diverts it back to the people around her or the places she's been to. So, take a few minutes to read over these posts and then we'll gather our thoughts," he announced.

I could hardly read my own words. They were blurry, and it seemed as though the words were dancing all over the page instead of forming coherent phrases or sentences. If I showed any expression on my face that possibly hinted at the fact that this was my writing in any way, it's over.

I gazed over the words again. Even though I had actually written this, I didn't know it by heart.

The ocean captures my imagination more than a picture can. A picture can tell a thousand words— as clichés go— but the ocean holds the memories and hearts of so many people. While we walked along the ocean today, I felt like I was home. I was several hours away from home. But my heart belongs here. You may say I'm absolutely mad, but that's okay. Because if you were here, you'd be thinking the same thing, too...

A cough at the front of the room drew everyone up from the pages of my words. My hands were shaking while I grabbed a pen, ready to analyse my own blog.

Mr. Henderson smiled down at us all. "Right, so this blogger is female— I'm assuming it's a girl, as her username is Blu Skyes. Presumably, her name being Skye. She never names the place, but in your minds, are you able to picture somewhere similar to where she's talking about?"

I looked around inconspicuously and noticed several nods. One girl put up her hand. Mr. Henderson nodded at her to speak.

"For me, it's the South of France. My family goes there every summer, but it feels like my second home," she told him.

He smiled. "Perfect, Sarah! That's exactly what I mean. I'm taken back to my days in Long Beach, where I had my first date with my wife. We go back there every few years."

Mr. Henderson went around asking some pupils about where it reminded them of, thankfully leaving me out. As I heard their stories and read back over my blog post, I realised how much my words resonated with the hearts of others.

As Mr. Henderson began to re-read my blog post, I smiled. People began to scribble down their analytical notes, but I just sat there. I didn't even know how to analyse something I had actually written.

"So, let's see what we have with this passage," he announced at the end. "I love these posts because they're so personal. You can feel everything that Blu Skyes feels. It takes a good writer to make you feel everything that they have felt. We need more writers like that in the world."

My peers began to analyse everything word-for-word, sentence-for-sentence, on whiteboards with different coloured markers to symbolise different themes: love, life, imagination. His eyes met mine and I swallowed hard, knowing I would have to answer something. "Olivia, what do you think of the second post?"

I looked down at the page:

His eyes gaze into mine and I don't want to escape it. The ocean is in his eyes. The moonlight is in his smile. As we dance on the pier,

my life is complete. This may be a blog post
that not many people will read, but it's where
I can finally spill my feelings. I know you'll
be reading this— know that on that pier you
changed me for the better. I don't want to go
on without you now. You may be an idiot at
times, but you're my idiot. I hope I'm yours,
too. When you get upset, please think of the
pier and the night that I slept in your arms,
listening to your breath soothing me to sleep...

He had cut my blog post short, but I didn't care. I smiled reading
back over it as memories of Wales flooded back to me, as if replaying my
favourite movie in my head.

I looked up at Mr. Henderson. "Well, I think it's a post about love.
How falling in love with someone can change who you are for the better.
It's about feeling one with the other person. Maybe you can't tell them
face-to-face, because you think you'll come on too strong, so this person
uses the blog post to express her feelings."

"Absolutely right. I couldn't have put it better myself," he admitted. Is this what it felt like to have your work appreciated by people? I
liked the feeling.

Mr. Henderson asked me to stay behind to clean up the extra
whiteboards and coloured markers he'd taken out for our analysing. I
helped to pick up the markers as he collected the whiteboards. When
everyone left the classroom, he chatted about things I had no interest in,
like my university choices.

"Which universities have you picked?" he questioned.

"Edinburgh, Cardiff, Oxford, Durham, and Bangor," I rattled off instinctively. I was still lying about Oxford, but it was easier for the time being. My other choice was Glasgow— not Oxford.

"You seemed to really relate to some of the words of those posts," he commented. I couldn't give away the fact that Blu Skyes was me. It was my secret— like Gareth half was. No one seemed to know my rumoured boyfriend was him. He was a secret in my heart. "You should look up her other posts. You'll like them. She's got quite similar views to you, but her personality is quite opposite."

"You mean she would understand me, but she's agreeable and very pleasant."

"I didn't say anything like that," he replied with a laugh and his hands in a surrender motion.

I picked up my schoolbag and smiled as I left the room. "Thanks, Sir."

"No problem. Good luck on your mocks."

I was going to need it. Boy was I going to need it.

Seventeen

People say that music brings everyone together. I don't deny it, but as I stood outside the exam hall, I could see that fear, anxiety, and worry brought people together, too. Everyone stood outside the assembly hall, nervously anticipating their mock exams. I fiddled with my pencil case, making sure I had brought six pens in case five ran out. Everyone was chewing and biting on their nails. Others were taking their blazers on and off, then back on and back off again.

Gareth had done revision with me last night at Sharon's house. His little girl was there, and I was happy I could spend the night with them both. Gareth was a great father. I knew he would be. We revised while he put on a movie for Poppy. It was my first mock exam, and I was burdened with the pressure of trying to get the best grades I could. Gareth could tell how much I was fretting, and his attempts to de-stress me had no effect whatsoever— from herbal tea to back massages— nothing worked.

Instead, we just had a casual chat between us. He was picking me up after my mock to treat me to pancakes (who doesn't love pancakes?). I told Gareth all about how Mr. Henderson had decided to pick two of my blog posts to analyse in class. No one knew it was me, and both of us were relieved at that. Gareth didn't want me to suffer at the hands of my classmates.

I hadn't been writing on it much due to my studies, but I had been checking it daily. I had even more followers now. Part of me knew I had to thank Mr. Henderson for that. But none of that seemed to matter as I stood outside the hall.

My hands were shaking as the doors opened to welcome us into hell. It was the Spanish written exam. My head filled with translations of every word I spotted on timetables that were plastered on the walls outside the hall. They were holding a French exam at the same time, which Molly and Louise were taking. I was tapped on the shoulder and turned around. The two of them smiled at me. "Good luck. You deserve to do well," Louise commented.

"Good luck, Liv. May you get the grade you need for Oxford," Molly told me.

I wished them luck, too, and proceeded to find my seat. When I sat down, I thought I was hallucinating— Molly and Louise hadn't been bitchy to me. But I wasn't delirious. I took a deep breath and took out one of my six pens.

The proctor at the front of the room called out the rules for the exam. I looked around at everyone. This was the last week at school before Christmas. I just had to get through it all. Get through this, and I was free from this hellhole for a month.

"You may begin."

SECOND SEMESTER

"Iceberg right ahead!"

Titanic (1997)

Eighteen

Prom. The one thing most girls are obsessed with and the one thing most guys are fed up hearing about. It was the first week back after Christmas, and it was all anyone could talk about. The mere thought of it made me so anxious and agitated that I couldn't stand on my legs and I couldn't sit still— I could have Irish danced my way to a seat in the common room.

Everyone was buzzing. It seemed like I was the only one suffering from the post-Christmas blues. In that moment, I would have much rather crawled myself into a ditch surrounded by hungry dogs than to go back to the hellhole I call "school." I took a seat and spotted Molly coming in.

I reverted my gaze to my phone and switched it on. The lock screen photo came up. I smiled at it fondly; it was a photo of Gareth and I at Christmas. He had spent Christmas dinner with us after spending the morning with Poppy. The Christmas tree illuminated the background of the photo, but I had put a black and white filter on it— everyone in my generation seemed to live in filters.

Molly came over and sat beside me. I smiled up at her, not wanting to be rude despite what she did, and then busied myself checking my email, which I had already checked five times that morning. It was awkward, but Molly wasn't one for giving up. She didn't sit there silently for long.

"Did you have a good Christmas?" Molly asked.

"Yeah. My sister's boyfriend spent the day with us," I told her. Molly smiled and told me how nice it must have been. It was nice, once Mum got over the awkwardness of Michael and Ava kissing in front of her. Dad was definitely the laidback parent.

"Mike came over to spend it with us, too. But families aren't all that they seem, I guess," Molly mumbled.

I looked at Molly and furrowed my eyebrows. Did she come to me because she had a family issue that she didn't know how to deal with?

"What do you mean?" I ventured to ask.

Molly sighed and showed me a Tinder profile. It was of her mum. I only could have been more shocked if it had been Grindr. "Mum's on Tinder."

"How did you find that?"

"Her phone. She's been flirting with men who are younger than my dad. She's even had a date from the sounds of the messages," Molly mumbled.

I felt sorry for her. Without the blonde sidekick in tow, I decided to hug her without the risk of being cat-scratched. Molly hugged me back and then pulled away. She dramatically fanned her face to stop tears from falling down her face to ruin her mascara. I was waiting for her to be blown around the room because she was fanning herself so much.

"I haven't told my dad about it. How could I?" Molly exasperated. "I couldn't do that to him."

I didn't exactly blame her for that. I wouldn't do it myself, if I was in the same position.

170

Molly continued to tell me about her "wonderful," backstabbing, two-timing mother. "She's actually telling people that she's going out to walk the dog with a pile of makeup on. How Dad hasn't noticed yet amazes me. They give everyone the impression that their marriage is perfect when it's not. It's really not."

As Molly was telling me all of this, I realised that people may flash a certain image of their life, but you don't know what's happening underneath. To anyone outside, it would look like Molly had perfect parents who were stinking rich. They were parents who loved each other and their daughter to pieces— along with their Corgis and garage full of Porsches. And no, I'm not joking about the Corgis, they have three of them! With Molly's confession to me, I felt like Jack Nicholson chopping the door in *The Shining* and poking his head through to see who's inside. I had the dirt on the rich girl in our school, but I knew I wouldn't tell anyone.

"Please don't let it out. I haven't even told Louise yet. If people like Lola got a hold of this, it would be plastered all over the school gossip Facebook page," Molly warned me. That, I knew. Over the holidays, someone had created a Facebook page all about the sixth form gossip of Willow High. The first post was about The Lucy Thing. It was obvious why Molly was now panicking that her mum's dirty Tinder laundry would be hung out to dry on the gossip page.

"I won't say a word," I promised. She thanked me.

"It's strange how we'll be getting university offers and interviews soon, isn't it?" Molly commented.

I nodded. The prospect terrified me.

"It's crazy. I hope you get Oxford. It's been your dream since Year Seven," I told her.

Molly smiled. "I hope so, too. I won't be far from home, but at least I'll be away from the mess that's about to get messier at home if Dad finds out."

"You'll get an interview. I bet you," I assured her. Secretly, I hoped no one would find out the truth about my interview.

When Louise came in, Molly went over to her. We were due at assembly in a few minutes to receive envelopes telling us our mock exam results. None of us wanted to get them, but we had to.

The bell rang, signalling our fate. We walked to the assembly hall like we were on a death march. It was an assembly just for our year. I knew that my results wouldn't be the best, but most of my offers would already be in the post. My phone buzzed when I got into the assembly hall. I looked down at the notification with a smile.

@LucyFelix: We need to meet up again! I'm missing seeing you. How about tonight?

I quickly typed out a reply before any teacher noticed I had my phone out.

@OliviaBernard: Sounds brilliant! Can't wait!

I put my phone away and quickly stood in line with the others. When we were requested to sit down, everyone dropped to the floor immediately. I cozied up beside the radiator, but I knew I would later regret it with the amount of uniform our school forced us to wear. Mrs. Turner came in with the dreaded box of our results. People began to mumble to each other. I rolled my eyes as Cynthia walked up to the front, and a unanimous groan went around all of the people in our year. I knew how they felt.

Cynthia went up on stage, as did Mrs. Turner. Mrs. Turner took the microphone first. At least we got a small amount of sanity before we entered the Mad Hatter's tea party.

"Your Head Girl will say a few words before I hand out the results. I want you all to know that you'll probably need a few shots of vodka before handing them to your parents— and your parents may need a few shots too," Mrs. Turner suggested. She really didn't beat around the bush this time.

Cynthia walked up to the microphone. We all prepared ourselves for another one of her so-called "motivational speeches." I would rather stick needles in my eyes than listen to her. Her bleached-blonde curls bounced around her shoulders as she got ready to speak.

"Well, we've entered a new semester. For those applying for Oxford or Cambridge, you should have already completed your interviews and are now awaiting your offers. For those who applied elsewhere, your offers will be coming really soon in the post," Cynthia reminded us. None of us were listening. Almost every girl was either twiddling with their split ends or looking at their nails, and the boys were either untying or retying their shoelaces or texting.

I couldn't blame them. Cynthia's nasally voice rang like nails on a chalkboard— you just wanted her to shut up and stop talking for good. Eventually, even Mrs. Turner got up and stopped the spectacle.

"Right, we'll call you by form class, so stay there until we call you," she mumbled down the microphone. Of course, no one listened. Everyone stood up and began to haul their way to the front of the assembly hall. I don't think our year had ever moved this fast, not even for the fire alarm going off. All of the teachers grabbed the boxes of mock result papers and climbed on to the stage to guard them from us.

Mrs. Turner called out the form classes, and each student climbed on to the stage to get their results. I was being pushed and shoved from one side to the other. Some people might say I had done a thousand steps just from navigating the crowd. I would say that I don't give a flying crap about exercise.

"Next, we'll have form class 7G!" Mrs. Turner called out. I piled onto the stage along with all of the other kids in my class. Cynthia was first up, of course, and stood proudly waiting to receive her envelope. Louise was in front of me in the queue. She turned around and smiled at me.

"Good luck," Louise told me.

I nodded and smiled slightly. "You, too."

You see, I could be nice at times. It took me some time, but I was learning. Finally, it was my turn. I swallowed hard and took the page from Mrs. Turner. It was already folded up, so I folded it again. I placed it in the inside blazer pocket, fearing that if I put it in the outside, one of the idiots in my year would take it out as I was walking past them and read it out loud.

I went to the bathrooms as fast as I could muster to open the sheet of paper. My hands were shaking.

A breath of relief escaped from my mouth as I looked down at the results.

AAA.

That was what I wanted, and I still had room to increase the grade to an A star if I got accepted to Oxford. That is, if I had actually applied for Oxford.

Nineteen

Gareth sat on my bed while I attempted to straighten the frizzy mess that was my hair. I couldn't wait to go out with Lucy tonight. We were going to the cinema, which I didn't mind in the slightest. I was socially awkward, and if someone invited me to go and see a movie or have a movie night, I was really happy— seeing as that meant there'd be less time to try to make conversation. These were the perks of being an introvert.

"Do you have Poppy tonight?" I asked him in the reflection of the mirror.

"I'm picking her up once I drop you off," Gareth told me. He kept smiling at me in the mirror. I frowned and turned around to look at him. Half of my hair was pinned up on my head and the other half was straightened.

"What?" I asked as I pointed the straighteners at him. He laughed. "I'm just… looking at how beautiful you are. I know you won't believe me, but it's true," Gareth replied. "Is that so wrong of me?"

I rolled my eyes and turned back to the mirror. "Don't be getting soppy on me."

"I won't."

We both smiled at each other. I went back to straightening my hair. I gazed at Gareth in the mirror. He was busy flicking through my Spanish folder and trying to pronounce the words; he was doing a terrible job. I began to wonder about asking him to prom.

In high school, there was pressure on asking someone to prom. For people like me, I found it difficult. My curvy figure, frizzy plum hair, and shyness weren't qualities guys wanted as a prom partner— nor a life partner. I had more rolls than a baker on a busy day. There was no way I could have gotten anyone if I hadn't met Gareth. I began to straighten the other side of my hair. He spotted me looking.

He grinned and held up my folder of basic Spanish vocab. He pointed to a word. "Banjos."

I laughed. "It's baños. There's no 'j' in it."

He looked at the page and nodded. He gave me the thumbs up. I smiled as I finished off my hair. Even on my bad days, Gareth could still make me smile just by being himself. I could understand now why Poppy was always such a happy little girl. Gareth could make anyone smile— he was still an ass at times, though.

"What are you looking at?" Gareth asked me. I didn't realise I had been staring. I turned off my straighteners.

"Nothing," I said.

Gareth smirked at me. "Tell me."

"Nothing."

Gareth came over to me after I safely put the straighteners on my table to cool off. He grabbed me from behind and began to tickle me. I laughed and pushed him off. We both fell to the floor.

"Fine, fine," I said as I sat up. "My butt hurts now."

Gareth laughed. "What is it?"

I sighed. I was worried about asking. "Would you go with me to my prom?"

"Of course. I'll see if Poppy's mum can take her for that night. Text me the date later, and I'll pay for both of our tickets."

"No, I need to pay. You can't always insist on paying for everything.

"I do because I want to. It's not fair on you to pay when I'm treating you."

"But you don't have to do this. Just let me pay. This is silly," I told him. Despite my protesting, he shut me up by shoving his leather jacket into my hands. He pecked my lips before we went down the stairs.

Getting good grades really pays off in my house. My parents let me out tonight without having an hour's worth of interrogation. My dad and mum came out of the kitchen and smiled at us.

"Dad, I'll text when the movie is almost over," I told him. I couldn't be bothered driving tonight, so Gareth had offered to drive me there.

"Sure, darling. Have fun," he said. I hugged him.

Gareth opened the passenger door for me. Soon enough, we were heading into town. Gareth took my hand when he didn't need both hands for driving. I smiled and held his in return.

Dating someone is strange. You fall in love with every single bit of them— their appearance, personality, their whole being. You don't know how long the relationship will last, or even if the person is the one. As Gareth's fingers entwined with mine, I began to question all of that. I couldn't say I was in love with him just yet. We had been dating for a few months now, but I didn't know if it was the real deal. I was too worried to say "I love you" to him, just for him to throw it back in my face at some point—even marriages are thrown back in at least one person's face.

How do people know if the person they're with is the one? You might want it to last forever, but the other person might want things to go in a different direction. Will the subject of marriage ever come up, or will the first half of the year be filled to the brim with meaningless dating? That's one thing I didn't understand about dating someone. If it's not for real, if it's not for life, what's the point? Maybe I was just naïve. Gareth smiled over at me as we stopped at a red light. He leant over and pecked my lips.

"You okay?" he asked me. I nodded and he smiled at me. I loved the way his dimples emphasised his smile even more, no matter how big or how little he was smiling.

"What?" I asked as he put the car into third gear when we got through the lights.

"I'm so lucky, you know that? I don't get much chance to speak, especially when you go off on a rant," he said. I faked shock. He took a quick glance at me, then looked back at the road before laughing. "You're so beautiful. I know you'll look stunning at prom, too. What's your favourite flower?"

"A rose. White roses, as a matter of fact. Why?"

Gareth winked at me. The way he winked at me should be illegal. We pulled into the cinema parking lot. I spotted Lucy standing by the doors. Her hair was pulled into a high ponytail and she had jeans on. No one ever seemed to dress up for the cinema.

I unbuckled my seatbelt and smiled at Gareth.

"Thanks for taking me," I told him.

He smiled. "You're very welcome, beautiful. Have fun and let me know when you get home."

"I will. Have fun with Poppy. Give her a hug from me."

"I will, gorgeous."

We kissed quickly before I went over to Lucy. Lucy smiled when she saw me. She pulled her pink hoodie around her waist as we walked inside. We were seeing a film about a girl growing up. You know, one of those coming-of-age films that are directed by middle-aged women who think that they know exactly what it's like for a teenager to grow up nowadays? You know, one of those trashy films. They don't represent my teenage years; I don't know about other teenagers.

As we sat down in the theatre, Lucy watched to make sure I wasn't eating all of the popcorn.

"You're going to bring some home for your dad, right?" Lucy asked.

"Yeah," I said with a smile. Any time Dad and I went to the cinema, we would always share the popcorn, mainly because it was the cheaper option. When I went to the cinema with my friend, Zoe, in primary school for the first time, I left a handful of popcorn at the bottom of my bag for him and took it home for him. Ever since then, when either of us have gone to the cinema, we've always brought home a handful of popcorn for the other.

"That's so thoughtful of you. I wish I could still do those little things for my dad," Lucy mumbled. Lucy's dad had passed away before she left Willow High. I was there for her during that time. I guess that gave us a special type of bond that we managed to rekindle after everything that happened.

Lucy wasn't the same after her dad died. Her grades began to fail and she would hardly talk. I had to do all the talking when the two of us were together. That wasn't like me. I hadn't experienced someone close to me dying, so I couldn't relate to her. It hurt when I couldn't help her on a personal level except to be there for her. She shut herself off from everyone, even her boyfriend.

"You and your mum share shoes," I attempted to cheer her up. The look Lucy gave me was between confusion and the question of, *are you being serious, Liv?* "It's a special bond."

Lucy smiled. That saved it. Phew. "I guess you're right. There's always one parent that you share a special bond with."

As soon as the trailers stopped, we stopped talking. Anyone who gave people a dirty look for talking during the trailers had a very sad life. From all of the glares Lucy and I got, I concluded that this included the man in the front with his wife. The movie began.

I rolled up the bag as quietly as I could manage and shoved it into my purse. Lucy was intensely watching the film, but I couldn't keep my eyes open. Maybe I was just as sad as the guy in the front, because I had paid for a ticket to be bored.

Eventually, I got into the film. The girl was struggling with friendships, family, and boyfriends— you know, the typical cliché of a teenage coming-of-age film. Then, she began to discuss having sex with her boyfriend.

"It's a natural part of growing up. Like, if you haven't done it by the time you're a certain age, there's something wrong with you," the boyfriend told the main character. The look on her face showed she wasn't sure, and she made an excuse to leave. I began to wonder whose reaction was right.

When the movie finally finished, Lucy and I headed to the bathrooms. As I was drying my hands, Lucy went to the mirror to reapply her pink lipstick. I gazed over at her. She spotted me in the mirror. "You okay?" Lucy asked.

I shrugged. "Just thinking."

Lucy frowned. She knew me too well. When I said "just thinking" it usually meant "I don't know how to talk to people about something."

"Spill it," she coaxed with a smile. I sighed.

"When do you think is the right time to have sex with your boyfriend?" I asked.

Lucy was taken back by my question. To be honest, so was I. I hadn't cared about relationships or sex until recently. I hadn't even kissed a guy until I kissed Gareth on the pier in Llandudno.

"I'm not sure. I guess it depends on how far you are into the relationship and if it's serious," Lucy replied. I didn't make any comment. She hugged me. "Don't worry, though. Don't put pressure on yourself to do it with your boyfriend. They should wait for you. Besides, it isn't all it's cracked up to be. Don't forget about condoms."

I laughed, and we went outside. Lucy began to tell me about her first time. She told me how she had expected something magical, something out of this world. But she didn't get it. It was just sex. Talking about something so intimate with Lucy made me feel like she had never left. I liked having her back. I didn't know who else to talk to about this.

"Lots of people think differently about sex. So, don't think you're weird for not doing it," Lucy reassured me as my dad pulled up. I thanked her and hugged her.

"See you soon," I called as she went to her car.

"You, too!"

Dad smiled at me as I got into the car. I closed the door and strapped myself in. He sped off out of the car park. We chatted about how everyone at home was. Ava was out with Michael again, and Harper and Mum had spent the night admiring Brad Pitt in some movie.

Dad was uncharacteristically quiet for his usual self. When we stopped at lights, he sighed heavily. I looked at him.

181

"Is everything okay?" I asked him.

Dad nodded. "Of course, sweetheart. It's just Mum and I are a bit concerned about how serious you and Gareth are."

Oh, balls. It was time for the sex talk. Please, Gareth hadn't even attempted to slip the hand yet. I didn't know if he ever would, or if I even wanted him to.

"Dad, please," I begged.

"Sorry, sorry," he replied. This was getting awkward. We both knew it.

I flicked on the radio. The radio filled the silence for a while. I wondered if people who presented on the radio ever thought about if anyone was even listening to them as they rattled on about their insight into buying cheap ice cream.

"Anyway, back to the music," the radio announcer said. "Here's one for all you lovers out there."

I inwardly groaned and rolled my eyes. I thought it would be some lovey-dovey song, like a classic "this is how I feel about you" ditty that talks about peanut butter and jam. Instead, we got played a sex song. I immediately switched it off and Dad couldn't stop laughing beside me.

"Seems like everyone is trying to hint something at you," Dad joked.

I stifled a small laugh. "I don't know what you're thinking, but I'm not planning on having sex with Gareth right now. I know you and Mum are trying to look out for me, and I do appreciate that, but I'm not stupid either."

"I know, honey. It's just with Gareth being older than you and being a dad, just like Michael, it's a bit complicated you know?"

I frowned and looked at Dad as we pulled into the driveway of the house. He turned off the ignition. "Michael's a dad?"

"Yeah, his fiancée cheated on him two years ago. He's got joint custody of his son and daughter. They're about five, I think. Twins," Dad told me. Ava never mentioned it. I didn't know why she wouldn't tell me. I just nodded and got out of the car.

Dad told me not to be annoyed at Ava for not telling me. Apparently, she didn't tell Mum either— Ava had given that job to Dad. I got inside, and Mum smiled at me. She was uptight; obviously, news had just broken out. She was sitting and picking the nail polish off her fingers. Harper was half asleep on the sofa watching the Brad Pitt film that she adored— *Mr. and Mrs. Smith.*

"Good time?" Mum asked.

"Yeah. It's nice to see Lucy again. I'm going to get a shower and then head to bed. Big prom dress shopping this weekend."

Mum smiled when I mentioned it. Out of everything she loved about having daughters, dress shopping was her favourite thing to do. She nodded, and I said goodnight to everyone before heading to the shower.

When I got out of the shower, I shut my door and climbed into bed. I grabbed my phone and messaged the two people I needed to.

@OliviaBernard: Ava, Dad's just told me. I understand why you didn't tell me. But I wish you had have told me. I hope you and Michael have a good night if you're staying over. If not, see you soon. Love you loads xx.

@AvaBernard: I'm really sorry for not telling you. You shouldn't have had to hear it from Dad. I'll make it up to you. I promise. Love you too xx.

@OliviaBernard: Hey, I'm home now and snuggled up in bed. So tired! I hope you had a good night with Poppy. Thanks for driving me and thanks for agreeing to take me to prom xx.

@GarethJohnson: Glad you're home safe, beautiful. I'm in bed, too—I swear Poppy takes too much out of me! You're very welcome. I can't wait to see you in your prom dress. Good night, get some beauty sleep— you don't need it and neither do I ;) Love you xx.

I swallowed hard as I read what Gareth had messaged me. It was the two words I'd been dreading since we began our relationship. I didn't know if this was a normal feeling. I didn't know if I loved Gareth. Weren't you supposed to feel something to let you know you were in love?

I sighed. Maybe I did love Gareth. If I didn't, surely I would have ended our relationship by now. Something had to come along to prove that I did love him, right?

@OliviaBernard: Love you, too. See you soon xx.

I guess that means I'm in love.

*

I wasn't sure when I had fallen asleep. I woke to my door opening a crack. My clock told me it was two in the morning. The last time I remembered was half past eleven. The door closed behind the person and they walked over to my bed. I was too tired to care who it was, even if it was a serial killer. Ava smiled up at me as I lifted my head sleepily off the pillow.

"You just get in?" I mumbled.

Ava nodded. "Yeah. Can I bunk with you?"

I pulled back the duvet to tell her that she could. Ava climbed in. She was in her pyjamas, so I assumed Mum and Dad knew she had got in.

Ava cuddled into me, and I wrapped my arms around her. Neither of us said anything. I felt Ava's hand stroke my hair gently like she used to do when I was scared of the thunderstorms when I was little.

"Thanks for your text," Ava said. I smiled in the darkness.

"You're welcome. Did you just find out, or have you known all along?"

Ava stifled a laugh. "I've known from the first day we met. I didn't want to try to be a step-mum. Like, I'm not step-mum material, we need to admit that. When he told me, I didn't speak to him for about a week. You'll think I'm petty for doing that. But hear me out: Michael should have been honest with me from the start. I didn't want to go back to him. But that's the thing about love – you fall for someone and if you do, you accept everything that comes with that person. His kids are so sweet, too."

"Poppy's sweet, too," I told her. "You know, Dad tried to give me a lecture about being careful if I'm having sex with Gareth." Ava snorted. "Same. He tried to tell me to be careful with Michael. That's when I broke the news to him. But, you'll think I'm weird."

"I won't. Tell me," I urged her.

"I don't want to have sex until I'm married. It's old fashioned, I know. But it's what I want. I've told Michael and he's happy for me. He respects my wishes."

Ava drifted off to sleep talking on about Michael. She truly was in love. I knew I wasn't like that with Gareth, not yet anyway. I didn't know if I held the same belief as Ava, either. I was too young to make life-changing decisions like this.

I wanted to be a kid again. As a kid, you don't have to worry about whether you should bring condoms to prom with you. Oh, how cliché, the possibility of losing your virginity on prom night. Well, screw that. I'm not a cliché— I'm just me.

Twenty

Mum and I drove into town. I sighed and laid my head against the window of the car. The neighbourhood became a blur. I looked in the mirror and saw the place I had grown up in get smaller and smaller. I began to wonder what it would be like to leave the place you had known your whole life and never come back. Part of me liked the sound of that.

The radio blared. Mum hummed along to old eighties tracks and gently tapped the steering wheel. I wasn't in the mood to do dress shopping. I begged Ava to come along, because I knew she would stay on my side with any arguments that broke out between Mum and I over dresses. Ava had to work and wouldn't cancel for me.

I switched off the radio and Mum glared at me.

"Why turn it off?" Mum asked.

"Why not?"

Mum switched it back on and ignored my annoyed sighing. This was part of the reason why I wanted to leave. Mum began to talk to me about how Lucy's mum told her that she wasn't going to prom.

"I don't blame her, after what happened," Mum said. I felt my hands clench into fists. I was trying not to get angry. No one likes to yell at their family. I hated it, but I couldn't help it sometimes.

"Good for her," I spat.

Mum looked at me briefly before looking back at the road. "I thought you and Lucy were friends now."

"We are, Mum."

"Oh, I just thought maybe you two weren't, from your sudden, nasty outburst."

I ignored the comment. If I didn't, I would scream. Neither of us spoke again for the rest of the trip to the shopping centre.

When we finally got there, I went straight to the dress shop. Mum tried to keep up with me, eventually yelling at me to slow down. I rolled my eyes and slowed off. She caught up with me as we went into Dress to Impress. The skirts hit you as soon as you went into the shop. There were enough dresses stockpiled that they were practically leaking out from cracks in the walls. For someone who normally never went dress shopping, it was pretty overwhelming.

A woman with a huge grin plastered on her face came over to us. "Can I help you lovely ladies?" she asked in a phony nice voice. Her black pixie haircut had so much spray on it that a white sheen was forming on it.

"We're just looking, thank you," Mum replied. I guess she didn't trust me to answer— to be honest, I didn't trust myself, either.

"Why are you so nice to them?" I whispered to Mum. "They just fake being nice to us so that we'll buy their stuff."

"This is why you'll never work retail."

Mum walked over to the section where they sold prom dresses in my size, fourteen. As Mum looked through all the dresses, I gazed over at the size eight and ten dresses. They were that sizes that Lola, Louise, and Molly would probably be looking at. I shrugged it off. I was determined to show a different, prettier side of me at prom.

"Right, you pick out some," Mum said to me. I nodded and began to look through the dresses. Mum went over to talk to the shop assistant.

I picked out dresses in different colours: blues, reds, yellows, golds, whites, and blacks. The most difficult thing about picking out colours of any clothes is getting it to match my hair. I rarely wore pinks because of the subtle clash of colours.

Mum came over and asked me about the dresses I picked. I showed them to her and she turned her nose up, but said nothing. The shop assistant sent me to a dressing room; that's where I hung up every dress and began trying them on.

I went out to show Mum every dress I tried on like I was modelling in a private fashion show, especially when the shop assistant came along to see how we were both doing. We didn't need anyone helping us. Believe me, Mum could advise the whole shop on what to wear.

"How about this one?" I asked as I came out in a black and white dress. The dress was mainly white with two strips of black down the sides, emphasising my curves.

"No, no, no," the shop assistant said, exasperated.

Mum nodded. "My sentiments exactly." I sighed and looked in the mirror at the end of the room hallway.

"What's wrong with it?"

"What's wrong with it?" the shop assistant repeated. "That dress makes you look fatter."

I glared at her. That was a sore point. Even Mum looked displeased at her comments. I laughed and walked closer in order to see the name on her nametag. "Listen, Julie. You're not exactly a slim girl yourself. I'm proud of my curves. Yes, this dress may make me look even curvier, but not fat. You got it?"

At that, Julie walked out. Mum sighed and gave me a sympathetic smile.

"We can try somewhere else, Liv," she said.

I shook my head. "No, Mum. It's okay. Look, I've got one more dress left to try. If that one doesn't fit, then we will go somewhere else."

Mum nodded in agreement. I went back into the changing room and got into the last dress. As I zipped it up at the back, I grinned in the mirror. This was the one. Out of every dress, this one was my favourite. Before, I had liked a black sparkly one, but because of my pale skin, I looked like death. Most people would say that girls with pale skin are just like Snow White. I disagree; when it comes to my own pale skin, I'm more like Casper.

I walked out of the room and smiled at Mum. Her mouth dropped open. Maybe it was from the shock that finally I didn't look ridiculous in a dress I had picked. Or maybe it was because a dress actually fitted me properly. I was shocked that this dress was perfect.

It had gold sparkles on the torso and the bottom of the dress was a gold, pleated material. The sequins had a fading-out effect halfway down the dress. The top had no sleeves and a V-neck showing the start of my boobs, but thankfully not exposing them altogether. There was a slit from the bottom of the dress up to the knee. I grinned at Mum.

"This is the one," I told her. She got up off the chair she was sitting on and came to study me. She walked around me several times, scrutinising me over and over again.

She nodded. "I think you're right. This is beautiful on you. There is a slight clash with your hair, though. I'm just thankful it's a dark plum colour."

"I can't help my hair, Mum," I said as I went into the dressing room to take it off.

"You shouldn't have dyed it."

"You allowed me to."

With no reply from Mum, I knew I'd won. Maybe it was just my family, but when you had an argument with either Mum or Dad and you got the last word without a response from them, it was confirmation that you had won the argument. I took off the dress and hung it up on the hanger.

Eventually, we left the shop with the dress bag over my arm. Mum made sure I carried it this way, so I didn't ruin it. Ava was going to lend me a pair of her shoes, as we were the same size, and I had already spotted a pair in her wardrobe that I wanted to wear on the night. The price for the dress was 250 pounds, but thanks to Julie being a judgmental bitch, it was now only 200 pounds. I was very grateful, but that didn't mean I was giving the shop a good review on Facebook.

When we got into the car, Mum complained about Julie. "That woman. She shouldn't have talked to you like that. You can bet that I'll be reporting her to her manager in the morning. No one talks to my daughter like that and gets away with it."

When Mum discovered that I wasn't listening one bit, she changed the topic to something she knew I would reply to. She's sneaky that way, my mum.

"Well, are you bringing Gareth to prom?" she questioned.

I looked out of the passenger window and nodded. "Yep."

"Are you staying with him overnight?" Mum asked. Before I could reply, she kept going. "It's just, Sharon told me that she would be out that night on a date with her new man. So, you and Gareth would be on your own."

I was trying not to laugh. I had the worst habit in the world—laughing at times I shouldn't. If I was in the army, I would be made to do enough punishments from laughing at inappropriate times that I would probably die from exhaustion. I coughed to try to decrease my desire to laugh at what my mum was hinting.

"He hasn't said anything to me yet, Mum, so I don't know," I informed her. She nodded and kept her eyes fixed on the road. "What sort of protection would you advise?"

Mum was so shocked by my comment that she almost ran the red light. She slammed on the brakes with so much force that I was almost flown forwards from my seat, the loose-fitting seat belt being my only crutch. Mum looked at me. I was grinning at her. Sometimes, I came out of my shell with my family. I had better days and I had worse days. Today was a better day.

Mum shook her head at me and put the car into first gear, getting ready to drive off when the lights changed to green. Mum couldn't help but laugh, too.

"I swear, you're going to be the death of me, Liv. Please tell me that you're joking," she said concerned. We began to drive off again.

"Of course I'm joking," I told her.

In truth, I didn't know whether or not I was joking. If Gareth wanted me to come to his place after prom, wasn't that the moment where most teenagers lose their virginity? Was I even ready for it? Ugh, I wish I had a virginity angel that could grant me condom-based wishes. Sometimes I hated being a teenager.

*

"Mum told me you almost caused her to run a red," Ava said as she painted her toes on the floor of the living room.

I laughed. "It was just a joke."

"Was it?" Ava asked. Ava could see right through me. I always thought that I would be one of those teenagers in PG movies that would never even mention sex, even when you had a boyfriend. She smirked and pushed her foot up to me. I groaned and blew air on the toenails. Ava grinned. "You know, sometimes I wish I lived a more fascinating life."

"Why?" I asked. It was a bit out of the blue for her to say that.

"I dunno," she admitted with a shrug. "I guess we all want to live more interesting lives, but we're stuck in the small little hell we call our town because we're too lazy to actually go out and change our lives for the better."

"I'm happy with my life. Mostly. Actually, okay, I'm not," I said. Ava laughed. She painted her other toes and threw the other foot up at me.

As I blew on Ava's other foot, she reached behind her and put in a movie. She smirked up at me. "Don't say I don't do anything for you, Liv. And don't say that I don't treat you, either."

"Why?"

Ava sat up beside me with the TV remote. She placed her feet on my knees and pressed play, bringing up *Titanic* on the screen in front of us. We both grinned at each other before Ava snuggled down on the sofa. I laid at the opposite end, causing our feet to be in each other's laps. It felt just like old times again. Only when I was faced with such nostalgia did I realise how much I missed the old times with my family.

I never told anyone, but I secretly lived for moments like these, moments where Ava and I could bond. Growing up, I didn't have many friends. Ava was always my best friend. We shared a room together after Harper came along, and before that, we were inseparable. When I wanted to do my hair in a plait, but my tiny arms couldn't reach the bottom of my hair, Ava would always take over and do it perfectly.

Ava used to be my role model. Part of me still thought she was. But at the same time, I was lost about who I truly was, and I couldn't look up to anyone until I knew *me*.

We watched as the movie proceeded to Southampton. Ava commented about how great it would be to move somewhere else to start a whole new life again. I thought about the same thing almost every day.

Every single day of my life, I had dreamt of moving away and starting over. I think that's why I had wanted to apply for universities that were far away from home. No one would know me there. No one would know what I'd been through. I'd be a whole new Olivia.

My depression and anger issues would all be in the past. Hopefully, the acceptance letters would get closer and closer to arriving at my door. I knew that I needed to decide, but was I prepared to leave everything I knew to start again?

Deep down, I think I knew the answer. I was. I was ready for a new start.

Twenty-One

What an idiot. That's the only word I had for myself at times. I clearly didn't get the "we're not coming into school on the day of prom" memo. Here I was, sitting in Mr. Henderson's classroom, waiting for him to appear. No one else was around. Boy, this was going be an awkward class.

Mr. Henderson walked into the classroom and noticed every single seat was empty, except for mine.

"Lucky you," he announced.

"I can sense your sarcasm," I responded. He laughed and placed his mug of coffee onto the desk. He looked at me and the four rows of desks between the two of us.

"Are you going to move to a closer desk?"

I shook my head and smiled. "I'm okay here, thanks."

Due to the fact that I was leaving at twelve, I didn't see the point in making a huge amount of effort. All of my hair and makeup appointments were in the afternoon, so Mum suggested I go in. To be honest, I think she just wanted to be rid of me for a while.

Mr. Henderson sat down in the row in front of where I was sitting and turned the chair to the side. He handed me a piece of work. I took it and looked down at the words. My words, yet again. I looked at Mr. Henderson. He was smiling at me. I knew there was more behind that smile than he was letting on.

"Read over the words and then we'll discuss it," he said. It was the post I had written while Ava was falling asleep during *Titanic* last week. I couldn't believe he was basically checking up on my blog. There had to be a catch.

I don't think we ever comprehend how alone we are in the world until we put ourselves into perspective. Maybe you had a whole group of friends. At that moment, you think life is wonderful— until you realise you're the one who walks behind the group, and when you need them to wait on you, they walk on and act as if they didn't hear your request. You could have a group of four friends, but you're always the one who gets left out of the conversation. Better still, you always seem to be "forgotten" when others make plans to hang out together. I've been there. I think that's why I've decided to start over again. I'm starting over where no one knows me or knows my name. I may be selfish. But I'd rather start again than be alone in the world where people who act like friends don't actually want me. Maybe that's what we all need to do— start over and live the life we all want to.

It will take guts from me. I'm the type of girl who lives her life in the shadows and waits for the world to move her. But it's now my time

to move the world for myself. It's time I took
life into my own hands. Watch out world, here I
come!

I glanced back up at Mr. Henderson. He was smiling at me. His
arms were crossed over his chest and he took a deep breath.

"Anything you want to tell me about this piece?" Mr. Henderson
asked. I shook my head. "Really?"

He looked at me and tilted his head to the side. He wore a half-
smile and had one eyebrow up. That was when I realised. He knew. Mr.
Henderson had known Blu Skyes was me this whole time. Had he been
taunting me with the first piece when he got our class to read it? Why
would he taunt me? All my life, I've been taunted by people in my family
and people in school. I never thought that he would have been one of
them.

I felt my breathing become harder, and I was blowing my breath
through my nose like an angry bull. My hands balled into fists. I looked
up at him.

"You know, don't you?" I asked. He nodded slowly.

I scrunched up the page and threw it on the floor. I proceeded to
pack my bag up, not caring about how anything went in. I just wanted
out of the place. I wasn't standing for it. Mr. Henderson stood up and
tried to stop me. I grabbed my leaver arch folder.

He stood in front of me so I couldn't leave. He could tell I was
angry. But I couldn't help it this time. I felt screwed over. My life is just
one big ball of screw-ups. I threw the leaver arch folder and my bag on
the floor. Mr. Henderson jumped at the loud thud they made when they
landed. Thankfully, they landed by my feet.

"Liv, calm down!" he told me.

"No! No! I'm tired of this happening to me! Can't I just live a simple life?" I yelled. All I could think about was the fact that Blu Skyes' identity was probably halfway around the school. He probably told every single teacher. Those teachers probably told the pupils. I couldn't escape it. "Everyone will make fun of me now for writing a blog. I'm lonely enough and depressed enough without having the whole school laughing at me over this. Do you realise what you've done by telling people?"

"Liv, I worked it out. No one knows except me," he assured me. But it was too late, I had already overreacted. He took my hands as I began to cry. I couldn't handle being more depressed. He held me as I cried into him. I had been bottling so much up that eventually I was bound to break at some point. I was glad it was this early in the semester and nowhere near my exams.

When I got angry, it felt like everything inside me had reached a boiling point. Right now, I thought my secret had gotten out. I could just imagine the joy the school gossip Facebook account would have with it. I was calming down. I felt my whole body relaxing. Mr. Henderson rubbed my back gently. He probably saw me as an emotional, tired, and angry toddler that needed a nap. I really needed a nap.

"H-How did you work it out?" I stuttered.

He smiled at me. "Your words. I've been in the same position as you in school. I know how you feel. When I read them, you were the first person I thought of. I've been checking out your blog every day. This one post hit me hard."

"I want to start over. When my university offers come in, I need to get away," I explained. He sighed.

"It's not up to me to persuade you. You do have a life here, too. I know you've got a young man now. I'm sure you two are very happy. Are you bringing him to prom tonight?" he questioned. I nodded. "I'm attending prom tonight as one of the chaperone teachers. I'm not really looking forward to seeing a pile of my students drunk, but 'perks of the job', as they say."

I laughed slightly. Mr. Henderson handed me a tissue and I dried my eyes. We both got up, and he picked up my folder and bag for me. I whispered a thank you and put my bag on my back. I wasn't sure how long we had been sitting there for or how long it took him to calm me down, but I was allowed out.

"Your secret is safe with me. Go and enjoy tonight without worrying," he called to me. I turned around at the doorway.

"Thanks, Sir."

*

Have you ever looked in the mirror and saw yourself, but it wasn't you? It was a version of you that you hadn't ever seen before. You touch your hair, and then your face, just to make sure it truly is you. A smile forms on your face. That was how I felt right then and there.

"Stop touching your face, you'll ruin your makeup!" Ava warned me.

My plum hair was curled and pinned up on the back of my head. Mum helped me to step into my dress. She zipped it up the back for me, too. She got me to turn around as I stood in Ava's silver high heels and the dress. Mum smiled at me.

"Perfect!" Ava exclaimed. Mum nodded in agreement.

The doorbell rang downstairs, and Mum ran to answer it. I grabbed my clutch bag. Ava helped me to walk down our stairs. I felt like I could conquer the world. It's amazing what a bit of makeup can do for a non-popular girl like me.

I took a deep breath. I could hear Dad, Harper, and Mum talking with Gareth in the living room. Mum had brought down my overnight bag. I was staying at Sharon's house after the prom. I was nervous, but right then, I was more nervous about Gareth seeing me. Even though we were together, I still felt like I needed to impress him.

Ava looked at me as we reached the bottom of the stairs. She grinned and hugged me before we walked into the living room.

For all of my life, I wanted to meet someone who would look at me the way that I look at pizza or pasta— that loving look in their eyes and that warm smile on their face that turned into a grin. That was what I had wanted. As I looked at Gareth's reaction when I walked into the living room, I knew then that I had found that person. His head shot up when he spotted me walking in. He looked me up and down, taking me all in. His mouth was slightly agape. He was speechless. Instead of saying anything, he put the corsage he'd bought me on my wrist. It was a white rose— my favourite. He had remembered. I smiled and thanked him. He leant down and pecked my lips gently.

"Y-You look amazing," he finally said.

"Thanks," I responded.

"Photos!" Mum announced. Dad ran to get the camera. After posing for what felt like a hundred photos, we made our way to Gareth's car. He put my bag into the back of his car and helped me into the front seat like the gentleman he was.

Mum and Dad waved at us as we drove off. Gareth waved back. Finally, we were on our way to the prom.

"What?" I asked noticing he kept glancing in my direction.

Gareth chuckled. "I just can't get over how beautiful you look tonight. I knew you would look beautiful, but you've truly just blown my mind. You're so amazing. Thank you for being mine. I mean, you really exceeded my expectations."

I smiled. Gareth reached from the gear stick to my hand. I held his hand and sat forward slightly so the headrest didn't ruin my hair. Gareth gently rubbed his thumb in circles on the back of my hand.

When he stopped at a red light, he leant over and kissed me passionately. I smiled against his lips and kissed back. Gareth gently placed a hand on the back of my neck to pull me closer to him. I desired to move closer to him, but I couldn't. The damn gear stick and handbrake were in the way.

A horn blasted behind us and we both jumped.

"Bugger," Gareth said. He attempted to put the car into gear and take off, but we stalled the car. I burst out laughing. The horns were blasting like mad. Gareth kept swearing, trying to start the car off. Finally, we drove off.

Gareth and I couldn't contain our laughter. The cars behind us overtook us and gave Gareth the finger in the process. I leant my head on Gareth's shoulder. He stifled a laugh again and placed his hand on my thigh.

"The stupid gearstick," I told him.

"The stupid traffic lights," he retorted with a smirk on his face.

We smiled at each other. I knew that no matter how crap prom might go for me, I wanted to be there with Gareth. No one else. He made everything that little bit happier no matter what I was feeling like.

We finally arrived, and Gareth parked his car into the hotel carpark. He took my hand and helped me out of the car. I was never ladylike, and I half expected that I would stand on my dress, rip the material and have my blue knickers on full display. They weren't even the nice knickers that girls my age wear. Aw, well, at least it didn't happen, and Gareth didn't have to see my granny knickers. For that, we are all eternally grateful. We made our way slowly across the gravel carpark. I leant on Gareth for most of it, as I couldn't walk well in heels.

We walked in, hand in hand. As soon as we stepped into the conference room that held the prom, we were amazed at the glitz and glamour of the place. Everything seemed to sparkle, and it was clear who had headed the prom committee. Lola came bouncing over to us and, with the wonder bra she had on, it was dangerous for her eyes. I didn't know how to help someone with a black eye!

I looked, out of curiosity, to see if Gareth was looking at her breasts, as most men do. But he wasn't. He was looking around the place and didn't even seem to notice that Lola had come over to us.

Lola's dress was stunning. It was black and had sparkles all over, just like the whole conference room— sparkles galore! Her hair was down in long angel curls. Her face was more made-up than usual, with grey smoky eyes and bright red lipstick. She smiled at us. For once, it wasn't a malicious smile.

"Welcome to prom! As Head of Prom Committee, I wanted to be the first to welcome you two and show you both to your table," Lola announced. We just smiled at her. "Photos will be taken just before dinner and you will be called according to surname... Have we met before?" I looked at Gareth. Gareth shook his head, but smiled uneasily. "I don't think so. Maybe through friends of friends, but I don't remember you. Sorry."

Lola shrugged. "My mistake, then. Anyway! Come right this way." Gareth took my hand, and we followed Lola to our tables. To my surprise, she had seated us at a table with Louise and Molly. Molly had brought her policeman boyfriend and Louise had brought Willie, or Stiffy. Gareth introduced himself to everyone.

Louise soon attached herself to Stiffy's mouth again. From the state of her lipstick, I could tell that it had already been a regular occurrence. Molly began to flirt and play "touchy-feely" with her man. I looked at Gareth, who gave me the most awkward face that had ever come into existence. Both of us hated the awkwardness of the couples at our table.

I stifled a laugh and Gareth kissed the top of my head. It almost felt like Gareth and I were third wheeling at a swingers' party— just observing and not taking part. I half expected someone to put their house keys on the table and pick up another person's.

Soon enough, more people arrived in a cloud of alcohol that could seemingly be only cleared with more alcohol. The smell made my eyes water. Even Gareth had to blink a few times. I wasn't judgmental— I just had opinions on people. That was my excuse, anyway.

Before we were called for our photos, Gareth went to the bathroom. The other guys went to the bar. Molly smirked at me.

"So Liv, you going to have a bit of fun later tonight?" Molly asked.

"What do you mean?" I asked confused.

Louise smirked at me too. "He's all over you. He's totally giving you the sex signals."

"Sex signals?"

Louise tried to explain to me what sex signals were, but I blanked her out.

"He'll touch your back, keep touching your arm – simple things like that."

I wasn't even paying attention to her ramblings anymore. When we got our photos done, Gareth placed his hand around my waist. We got one where he was holding me close and we were facing each other. I couldn't stop thinking about Louise's "sex signals" comment. When I looked into his eyes, I could only see love. Maybe I was too naïve to see the sex, if it was even there.

Eventually, dinner was over. Believe me, the food was amazing! The hot chocolate fudge cake was heaven in your mouth and melted into the sauce on your tongue. I don't think I've ever had a chicken salad as tasty as that, either. I would gladly go home right at that moment, but I decided to stay a while. I cuddled into Gareth and he wrapped an arm around me. It's fascinating how simple things like a prom can bring people together again. Molly, Louise, and I were getting along like we hadn't ever fought one bit. The three guys were getting on well, too.

Louise was just as tipsy as she ever was. Have you ever been in a situation where you weren't drinking, but the alcoholic fumes in the air were so strong that you could have gotten tipsy on them? Yeah, that was me right at that moment.

"Remember when we had that full-on cat fight and Mr. Henderson had to pull us apart?" Louise asked. She had a glass of wine in her hand, threatening to spill it at any moment. She took a sip of it.

"Yeah, good times," I responded. Molly smiled at me. We were both humouring Louise until she either passed out or until someone came to pick her up from prom.

After Mrs. Turner gave her speech— which resulted in more people running to the bar— all the teachers were making their way to the door of the room. Louise spotted Mr. Henderson.

"Ah!" she squealed. "Just the man we were talking about." He laughed and came over to our table. "Having a good evening?"

"The best, we're having the absolute best time, Sir," Louise said, almost crying.

He shook his head and looked at Molly and I. "You must be Gareth?" he asked. Gareth nodded and shook his hand. "Nice to meet you."

Molly introduced him to her boyfriend. Louise was crying into Stiffy's shoulder. She was an emotional drunk, if that wasn't obvious by now.

Gareth looked at me. "Fancy a dance?" He asked.

I gazed at the dance floor. Couples were dancing with their arms around each other. I knew Stiffy wouldn't risk taking Louise over there in case he had to carry her back to the table. Before I had met Gareth, I never got up to dance because I never had anyone to dance with.

"Of course," I told him. He stood and took my hand. I was aware people were staring and probably wondering how someone like me could ever have a boyfriend. But I didn't give a crap at that moment. I wanted to be dancing to Ed Sheeran in Gareth's arms.

Gareth pulled me closer to him. I smiled and laid my head on his shoulder as we danced. He kissed my head every so often, bringing an illuminating smile to my face. My mind brought me back to when we were dancing in the pouring rain. Neither of us cared then, and we didn't care now.

I felt Gareth's hand pull me gently closer to him even more. I looked up at him.

"You okay?" he asked.

"I am now that I'm with you," I replied without even thinking. A smile formed on Gareth's face. In the dim light, I could see the black stubble beginning to form again on his face. He leant down and kissed me. His lips were slightly parched, but that didn't stop us. I placed my hand on the back of his neck.

Eyes were probably bulging at the fact two people would be practically making out on the dance floor. When you're in love, you don't care about things like that. Love. I was in love? I was in love with Gareth? I wasn't ashamed of it.

"I love you," I told him. Our foreheads were pressed together, and we just looked down at each other's lips. Everything around us was a blur. Gravity pushed our lips together. We kissed again, but slowly, passionately.

"I love you, too, Liv. My gosh, do I love you," he admitted when we pulled apart. I smiled at him.

Molly came over to us to tell us that a drunken Louise was leaving with Stiffy. I went over, and Gareth followed close behind me. Louise had mascara running down her face. She hugged me tightly. I was almost knocked off my feet. She hugged Molly, too. I began to wonder whether she would remember the night or not, but that wasn't my issue to deal with.

Lola came over after Louise had been helped out of the room. "The minibuses are here to take us to the nightclub," Lola told us all. Molly and her man went to the bus. I walked over to the table to grab my clutch bag.

I looked at Gareth. "Do you want to go to the nightclub?"

"It's your call. To be honest, I'm not too fussed."

I took his hand and smiled at him. "Let's go back to your place."

Gareth took my hand and we went out to his car. I knew this night could make or break us. But, like a game of chess, you don't know how it's going to turn out until you see how the other person moves their pieces.

At that point, I felt it was checkmate.

Twenty-Two

Sharon had left Gareth a note when we got to the kitchen. She was out on a date tonight and wouldn't be back until late— just as Mum had predicted. Gareth smiled and looked at me.

"Want anything to drink?" he asked. I shook my head. It was already two o'clock in the morning, and to be honest, I needed to sleep desperately. Gareth could even tell seeing as I kept yawning audibly.

"Let's get you up to bed," he told me. I yawned at that moment, as if confirming what Gareth had already suspected. He chuckled and took my hand.

I didn't get to go into Gareth's room at first. We went to the bathroom, as I wanted to wash the hairspray out of my hair. Embarrassingly enough, I needed Gareth's help to take out the bobby pins, as well.

While I washed myself in the shower, I kept thinking about Gareth and his room. I think that a bedroom can tell a lot about a person. Someone you know quite well could show you their room, and you'd learn a whole different side to them.

When I was dressed in my pyjamas, I wrapped my hair up in a bun and went into the room. Gareth had hung up my dress for me. He smiled from his bed. That smile would be one thing I would always want to remember about Gareth. I put my bag on the floor, near my dress hanging up on his wardrobe.

I took that opportunity to take a quick glance at his room. His walls were pale blue, and all of his furniture was pine. In the corner was a crib. It was pink and filled with various blankets and stuffed toys. I walked over to his bed. He smiled and pulled back the duvet for me. I curled up beside him. My arm instinctively went around his torso. He had on the same pyjamas he wore at Llandudno. Don't worry, he washed them.

Gareth began to rub my side as I laid in his arms. My head was rested on his shoulder. I looked at him and sat up on my side slightly. I leant down and kissed him. He kissed me back hungrily. I pulled myself closer to him, and he kept me there with his arms securely around my back.

I pulled away quickly. "I don't want to have sex, yet!" I yelled. Gareth jumped in shock. His eyes bulged at me. Out of fear, I closed my eyes tightly.

When I opened my eyes, I saw Gareth desperately trying to hold back a laugh. He sniggered, then coughed to try to cover it up.

"You do know that I wasn't going to suggest it?" Gareth asked me.

I bit my lip and looked down at the duvet. I was embarrassed. In fact, I had been less embarrassed when I had wet myself at school when I was six. Gareth sat up beside me on the bed and rubbed my back gently.

I smiled and laid my head on his shoulder. He began to chuckle again.

"What?" I asked without looking at him.

"You should so put that in your blog," he replied with a laugh. I shoved him playfully.

"Sod off!" I snapped. He laughed and pecked my lips.

We laid down again, and Gareth pulled the duvet over us. It was three in the morning. I yawned. Gareth kissed my head.

He eventually dozed off. I couldn't sleep. Part of me was slightly disappointed that I didn't want to go further. Wasn't it a huge deal to actually lose your virginity? At least, some people thought it was (by some, I meant Lola).

Had I missed out on something? As I looked at Gareth's face while he slept, I smiled to myself, because right there was the one person who had changed my life. I was blessed, and I was happy. Gareth made me happy.

Twenty-Three

If these were the last words I was to write, I would be happy. I'd be so happy. In fact, that's all I'm feeling right now. Depression can suck at times. It can feel like you're so alone and lost in the world, in your own mind. But somehow along the way, you can find a piece of happiness. He is my happiness.

Prom was last week, and I'm still reeling from it. My heart could burst with hope and joy. At the tender age of eighteen, I think I've finally found someone I want to be with for the rest of my life. I'm pathetic, I know, but he makes me happy. I love him. People of the internet, I love him.

I smiled as I closed down my laptop screen. I was in the coffee shop in the library. It was Saturday, and I was happy. My family couldn't believe the change in me. To be honest, I couldn't either.

Ava and I talked about prom night. I had the balls to tell her about my embarrassing moment. She laughed at me— as Ava would— and told me that Gareth's reaction was a good sign. Maybe I was crazy, but I felt tipsy on love. Gareth just made me so full of joy and contentment. I didn't think he would ever leave me. At least, I hoped he wouldn't leave me.

I picked up an iced smoothie I had got in the café. I had just uploaded the post to my blog page. My phone buzzed as I was packing up. My face paled as I read it walking to my car.

"No, no," I mumbled to myself. I found myself sprinting to the car and reading the text at the same time.

@AvaBernard: Liv, don't mean to alarm you, but Mum and Dad are on the warpath for you. Letters just came with your names on them. They haven't opened them, but they have writing on the front—Ava xx

When I got home, my heart was in my throat. I couldn't swallow properly, and I felt like I couldn't breathe properly, either. Mum and Dad had gotten to the post before I had. I had packed up early from the library, hoping that I would get home as the post arrived. I was wrong.

Many people couldn't see why my parents would be so angry. I knew they would be. I hadn't applied for Oxford like I told them I had. I had applied for Bangor University along with other ones in the U.K. All their acceptance or rejection letters were arriving around the same day— today. Mum would flip more than Dad would, but that was okay, I was used to it.

I sat in my car with the engine turned off. I looked at the house and could almost see the anger oozing from it. I was glad Ava had warned me, but I didn't think anything would change their reaction. Finally, I managed to urge myself to get out of the car. My hands were shaking as I grabbed my bag from the back and locked up.

With every footstep I took, I felt as though I was on a death march. I didn't want to go inside. I didn't. But I had to. When I closed the front door, Mum marched out to me and skidded to a halt, arms by her side and hands in fists.

"Kitchen, now," she spat.

I nodded, trying to radiate with confidence to block out most of Mum's anger rays. On the kitchen table were all my letters. They had opened them in the space of time between Ava's message and me getting home. Dad didn't even look near me.

"Sit down." I could hear the disappointment in his voice. It felt like a knife to my chest. I had always been a disappointment to my mum— middle child struggles and all that— but I hadn't ever been a disappointment to my dad.

I sat down. I placed my bag on the chair beside me, so no one damaged my laptop. My car keys were placed gently on the table in front of me. Mum sat beside Dad. Finally, they both looked at me.

"Explain what this is," she said. She showed me an acceptance letter from Bangor University. I took it from her and smiled.

"I got in. Shouldn't you be happy?" I asked.

Mum scoffed. "Happy? You aren't even aiming for the top chart universities."

"You think I want to go to Oxford?"

"Is this because you're scared that you might not get it?" Mum asked me, concerned. "I just know they'll let you in once that letter comes in."

"We aren't getting a letter, Mum! I didn't apply!"

Mum's face shattered, probably along with her heart. I sighed and picked up all the acceptance letters. Most parents would be proud at all of the universities I got accepted into. Not mine.

Mum couldn't even speak. Dad rubbed her hand sympathetically.

"You went for an interview," Dad stated.

Have you ever tangled yourself so far up in your whole web of lies that you couldn't find even a tiny loophole to escape out of it? Well, I had. It was that moment. I had no more loopholes left to get out of. Everything was tangled. My brain felt like the scribble I made back when

Mr. Henderson discovered my anger issues. I was getting angry, but then the anger faded. I felt guilty.

"I lied," I stated back to Dad. "I didn't attend an interview." From the look on both of my parents' faces, neither of them had expected that.

"Where were you?" Mum asked. "Gareth took you to Cardiff, and he said on the way back, he was taking you to Oxford for an interview."

"He took me to Wales. He took me to a place that I fell in love with. That's why I applied for Bangor. They have the course I've always dreamed about, and there's this amazing town close to it that has all of these amazing places. I can travel by train to university every day. It's what makes me happy." I told them. I didn't know where I had gotten the balls to speak like this, but I had found them, and I wasn't letting go of them. Not yet. Not now.

"So it was Gareth who did all of this, Bill," Mum said. She put her head in her hands and shook her head. "And to think I thought he would be good for her. Look at what he's done now. Ruined our daughter's future and filling her head with lies!"

I stood up and glared at the two of them.

"Don't you dare," I spat. I was angry. "He made me realise that there was more to life than what you dreamt out of me."

"You've always wanted Oxford!" Mum yelled.

"Because you kept hammering in the fact that I always wanted Oxford!" I yelled. Ava and Harper were standing at the door. I held my acceptance letters so tight in my hand that they began to crumple. "It was always you. And I love Gareth!"

"He's ruined your life!" Mum yelled. I shoved the empty envelopes off the table in one quick sweep of my hand. Everyone jumped.

"He showed me the life I should have! The life without the pressure of matching up to the perfections of my sisters, without living up to your expectations, and without ever apologising for having a dream of my own," I told them firmly.

Mum stood up on the other side of the table. The two of us locked eyes. Mum's hard orbs bore into mine. Finally, they softened.

"You're not to see him again, understood?" Mum asked.

"I agree," Dad said. Ava gasped from the doorway. Her shock was exactly how I felt in that moment. How could they do this to me?

I looked between Mum and Dad, as if watching a tennis game. I wish I had been. I expected this from Mum, but not Dad. Not Dad.

"Dad?" I whimpered.

"No, Olivia," Dad said, raising his voice at me.

I grabbed my car keys and ran out of the house. I could hear everyone shouting after me, but I didn't care.

I locked the car once I got inside. I threw the acceptance letters on to the passenger seat and started up the engine. Dad came running out to me, but I sped off before he got near the car. Tears rolled down my cheeks.

I didn't know much about love. At eighteen, I hadn't dated anyone or even had my first kiss until Gareth came along. I wasn't prepared to give up all of that just because my parents thought I had made the wrong choice about university. My phone kept buzzing on the console as I drove. I didn't look at it— I wasn't stupid enough to lift my phone while driving. Also, it would probably be my family.

Luckily enough, I remembered Sharon's address. I pulled up at the house and ran to the door. I didn't even have the sense to see if Gareth's car was there. My hand kept hitting the doorbell. The sound vibrated outside. My mind felt elsewhere, as I didn't even realise Sharon had opened the door until she took my hand off the bell. I looked up at her. Tears were streaming down my face, and I sniffed before I spoke.

"I-Is Gareth in? I need to see him," I breathed out. I found myself walking inside as I spoke. Sharon took my arm gently.

"What's wrong?" she asked me.

"I just need to see him, please," I begged.

Sharon nodded. "That's okay, sweetheart. Before you go into the living room, you need to hold on a minute. I have to explain something to you."

"As much as I like you, I don't have time to listen to explanations."

I pulled away from Sharon's soft grasp and stormed into the living room.

"Gareth, I need to talk to—"

My speech stopped. I couldn't move my lips, but my eyes had no problem moving. I didn't know whether what I was seeing was a dream or if it was real. Gareth was sitting on one sofa. Across from him sat Poppy and Lucy Felix.

"Liv, I can explain," Gareth said. I looked at him, waiting. "Lucy is Poppy's mum."

Twenty-Four

I began to back out of the living room. Everything was blurred. I couldn't hear anything except for my erratic breathing. When I got outside, it was starting to rain. The rain was pouring down, but I didn't care; it didn't even register with me.

Someone grabbed my arm. I twirled around to see Gareth. He sighed. Rain was pouring down his face and droplets were slowly trickling off his nose. I could feel the rain hitting me, but I didn't care.

"Don't walk away, please. I'm sorry I didn't tell you. How did you expect me to tell you something like that?" Gareth asked. He sighed and let go of my arm. "You'd think I was using you or something."

"Were you?" I whispered.

I was hoping Gareth hadn't heard me over the rain, but he had. "Was I what?"

"Using me?" I asked. His mouth formed words, but no sound came out. "All those times you asked me about what happened to me last year, you already knew. You came to my school open night, and I had hoped you were going to see me. Then you convinced me out of Oxford, which my parents now hate me for! Was that all for her?" I found myself yelling every single word.

"N-Not all of it."

I scoffed and walked off to my car. I opened the door. Gareth put his arm in front of the door to stop me getting in.

"I'm sorry. I love you!" Gareth begged me. "You know I love you. Yes, I admit it, I should have told you about this, but I didn't want you to find out this way."

I couldn't look at him. If I looked at him, I would fall for him all over again. The rain couldn't wash away my pain this time.

"You can't expect me to love you when you hid something like this from me," I told him.

"I wasn't the only one," Gareth informed me.

My head shot up as soon as Gareth said that. There were streams of water over his cheeks. I couldn't tell if he was crying or if it was just the torrential rain.

"Who else knew?" I asked.

He sighed and stepped away from my car. He ran a hand through his hair and looked at me. "Your parents. Molly. Louise. Lucy— you can't just be angry with me."

Have you ever felt like your whole world had collapsed in around you? At that moment, I did. I got into my car and slammed the door shut, locking it yet again. I turned on the engine and put my seatbelt in.

Out of the corner of my eye, I could see Gareth's pleading face staring at me through the window. Sharon and Lucy were at the front door, calling my name, too. But they were all muted because the sound of my heart breaking into a thousand pieces was loud enough. I drove away from them.

All I could hear was my heart beating in my ears. Everything Gareth and I had been through came back to me in my head: Llandudno, our first kiss, our dance in the rain. I stopped at a red light and looked at the rain before my window wiper washed it away. The last time Gareth and I were caught up in rain was when we fell in love. I wanted to scream and cry even more, but I was numb. Every ounce of strength in me was needed to drive the car again when the light changed to green.

As I approached the house, Dad was looking out the window. He pulled away from the curtains when he saw me. I turned the car off and threw my head back against the headrest. I slammed my hands against the steering wheel.

"I love you so much, Olivia. Rubbish!" I spat before getting out of the car.

I walked inside, and Dad kept asking me where I'd been. I couldn't speak to him. He knew. He knew, and he didn't tell me. Aren't parents supposed to be the ones to protect you from everything? Why didn't they warn me? I wouldn't have minded if I had have known before now, before months of dating him!

As if by instinct, I grabbed a suitcase and a backpack. My parents had left my bag with my laptop on the bed. Dad ran up as I began to fill my suitcase with all the essentials.

"What are you doing, Liv? We're sorry for what we said. Don't leave," Dad pleaded. I zipped up my backpack and suitcase before glaring at him. He could tell how angry I was. My whole body felt like it was shaking. If I ground my teeth any harder together, I'd have none left.

"I'm leaving," I stated, grabbing my laptop and phone charger. My phone was still mindlessly buzzing. I didn't dare look at it this time either. Instead, I shoved it straight into my bag with my laptop.

"Why?"

I laughed sarcastically. "You seriously asking me that when you have all damn well lied to me?"

"No one has lied to you."

"I know that you have been lying to me!" I screamed. I pulled my suitcase onto the floor with a thud. I pulled up the handle.

"About what?"

"Gareth and Lucy!"

Dad stayed silent for a while. He let out a loud sigh and ran a hand over his bald head. He pushed his glasses onto his head and rubbed his eyes. When he refused to say anything, I pushed past him with all of my things. Dad came speeding down the stairs after me.

"We were all just trying to look out for you," Dad said.

"Well, you can tell them I'm leaving again. I'll return when my whole family stops keeping secrets from me!"

Dad shook his head. "Your sisters had no idea about this. Just your Mum and I."

"Is that meant to make me feel better?"

"You know what?" Dad asked. "You seem to harbour this deep anger and resentment against anyone who has ever been there for you!"

I scoffed. "You lied to me! All of you knew, even Lucy, Louise and Molly knew. How long was I being laughed at by people in my own town?"

"We were just trying to protect you."

"Protect me?" I yelled. It was as if he just swore at me. "Is that what you and Mum were trying to do when I was diagnosed with depression? When you both told me all the feelings I had would go away, I believed you! Guess what, Dad? They still haven't gone. I'm still bloody well depressed!"

Dad looked hurt. Sometimes I didn't have a filter on my mouth. I wished I had a filter, especially at moments like this. But I couldn't act like things were all okay. The whole atmosphere had changed. It felt like I was drowning and couldn't breathe.

"I-I thought Gareth was making you happy Liv," Dad mumbled. He couldn't even look at me. It sounded like he was in tears. I hadn't seen my dad cry, and I didn't ever want to.

"He was making me happy," I told him. "But that doesn't mean that my depression just disappeared. Just because one person makes me smile and makes me happy doesn't mean that my mental illness is gone. You need to understand that."

I dragged my suitcase over to the front door, my bags over both of my shoulders and my car keys in hand.

"Where are you going?" he asked.

It was my turn not to look at him now. "I need a break. I'll be back when I'm ready."

I didn't wait for a response. If I waited and he pleaded for me not to go, then I knew in my heart that I would stay. I needed to get away. I needed to be away from here so badly. As I drove off again, I knew how Lucy felt when everything in her life went wrong and everyone was talking about her. She just wanted to escape the town. I couldn't blame her, because it was now my turn to do the same. I needed to go somewhere that no one would every expect to find me.

*

"What are you doing here?" Michael asked me. I pulled my suitcase in past him. My bag hit him.

"Sorry," I mumbled. He closed the door.

"Don't be. It's okay. Why are you here, Liv?" he asked me again.

I dropped my bags and let go of my suitcase. I broke down on the floor crying. I began to scream through the tears. I couldn't control the pain any longer. Michael ran to me and held me. I laid in his arms and screamed into his chest. He kept trying to calm me, as if I was his child.

"Shhh, come on now," he whispered as he rocked me gently. I could feel my whole body jerking up and down as I cried.

Why did I run to Michael? Because it was the one place out of town that I knew I could still see Ava. It was the one place I knew I could count on to feel welcomed. He rubbed my back and pulled me closer. Nothing was helping, despite how much Michael was trying to help me. I wanted to forget about Gareth, but how do you forget about so much of who you have become?

Nothing made sense. Nothing. Michael heard my phone buzzing and handed me it. I looked at the screen as I continued to sob.

Page: @Willow High Gossip has just mentioned you on their wall post.

@LouiseKillen: Olivia, I've just spotted the gossip page. I'm so sorry. Message Molly and me soon.

@GarethJohnson: Please reply to me. Don't give up on us. I'm sorry.

I grabbed the phone off Michael and flung it down the hallway. Michael didn't ask. He just kept holding me and trying to calm me down. I didn't even know someone could feel this broken. If love destroys us this much, then why do we keep falling in it? Why?

Michael made the two of us some dinner. It was pasta with grated cheese and some tomato sauce over it. I poked the pasta shells with my fork. Michael spotted me.

"Enjoying your dinner?" Michael asked. I glared at him.

"No.

He chuckled. "You're the one who caused me to overcook the pasta."

I couldn't believe him. I put the bowl down on the coffee table.

He was smirking at me as he ate some pasta. I squinted at him.

"What?"

Michael sighed and set down the bowl on the coffee table, too. He looked at me. He wanted to say something but didn't. He ran a hand through his short hair. It reminded me of how my dad runs his hand through his hair. Well, his non-existent hair.

"Don't you think that you kind of…"

"Kind of what?" I replied, enraged.

"Kind of think you deserve a bit better than everyone else?" Michael questioned. I was a shy type of girl who didn't say a single word to most people, but at times thrived on the thrill of making my opinion heard. There were very few times that I could actually be made speechless. This was one of them.

"What the actual…" I trailed off. "Explain."

Michael sighed. I was making him feel awkward. The inane wringing of the hands and tapping of the feet on the wooden floor was enough to drive even someone without anger issues mad. "You think you deserved not to be lied to. Everyone is lied to. I was. My wife was having numerous affairs behind my back. Everyone in life is lied to. You're nothing special to think that you shouldn't receive that. No one deserves it, but everyone receives it whether we like it or not. And let's not forget, you lied to Gareth too."

"How?"

"Ava told me."

That shut me up. My anger. I sniffed and wiped away a few tears that had fallen. I stood up and picked up my bowl.

"You know, I'm not quite hungry anymore. Thanks for dinner," I mumbled. Michael called me back, but I took my bowl to the kitchen. I left it on the worktop and went upstairs to the spare room.

Michael came up a few minutes later with my suitcase. I couldn't manage to carry it upstairs with my measly, weak arms. I smiled slightly.

"Thanks."

Michael sighed and put his hands on his hips. "Now, I'm allowing you to stay off school tomorrow. It's a Monday. We all hate Mondays. I'm off work for a *completely different* reason. I know you brought your school uniform with you, as it's sticking out of your extremely badly packed suitcase. But tomorrow is a chill day. And heck, who knows, we might have some brother-in-law, sister-in-law bonding."

"You're asking Ava to marry you?"

Michael began to walk towards the door. "I've bought the ring, but who knows when I'll do it. Now, if you are actually hungry soon, come down and I'll make you frozen pizza."

"Always the chef."

"You know it!"

With that, Michael left the room. I sat on the bed with my laptop on my thighs and my legs spread across the bed, enjoying the comfort of an oversized bed in a spare room. I didn't dare to look at my phone, which surprisingly still worked after being battered against a wall.

Deep down, I knew Michael was right. I had treated Gareth the exact same way he had treated me. Admittedly, maybe not just as bad as he did to me, but pretty close. Any sensible person would message him and apologise and admit their own fault. What did I do? Well, being the selfish person that I could be, I did nothing.

Twenty-Five

I have so many regrets. Not just because of people who have come and gone through this life, but because of how I have treated them. If you lie to someone, why on earth should you hate that person for lying to you? Tit for tat *never* wins. People have passed through my life, and those who have either haven't given a flying stuff about me, or we had a fall out that we never made up from. Is it worth it? No. But that doesn't mean I can forgive someone and act like nothing happened. I'm not that type of person. I'm sorry that I'm not.

I smiled slightly and hit post on the blog. I had made peace with what had happened between me and Gareth, but Ava was worried about me. To Ava, my behaviour wasn't normal compared to how others would react in my situation. Talking things through with Michael had helped me. I tried to tell her that, but Ava was stubborn. She was smart, too.

More than anything, I was learning to accept what had happened. But I hadn't moved on, I truly hadn't. In my heart, I was still waiting for Gareth to stand outside Michael's house throwing rocks at the window and screaming "I'm in love with you. Forgive me. Please." But that's the kind of thing that happen in movies, not in real life.

Ava looked at me as I closed down the laptop screen. She was cuddled on the sofa with Michael, mindlessly stroking his chest. It was clear that those two were in love. I wondered if Gareth and I had looked so in love to the people around us.

"What's wrong?" I asked.

"Nothing. Don't worry about me," Ava told me. "I'm more worried about you."

I had to resist the overwhelming urge to roll my eyes. Ava meant well, and I knew that. But sometimes it was too much for me.

"I'm fine. I've told you that. Michael has told you that, too," I reminded her. Michael shrugged, as if to say, "keep me out of it."

I sighed and got up. I needed a drink of water. As I went to the kitchen, my phone buzzed. It was a notification from my blog. While it probably sounded pathetic, the blog made me happy in times like this. I could vent my anger and frustration without affecting others— it was my outlet.

"Hey," I heard Ava say. I turned as she walked over to me. "I know that Gareth is half out of your life now. But you're going to meet someone who will be amazing to you."

Ava patted my shoulder, like a puppy dog, before walking back to the living room. I understood that she was worried about me. But I just wanted everyone to leave me alone. I put my phone in my pocket as I heard the doorbell ring. Michael called that he would get it.

"Okay," I replied back. I decided to do the dishes, humming to myself as I put the plates into the drying rack.

"At least your sister was right," a male voice said. I turned around and saw Mr. Henderson.

"Oh, crap."

He smirked. "I'll take a coffee while you're making one."

I dried my hands and began to make a coffee for him. He sat down at the kitchen table. I knew why he was here. I was supposed to be in school two days ago. I didn't go. When Michael tried to persuade me, I blanked him out. Needless to say, he gave up in the end.

I sat down the coffee. Mr. Henderson smiled at me and indicated for me to sit down. I didn't exactly want to, but I did.

"So, you've been avoiding school," Mr. Henderson stated.

I nodded and looked at the time on the cooker. "And so are you. How ironic."

"Why have you been avoiding me since formal? You were happy at prom and—"

"And things change. If that's all you came here to ask me about, then you can go and sod off," I spat. I wasn't in the mood to bring up the fact that the whole school was probably laughing at me right that very second.

Mr. Henderson sighed and shook his head. He took out his phone and showed me the gossip page for the school. The latest post was about me and Gareth. I swallowed hard and sighed.

"Look, I don't care," I lied.

He stifled a laugh, knowing I was lying. "I know you well enough now. You can't allow this to set you back. I take it you're not speaking to Gareth right now?"

"No," I admitted. "He broke my heart. How do I know what he said to me was true or not?"

Mr. Henderson ran his hands through his hair. "I don't know. But I do know he loves you very much."

I didn't reply.

"Seeing as you're not in the mood for talking, I suppose this would be the time to tell you that we caught the person who started the gossip page. The staff are going to confront them tomorrow. You can put in your guesses for who it is. But I can assure you, you won't guess it right. I didn't."

"You take bets on which students get into trouble?" I questioned.

Mr. Henderson smirked and then shrugged. "It makes my job a little bit more interesting. But you'll see what I mean tomorrow when we announce it in assembly."

I knew he was trying to persuade me to go into school, but all that my mind could think about was Gareth. I needed to move on. I just didn't know how.

Ava came in at that moment. I excused myself from everyone and left the room. I knew what I needed to do, but I couldn't do it. How could you seriously forgive someone for not telling you who gave birth to their daughter? I didn't care that Lucy was Poppy's mum. I just wished Gareth would have told me the truth from the start. None of it would have mattered because I loved him. I knew it now. I knew it was too late, though.

I sat on the bed in the spare room and stared at the four walls. I didn't know what to do. It was a battle between my head and my heart. Boy, did I sound philosophical. No one ever prepared me for heartbreak. You learn about algebra in school and all sorts of other pointless things.

What about the real-life issues? I knew that I couldn't keep running away. But just once more, I needed to.

Twenty-Six

I was running away for the second time. I promised myself it would be my last time, at least until maybe I had an illicit, sexy affair with some billionaire. I wanted to get away from Gareth and school and the prospect of picking university choices. I wanted to go to university eventually, especially Bangor University. It was beautiful and ideal for me. I didn't even know if my parents would allow me to go.

But that was the least of my worries. Of course, I wanted to know who was running the gossip page at school, the person who had single-handedly ruined everyone's lives, including mine. Whoever it was had to be some sort of genius. But despite Mr. Henderson trying to persuade me to go back to school with the bait of finding out who this mad genius was, I decided to leave. I was going to the one place where I felt at home. The irony was that Gareth would be the only person who knew where I was. Yet somehow, I wanted it to be like that.

The plane flight felt lonely without him beside me; I even missed him annoying me by pulling out my earphones. I sighed and gazed out of the window at the land below me. I expected music to play like in the movies. If we haven't looked out of the window at least once and pretended that we were in a movie, are we even human?

There was no going back now. I promised I would return when I was ready. To be honest, the only reason I promised that was because Michael and Ava refused to take me to the airport unless I did. But I knew I couldn't stay away forever— not that I didn't want to, though.

I noticed the woman beside me was reading Jane Austen's *Northanger Abbey*. That Jane woman had been following me around since I first read *Pride and Prejudice*. Now, she had decided to appear at the most pivotal moment of my life— running away like seven-year-old me had always wanted to. The woman looked at me over her purple-rimmed glasses. She reminded me of a middle-aged Molly, only with blonde curly hair. The engagement ring on her left hand sparkled, telling me that she had found her "hero", as our Jane would have called him. How lucky— she's falling into the trap we all do. Why do people allow themselves to fall in love over and over again, even though they know there's a chance of heartbreak at the end?

"Have you read it?" she questioned me.

I nodded, relishing in the moment of, for once, being able to talk about my love for Jane Austen. "Yes, I have. I'm a huge fan of her work."

A grin formed on the woman's face. She placed her hand-crafted bookmark back into the pages of the novel. The bookmark had flowers hand-painted on it, pink roses from the looks of it, and a white lace trim around the edge.

"Me, too! Don't you just love her depiction of romance? I've never seen anything more accurate than this novel," she commented. "I wouldn't call that accurate anymore." Okay, I let my own heartbreak cloud my judgment. But we've all done that before.

The woman frowned at me. I wanted to tell her it was my pessimistic alter ego, but negativity seemed to be such a dominant trait of mine lately that I wasn't entirely sure it was an alter ego anymore. The woman sighed and shook her head at me. "I would— they're not instantly in love. In *Northanger Abbey*, Henry goes back to Catherine and forgives her all the time. Maybe if we spent more time forgiving the ones we loved rather than judging them, we all might get along a bit better. We might even fall in love again."

That shut me up. Obviously offended, the woman went back to reading and ignored my existence for the rest of the flight. No matter what I tried to do, all I could imagine was Gareth standing in a cravat, calling himself "Mr. Tilney" and asking me to forgive him for our grave misunderstanding. In any other circumstances, this would have been creepy. But right then, I knew it was my mind telling me that I needed to consider forgiving him. After all, I never told him the full truth about me.

Despite having travelled the entire journey before, it seemed longer this time. The train ride to Llandudno was the loneliest, with people sitting by themselves at every single table on the carriage. It was as though the train had personified the terms "loneliness" and "heartbreak"— Mr. Henderson had clearly taught me well.

I opened up my laptop and went to my blog. Ava had discovered it after she asked me why on Earth I kept carrying around my laptop with me in Michael's house. The night I told her about it, she religiously sat and read through every single blog post I had ever written. In essence, she was reading my diary. Only when she finished it did she understand exactly what I was going through.

There were only three people who knew it was me behind the blog. That's how I wanted it. When I was growing up, I always got mad at my parents for reading my diary, or even Ava. Now, we get mad when people don't read personal things about us online. It's crazy. But let's face it, I fell into that trap, too. We all did.

I'm going away to the place I call my "home." It's a place I hope to someday settle down, either by myself or with some poor soul who wants to spend their life with me. No one will know where this is, but that's the amazing part. I'm alone and I need to discover everything before I go back to my real home. Until I get that far, I won't be posting any more on this. This is time for me and time for me to see where everything went wrong. I'm as alone as I was before all this started. People never stay in my life, and I'm used to that. But never did I imagine this would happen. It's something I need to adapt to, whether I like it or not. This is the time I'll take for adapting.

Until then,

Blu Skyes

I posted my blog entry and shut down my laptop. It was all I could do to make the train journey go by faster. Despite always having been alone, only now was I feeling the isolation that came with it. I had no one. I let go of the one person who had actually meant something to me over a stupid lie. Loneliness was all that I knew now.

A taxi driver was waiting for me when I got out of the train station. He was driving me down to the hotel Gareth and I had stayed in. All I wanted was for him to shut up. I was the type of socially awkward person that hated talking to strangers, especially taxi drivers. It seemed as though he wanted to know everything about me. I knew he was just being friendly. I rubbed my forehead out of annoyance at him and at myself. When I looked up, I saw him looking in the rear-view mirror.

"Just remember to enjoy yourself here. It's great for making memories," he told me with a sorrowful smile. I didn't think it was that obvious that I was hurting. Maybe I should have worn a temporary tattoo on my forehead saying "HEARTBROKEN" to make it easier for people.

When I got to the hotel on Vaughan Street, I went straight to my room. All I wanted was to feel the warm water of a shower over my body. I needed to feel something. When I was taken to the room, I realized I had been given the same room I stayed in with Gareth. I never requested it. Fate liked to laugh at me in that way. The room was a lot smaller than I had remembered it. But despite this, the small desk was still perched at the window, looking out at the promenade and the pier. A smile began to form on my face as I reminisced over the times that I had with Gareth here. I did miss him, despite refusing to admit it to myself.

I set my suitcase down on the floor and placed my bag on the chair at the desk. My face was soon plastered against the window, looking out at the sight before me. I was sure that I looked like one of those kids who put their nose up against the window when they're bored. The waves came in languidly, like they were in a slow-motion sequence in a film. Seagulls flew overhead and squawked with every glimpse they had of food. People walked about and sat on the promenade. I wondered if they had felt what I felt or had been through what I had. Well, maybe not the guy you were in love with having a daughter with your ex-best friend who left town for a year and only came back to be close to him again— not everyone has had that pleasure.

The hot water of the shower soothed every aching pain I had. I was relaxed, and I was ready for dinner. All I could remember about the hotel was that the food was delicious. Was that bad? Probably, but I didn't really care. I tied my wet hair up into a ponytail and pulled on my sneakers again before making my way back down the stairs.

People were gathering around tables with beers and wine. My desire to have a glass of beer was ridiculous, even though I didn't drink beer. Welcome to the insane mind of Olivia. The waiter smiled at me in a sympathetic way when she discovered I wasn't having a guest for dinner.

"Table for one?" she asked. Her tanned skin was flawless, and her straight black hair fell half-way down her back. She was beautiful. My poor skin and frizzy hair weren't beautiful to me. That was when one thought came into my mind: it was beautiful for Gareth. I pushed the thought to the back of my mind.

I swallowed hard and nodded. The waitress took me over to a table which had two chairs at it. I sat down and looked over the menu. Everyone around me had others eating dinner with them. The chair across from me seemed so lonely that I half expected it to go over to the table of ten people just for company. I placed down the menu, and my gaze caught an elderly woman looking over her own menu. She caught me looking and waved over at me.

A smile formed on my face as I waved back. She got up with her walking stick and came over to me. Only I could manage to make someone feel so sad for me that they had to join me for dinner. Thank goodness the chair didn't leave me.

"Is anyone sitting here?" she asked. Her voice was sweet and soft. I shook my head.

"Unfortunately, I'm on my own. Or maybe it's unfortunate for you to have to sit with me," I replied. Yeah, I'm such a charmer. It makes you wonder what Gareth ever saw in me.

The woman laughed and sat down with me. She placed her walking stick against the wall. A sigh of relief escaped her mouth.

"I'm here alone, too. It's nice to find someone else who isn't having any company," she told me.

I wanted to ask why she was on her own, but I knew it was rude. I wasn't rude— contrary to what many people thought. My parents might have favoured Harper and Ava over me, but they always taught us manners. I nodded in agreement; after all, I did feel the same way. As many elderly people do, the woman went on and on about her stay in Llandudno. She mentioned how she and her husband used to travel here from Liverpool ever since they got engaged.

I smiled, hearing the story of her love life. At least someone's love life was going well. Well, I thought that, until she told me her husband had passed away. Despite that, she continued to come here religiously. I watched her face as she spoke of her husband. Her eyes lit up in the most beautiful way, as if seeing a child being born for the first time. "You were so in love with him," I commented.

She smiled. "I was. I still am— don't mistake that, my dear. He may have passed on, but I still love him as though he were right here with me."

I sighed and played with the spoon as the waiter sat down our starters. The tomato soup rolled gently in the bowl, and I half-expected Moses to come along and part it like the Red Sea.

"How did you know you loved your husband before you two got engaged?" I questioned. It had been a question I'd been wondering for a while. I was asking for a friend... Yeah, that lie never worked.

The woman took a spoonful of soup into her mouth and smiled at me, dabbing her lips on the napkin. "You just know."

I shook my head. It was *never* that simple. If it was, that little guy I went to nursery with would have been "The One." I thought I was in love with him, too, but that was my younger, insane self. I can't say that I've matured much since then.

"It can't be that easy," I protested. "You can't just spend a day or two with someone and know that they're about to mean the entire world to you. You could start out hating the person and wanting nothing more than to be away from them. But then you fall in love with them. So, it's never easy."

A smile of recognition flashed over the wrinkled features of the woman.

"I guess not, then. You know, my Trevor used to always say, 'Betsy, you're one cow when you're mad. But I think that's when I realise I love you more,'" she told me. I frowned, not quite understanding what she meant. A laugh escaped from her pink lips as she remembered it. "He used to fight with me, before and during our marriage. We used to bicker until the neighbours would leave their houses just so they didn't have to listen to us through the walls anymore. He called me wicked names, but I called him them back."

She winked at me, and I stifled a laugh as I took a spoonful of soup. She laughed again at the memories of her husband before telling me more. If I ever become that in love with someone, I'd like a photograph, just to prove it.

"When we fought, he realised he loved me more. I was the one person that he fought with and didn't walk away from."

I set my spoon down gently in the bowl. "But what if you do walk away from the person you're fighting with?"

She shrugged, as if what I had said was nothing new to her. "If you love them, you'll always find your way back to them. Whether they come to you or you go to them."

I smiled slightly and that was it. Silence filled the rest of our starter course. Only halfway through the main dish of chicken and mashed potatoes did Betsy ask me about my love life. The topic was one which I had refused to go near for the last two weeks. I mumbled something about a guy I thought I liked until something went wrong. I wished it all ended like that. If movies have taught me anything, it's that love ruins you. Love ruined Jack so much that he died to save Rose. But then again, that wouldn't have been my view a month ago. For me, that would have been an undying symbol of a love that would never be broken.

The noise of people gathering in the dining room was deafening to anyone who sat in silence. I laid down my knife and fork before wiping my mouth on the napkin.

"Do you love him?" Betsy asked suddenly. I looked up at her. I didn't know how to answer. It wasn't a question I contemplated extensively. "Think about it, and then maybe you'll discover what you should do."

Betsy finished her dinner and got up before I could form a reply. She hugged me gently, as if I might break, before leaving back to her hotel room.. I sighed and sat back in the chair. This wasn't what I expected from a night of eating food in a hotel. All I wanted was peace of mind. Since I walked away from Gareth, that was something I was lacking.

I got up from the table and walked outside. The light hoodie I wore to dinner was instantly wrapped around me. My breath was forming kisses from angels in the frosty air. The thing about summer in the U.K. was that you always had to wear a jacket when going out— unless we got a heatwave, which only ever happens after a harsh winter. You see, always cold at one point in the year.

Going outside for me was a relief. The fresh sea air filled my lungs as I walked towards the promenade. The sun was just setting. A blue and pink glow reflected on the ocean. The lights lit up the promenade as I walked along it. It reminded me of Times Square at night— the only light in the darkness. I guess that's what Trevor was to Betsy and vise-versa. They lit up each other even in the darkest moments.

As I walked along towards the pier, all that was on my mind was Gareth. From the moment I met him, he irritated me so much that I would have preferred to shove my head in a fire than to sit with him. He was as pass-remarkable as I was. Yet, when I was down and when I needed help to start up my blog, he was there. When I needed someone to cheer me up, Gareth was the first person who managed to put a smile on my face.

It didn't matter to him whether I had depression or anger issues. None of it mattered to him. It didn't matter to me that he had a daughter. Deep down, I didn't think I even cared that he had been with Lucy or that Lucy was Poppy's mother. As the sun set and the streetlights got brighter, I realised exactly why I didn't care about any of it— I truly, madly, deeply loved Gareth.

I walked along the pier and looked out towards the sea. No one else was about. My mind had drifted to the night that Gareth and I danced on the pier in the pouring rain. I didn't just fall for him then. I already loved him. I had already fallen in love with Gareth. Who takes someone like me to a place like Llandudno? Only he did. He knew I would love it because he loved me enough to know me inside and out.

I reached the end of the pier at the old Victorian building that Gareth and I had danced around. I stopped and looked out. "I love him. I still love him," I whispered to myself. My breath danced in front of me.

Despite the cold, a smile formed on my face. I loved Gareth more than I had ever loved anyone. He didn't take away my mental illness— he made me happy, but that didn't mean I didn't still have my depression. He just accepted me for it. That was all I really needed from someone. I was glad it was Gareth.

I closed my eyes and could picture him calling my name, wanting me back again. A sigh escaped my lips as I thought of it. I messed it all up. Even though my imagination could hear him calling for me, I knew nothing could ever be repaired again. I needed to go back to him. It was the only way to make things right.

"Liv! Olivia!"

I could almost hear his voice in my mind wanting me back. As I turned and gazed back down the pier, I realised that the voice wasn't in my mind. It was here in Llandudno, and it was running up the pier towards me.

Twenty-Seven

Gareth ran up the pier towards me. I didn't think this was real. Ava told me she wouldn't say where I was if he asked, but here he was. I knew she wouldn't have broken her promise, so how did he know where I was? Maybe he was just here to see if I was still okay but didn't want me any longer. After how I treated him, I couldn't blame him for no longer wanting to be with me.

"How did you know I was here?" I asked him.

A smile appeared on his face. "Your blog post kind of gave it away. It wasn't that hard to put two and two together. Well, at least I hoped that was the case, and I'm glad it was. I saw you walking towards the promenade and I just had to catch up to you."

"You followed me all the way out here?"

A chuckle escaped Gareth's lips. "I guess I did."

I wanted to ask him why, but I didn't know if I had the lady balls to do it. His eyes were burning into my cheek, willing me to look at him. I couldn't. He sighed, taking my hands in his.

My head spun around to him. He smiled slightly.

"Can you let me talk for at least a minute without being pessimistic, arguing with me, or back-chatting?" he asked. I could tell he was hiding a smirk under his beard.

I nodded and gazed down at our hands. I pulled mine away from his.

"Ever since I met you, I thought you were beautiful. I'm not going to lie, you're a brat sometimes. But I love you. Every single morning, I wake up excited to see you, because it's another day I get to spend with you. I told Lucy I liked you. She was the one encouraging me to keep talking with you. I know you found out about us in the worst possible way—"

"You got that right," I mumbled.

We both looked at each other. I smiled down at the wooden pier.

"Sorry. I'll keep quiet," I replied, unable to hide the grin any longer.

"I'm sorry you found out like that. All I want to do is make it up to you. The only reason I couldn't at first was because you wouldn't let me. I came all this way because... because when you love someone, you don't want to let go. You keep running to them and trying again. I can't let you go now. I love you. I think you know I always have. I've been mad about you from the first moment I met you. Your wild plum hair, your 'charming' manner, and your smile. Your compassion for people around you, even though you have disagreements with them. I have and I will continue to love everything about you. If you don't feel the same way, then I'll leave now. But if you do, then please know that you have my heart. You have every inch of my heart— the heart that has been yours since I first clapped eyes on you," he admitted.

His eyes searched mine, willing and waiting for an answer. I stepped towards him and placed a hand on his bearded cheek. I rubbed the stubble that was there and smiled slightly.

"You never shaved the beard," I whispered. Our breaths lingered together in the cold night air of Wales.

He shook his head. "No, I never did."

"That's good. I always loved it on you," I told him. I finally looked up at him through my eyelashes to find he was still looking at me.

I hadn't seen anyone's eyes filled with so much love before until I looked into his. His eyes shone under the lights with hope. He was hoping I was going to return his feelings. I smiled slightly and took his hand. Gareth intertwined our fingers together.

I hadn't told anyone I loved them before, except for my family, of course. Gareth was the first person. I didn't even know where to start until I was sure I loved him. Now, I had to be sure I did again.

As he gazed into my eyes, something inside me snapped a bit. His warm eyes looked into mine with nothing but love. I could see he wanted to be forgiven, that he truly was sorry. The eyes never lied about anything. You could tell someone that you were happy, but when someone looked into your eyes all they could see was sadness. Gareth loved me. It was plain to see. And perhaps, I just needed to tell him I felt the same, because I did. Butterflies came back to me and the desire to wrap my arms around his neck and kiss him was overwhelming. Despite what he did, I don't think I ever stopped loving him. "I love you."

Gareth sighed in relief. "I thought you were never going to say it. Thank you. Thank you for giving me another chance, for giving us a chance."

"You don't have to thank me. I always have, I just couldn't accept the fact that everything in my life was changing, all because of you," I

245

told him. "Everything I've believed and fought for wasn't for me. How can one person change that for me?"

"Because you needed someone to help you get the life you wanted. You always knew what you wanted. You just needed someone to pull it out of you and help you to achieve it."

He leant down and took my chin with his finger. Gently, he pulled my face closer to his and kissed me. I kissed him back, wrapping my arms around his neck. He pulled away, breathless. Our foreheads touched, but our eyes were closed. We didn't need to look at each other because, in that moment, being together was all that we needed.

*

I opened up the door to the hotel room. Gareth couldn't stop laughing. I spun around and looked at him.

He smiled, closing the door behind him. "You got the room we stayed in."

"I know. I didn't choose the room, though," I told him. He laughed about the coincidence and flung his backpack on to one of the beds.

I pulled the curtains closed in the room and took off my jacket. On the desk sat my laptop. The blog had connected Gareth to me from the start. It was the one thing that helped us grow closer. Without it, Gareth wouldn't have been able to come after me.

I felt Gareth's arms wrap around me. I grinned and laid my head back on his shoulder.

"I know what you're thinking about," he told me.

I laughed, wondering what on earth was going through his mind. "Go on, what's that?"

Gareth turned me around in his arms. A grin was plastered all over his face. Any time we were together, he was always grinning.

"You're thinking— 'why didn't I bring *Titanic* to watch it again in the hotel?'"

"Oh yeah, that was totally it."

"Your sarcasm amuses me. But this will amuse you further," he assured me.

He let go off me and ran over to his backpack. He aimlessly searched and looked up at me, before pulling out the DVD of *Titanic*. I burst out laughing. I couldn't believe I loved someone who was clearly this insane. Then again, he was probably thinking the same thing about me.

I took the DVD from him and pushed it into the player on the TV. He pushed the beds together and laid down. I stared at him from the TV. He glanced up at me, scratching his beard in embarrassment.

"Oh, ehm... I can move them apart again if you don't want us to, you know, sleep close to each other. I don't mind. It's whatever you're comfortable with," he mumbled.

I laughed, catching him off guard. "I wanted to see how long it would take to get that inane smirk wiped off your face."

Gareth grinned and laid his head on the pillow. I couldn't get over how much I loved him, or how long I had been denying it. He gave me his goofiest smile. If anyone wanted to see what a modern-day Mr. Tilney looked like, here he was, lying on his hotel bed that was pushed together with my hotel bed. How darn romantic!

I laid down with Gareth and he took me into his arms. I'd missed this, even if I couldn't admit it to myself. I knew if Mum had walked in on us that she would have freaked out, thinking we were about to have sex. It would be like the Ava and Michael incident all over again. Isn't my mum just something?

Gareth nudged me gently. I looked up at him.

"Yeah?"

"I finished *Pride and Prejudice*," he told me with an air of pride about him— fitting, I know.

I laughed. "Really?"

He nodded and showed me the book that was in his bag. It was the paperback I had bought him when we were last here. It was battered, and the front cover was irrevocably ripped and torn in various places. He had clearly loved it as much as I did.

Gareth handed me the copy, and I flicked through it mindlessly until I spotted a highlighted page. I frowned and read over it out loud.

"In vain I have struggled. It will not do. My feelings will not be repressed. You must allow me to tell you how ardently I admire and love you," I read. It was Darcy's confession of love for Elizabeth.

When I tried to hand the book back to him, he shook his head. "I'll keep it on one condition," he replied. I frowned, not quite understanding him. "I'll keep the book, but you must keep the page. It says your name on it."

I scoffed. "No, it doesn't."

That was when he pointed it out to me. He had written my name at the top of the page in his messy handwriting. He grinned at me, catching me out.

"I wrote it because… it's how I felt about you. I love you and admire you, Olivia."

A warm blush appeared on my cheeks, which hadn't ever appeared before, at least not of the intensity that it was now. He leant over and kissed me gently. I wasn't able to restrain myself and ended up returning the affection.

When he pulled away, he tore the page from the book and handed me it. I attempted to argue with him about rereading it and not knowing what happened, but he fought back with me.

"I will know, because you'll have the page. You have the page that describes my feelings for you in such a beautiful way," he replied. I smiled and cuddled down with him on the bed.

"What if something happens between us that means we won't be together anymore?" I asked. Yes, I really was this worried about the page.

"Then you'll always have a memory of me, and I'll always have a memory of you. We'll never forget each other for as long as we live."

Titanic began to play again. It was like deja-vu, but in a good way. This was how I wanted to spend my time in Wales. After all I had done to Gareth and he had done to me, he came after me. Betsy was right; you never give up on the people who you love.

That was when I thought of my family— Mum, Dad, Harper, and Ava. I had left them all over again. I needed to do a Mr. Darcy and swallow my pride. I needed to go back home. It was where I belonged. Someday I would return back to Llandudno, and it would be a happy moment for me. But I couldn't be truly happy without fixing things with my family.

When the movie ended, I sat up on the bed, facing Gareth. He smiled and sat up, too.

"I want to go home. Can we go home tomorrow?" I asked. Gareth nodded and kissed my lips. I didn't want him to stop kissing me. I pulled away and he laid a hand on my cheek. My head fell into his hand out of instinct.

"Of course, we can."

As I looked at him, I didn't understand how anyone could survive love. It took every inch of your being to love someone so much. Yet it was destroying me in the most beautiful way. I didn't want it to end. I wanted to love Gareth for as long as he loved me… and more. Because if you love someone, you never really get over them. They'll always have a piece of your heart; I happily gave mine to Gareth. No one else would love this goofy idiot as much as I ever did.

Twenty-Eight

The next morning, Gareth went to Starbucks to get us breakfast and coffee while I got packed. I didn't remember much of last night except falling asleep in his arms. I liked to think that Jane Austen would be proud of me for finding my hero, if she were still alive today. When I got dressed, I let my hair flow down my back, knowing that I looked similar to Miss Trunchbull with it up in a bun.

My phone buzzed as I finished packing. It was Gareth. After finally turning on my phone last night, I was welcomed by floods of texts from Louise, Molly, and my parents. Louise and Molly were telling me who set up the gossip page. I was going to confront them about it when I was back at school tomorrow.

Gareth: Waiting outside for you. Come on down when you're ready xxx

I immediately grabbed my bags and checked over the room, making sure I hadn't left anything. Finally, I made my way downstairs. For once, I was looking forward to going back home. This whole trip away was supposed to have been for me to discover who I was, but I already knew.

I was Blu Skyes. I was the girl who wrote an anonymous blog about her life and her love life. I was the girl who didn't want to go to university and was heading home to tell her parents the harsh reality. I didn't quite know what to do with my life, but I knew that I would figure it out eventually.

Gareth sat in his car waiting for me. I threw open the back door and put my bags in beside his backpack. When I got in the front seat, a coffee and a ham and cheese toastie were greeting me. I grinned and kissed his stubbled cheek.

"Thanks," I replied.

He chuckled and pulled away from the curb. "You're more than welcome."

*

It took us a while to get onto the main road. Gareth was holding my hand whenever he wasn't changing gears. While I was with him, everything else was irrelevant. I didn't care if the gossiper was announced or if Lucy was Gareth's ex or even about the trouble I had caused at home. All I wanted and cared about in that moment was Gareth.

He kept looking at me out of the side of his eye as we got on to the main roads.

"You're giving me a complex, looking at me constantly," he told me in his usual joking manner.

I blushed and looked down at our hands. "Sorry. I'm just… I just can't believe that you loved me enough to come back for me. I do love you and I think you're an idiot for lying to me."

"Well, I'll let you know that I feel the exact same way," he said with a smirk plastered on his face. Gareth lifted my hand up to his lips and kissed it. We pulled to a stop as a queue of traffic was building up.

"Would you stop thinking about the whole situation of what happened between us?" Gareth asked. He must be some strange magician; he always seemed to know what I was thinking without saying anything.

"How did you know what I was thinking?" I questioned. He winked at me and continued to drive on as the traffic moved. I missed spending moments like this with him. I didn't know why we ever fought. It was stupid.

I laid my head gently on his shoulder as we got up to the national speed limit. He drove the whole way to see me. If Gareth hadn't have come after me, I knew I would have gone home to him. Even if he'd rejected me, I still would have tried. You don't just give up on someone you love. That was something I had to remember next time we fought.

Halfway home, I woke up and Gareth pulled into a service station. He smiled at me and gently unbuckled my seatbelt. I looked at him out of one eye.

"I'm awake, you know," I told him.

He laughed and nodded. "I know. But I didn't want to wake you if you decided to sleep again."

It was lunchtime, and I was hungry— as usual. We went inside the service station and walked over to the restaurant area. The smell of chips, burgers, and bacon filled my nostrils. I grinned at Gareth. He knew exactly what I wanted: a huge plate of chips and a burger. That's the only way to my heart.

I took a seat while he got the food. It was a quiet day with only businessmen and truckers in the restaurant. No families were about. That was when my mind went back to Lucy and Poppy. They were Gareth's family as much as his parents were, yet Lucy had let him go to see me.

Instinctively, I took my phone out of my pocket and rang Lucy. I needed to thank her. While the phone was ringing, I looked over at

Gareth. He was stuck in a queue of truckers who couldn't decide what they wanted to eat. He waved over at me as I heard a reply on the end of the phoneline.

"Hello? Olivia?" Lucy's voice came. It sounded urgent.

"Yeah, it's me," I replied.

A sigh of relief came from the other end of the phone. "You're still talking to me, then?"

I smiled slightly. I didn't realise how much I had hurt Lucy by walking out on them that day. It wasn't fair to her.

"I am. I'm sorry about what happened that day, I should have never caused you so much trouble," I admitted.

Lucy laughed on the end of the phone. "I'm glad to hear that, and while yes, it did hurt, I'm not annoyed. You should have seen Gareth; he looked like a miserable puppy when you left. I had to send him your way. He wanted to go, but he was scared that you'd probably reject him. I know we all should have told you. I do regret that. Believe me, but I wanted to do something nice for you by telling him to go. It was my fault for not telling you. When Gareth told me that he was seeing someone who knew me, I should have talked to you myself."

"So you encouraged him, then?"

"Of course I did. He loves you. Gareth and I weren't in love like you two are. Poppy would love to see you again when you're back."

I grinned as Gareth sat down with our food. He had ordered the same as me. "Well, that will be sooner than you think. We're about half-way home now."

"Is that Lucy?" Gareth asked before Lucy could respond. I nodded and handed my phone to him.

He began to chat away to Lucy while I poured tomato sauce onto my burger. The cheese was stringy and melted— just perfect. Gareth laughed and smiled at me before thanking Lucy for encouraging him to go after me.

I held his hand across the table. His laugh was so perfect. I knew that he wasn't perfect, but parts of him were. He most certainly wasn't flawless, but he was flawless enough for me.

I ate my chips as he finished up talking. He hung up the phone and handed it back to me. I put it down on the table. Gareth kissed my cheek before starting to eat his burger. Lucy didn't hate me like I thought she would. Sometimes we needed to see that people still loved us, despite our mistakes.

"This is good food," Gareth said. He put a chip in his mouth.

"It is. You okay?" I asked.

Gareth nodded. "Yeah. Lucy can't wait to see us when we're back. She wants to let you spend some time with Poppy again."

"Yeah, she told me all about her plan."

Gareth smiled at me. As I looked into his eyes, I knew what love meant. It wasn't that everything was perfect with the person you loved. It was perfect when you were with them, because they made you so happy that nothing else mattered. That was how I felt with Gareth. That was what kept me going in the dark times. I knew that with him, I had happiness despite my depression. He taught me that it was okay to have depression and other issues. All that mattered was that I kept going. Gareth helped me to keep going because he made me smile.

At least Dad realised that before I left. He got it wrong, though. Gareth didn't take away my depression; he just made me smile, despite everything that was going through my head. He gave me hope.

When we got back on the road, the sun was shining high in the sky. It was mid-afternoon, and the sun was at its peak, creating a glow across the sky. Everything looked so much brighter in the sunshine. Suddenly, I was brighter. My soul was happier, and I grinned at Gareth.

"Can I do something?" I asked him with an inane grin on my face.

"I dread to think, but sure," he said, uneasy at my suggestion.

I wound down the window. The blast of air hit me straight in the face, making it hard to breathe until I got used to it. Gareth looked over at me as if there was something wrong. I smiled and put my head out of the window. My hair whipped around my face before being whipped right back.

For once in my life, I felt alive. I was in love and I knew I wanted to get better. I couldn't live with my issues like this again. I let them get too bad. I wanted to change.

"Woo!" I screamed out of the window.

I heard Gareth laughing. He took my hand in his, and I put my head back in. He smiled at me. I knew I loved that sight, because every time I looked at him, I saw a hope for the future. It wasn't in the love he gave me, but how he showed me that there was so much more to life than what I thought.

"I didn't realise life could feel this good," I admitted.

"It can. Have you thought about, you know, help?" he questioned.

I nodded and sighed. I squeezed his hand gently. "I'm going to get some help after my exams, during the summer. I'm putting off university to get the help I need. It's more important than education for me."

He nodded while keeping his eyes on the road. "Definitely. I think I better go into the house with you to explain everything to your parents."

*

Gareth went in with me as soon as we arrived home. Mum ran out to me. She engulfed me in her arms and held me close to her. I hugged her back, knowing that how she acted wasn't out of malice, but because she wanted the best for me.

"I'm so sorry," she said.

I nodded with my chin on her shoulder. "I know. Me, too."

She kissed my cheek, and we turned to see Gareth standing awkwardly at the car. She ran to him and hugged him, too. I laughed, wiping away stray tears that I didn't know were falling. Mum took us both inside. Dad, Ava, and Harper were waiting for us. I hugged each of them, too. Gareth shook my dad's hand before hugging my two sisters.

We went into the living room where Gareth and I had first met. We sat down beside each other. Gareth started to explain everything for me— his actions, my running off, and my university issue.

"I'm sorry for not telling Liv about Poppy and Lucy. If I told her, I knew that she would leave, because Lucy was her best friend. Liv is a good person and wouldn't take her best friend's ex. I know her too well now. I should have told her. But when she found out, she felt like she just needed to get away."

I tried to keep Gareth quiet because I wanted to do the talking myself. I needed to stand up for myself in front of my parents. If I didn't do it now, I would be pushed around for the rest of my life. My parents had emotionless faces when I got to the part of not wanting to go to university; I was picking my mental health over my grades and over a degree.

"I want to focus on my mental health first. When I get better, I'll go to university, because I believe I need to do this for myself. I need to put myself and my health over grades and education."

Mum sighed. "Will you go to university eventually?" she asked.

I shrugged. "I want to go to Bangor University eventually. I don't know when. But what I know now is that I want to get better, and that's all that matters to me. I wish I was going to university to make people proud, but I'm making this decision for my own wellbeing."

The room was silent. Gareth squeezed my hand to reassure me. It was the first time I had properly stood up for myself. I liked the feeling. I hoped I had that courage tomorrow in school when I confronted the person behind the gossip page about the crap that they wrote about me. Mum and Dad smiled at each other before smiling at me. "Good for you, Liv," Dad said.

I got up and hugged him tightly. "Thank you. Thank you both so much."

"You should have just told us," Mum said to me.

"I know. But I'm telling you now. It's not too late. I'm still going to revise for my exams and try to do well, but university isn't the focus anymore."

They understood, which was something I didn't think they would have done. It felt good to finally be doing the right thing for me, rather than what others wanted of me. I knew I would still make my parents proud, just not through university. I was okay with that. I was okay.

Twenty-Nine

The next morning, I was ready for school. Mum and Dad had their reservations about letting me go back so early, but I reassured them I'd be all right. Nothing was different about me except for my inner self. I needed to work on that for a while.

No one knew I was going back to school except for my family. Ava was dropping both Harper and me off today. They smiled at me as I came downstairs.

"Jeez, don't change your attitudes for me," I told them. They laughed, and Dad went back to his newspaper. Ava and Harper went to their phones, and Mum to her recipe book. That was it, back to normal, just what I wanted.

I sat down to toast and bacon. I grabbed the tomato sauce and poured it over the bread and the bacon. Ava looked at me out of the corner of her eye.

"You're disgusting," Ava mumbled with a smirk.

"Oh, shove off," I told her.

"Liv!" Mum and Dad shouted. Ava and I grinned at each other. Nothing had changed.

Finally, we were going to school. I was nervous, which was obvious to Ava. My leg kept jiggling like something strange. She rubbed my arm affectionately as we pulled up to Harper's school. Harper said a cheery goodbye to us and left the car.

Ava looked at me with concern. I knew what she was thinking: *is she ready for this?* I didn't comment. I didn't know if I was ready to go back to school, but I was trying not to mull over it in my mind too much. She tried to talk to me the whole way to the school, but nothing helped.

"You'll be fine, won't you?" Ava asked.

I nodded and unbuckled my seatbelt as she pulled up outside the school. "I'll be fine, trust me."

She didn't comment. I couldn't blame her. I was nervous. In fact, I wasn't just nervous; I was going to puke. But I had to face it sometime. I wanted to confront the one who had done this to me. The person behind the gossip page had ruined so many people's lives. Everyone knew who it was, but I needed to speak to them directly.

When I walked into the common room, I was aware that everyone around me was as alert as a ferret on E numbers. Louise and Molly ran over and hugged me. I smiled slightly before hugging them back.

"We missed you. Are you okay?" Louise asked.

I nodded and sighed. "Yeah. I just needed to be away. But I think I worked out everything I needed to work out for myself."

They led me over to our usual sofa by the microwave. It was the handiest place to sit for lunchtime, because we were always first in the queue for the use of the microwave. Sometimes we would take our time on purpose, knowing that everyone was desperate to eat their lunch and skive off the next lesson.

Louise and Molly tried to keep talking to me to see if I was okay, but I was more concerned with the evil mastermind behind the gossip page.

"Where are they?" I asked.

"Not in yet. You did get our text that it's—"

Molly couldn't finish her sentence. The common room door opened, and everyone went silent. They all glared at the person who had just walked inside. With the click of a button, they had posted something about every single one of us to ruin our lives.

It was Cynthia.

She looked around the room and smiled over at me. Because I'd been out for so long, she assumed no one had got around to telling me. I got up and went over to her. I wanted the truth from the horse's mouth.

"Hey," she said.

The whole common room was silent. I stood in front of her. She looked as perfect as ever. Her blonde curls bounced with confidence—normally, it was just my boobs that bounced with confidence. I folded my arms across my chest.

"Why did you do it?" I asked. "Why did you try and ruin everything for me?"

Cynthia laughed and shook her head. "I didn't do any of that."

"Yes, you did! You ruined everyone's lives through that page. It got you nowhere. So why ruin it for me? What was your motivation there?"

Cynthia shook her head and flung back her curled hair off her perfectly shaped shoulder. Only then was I aware of how small she was. I could almost hear Gareth calling her a poisoned dwarf.

"I didn't ruin your relationship. I simply put up that you had a boyfriend who was a father. Everyone already knew. What makes it worse is he's your ex-best friend's ex-boyfriend. That's awful to do that to someone. It was never going to work. You knew that yourself, and that's why you ran. You broke it off with him because you found out everything and realised how much it was a bad idea to even be with him. I didn't do anything to your relationship; you did it all yourself," she said.

"Why make the page?" I questioned.

Cynthia laughed. "Because no one would have suspected it was me. Everyone would have pinned it on one of the so-called 'Classic Mean Girls', like Lola. But not me. Being head girl meant that I knew every-one's dirty little secrets — I heard everything that was said between pupils gossiping about each other. I just used that to my advantage."

"But it got you nowhere!" I screamed in frustration.

"Maybe not, but it managed to get the truth about everyone out there," Cynthia reasoned. "Besides, your life could have made a whole gossip page in itself. It's so fun to hear about every single dirty secret you had."

I swallowed hard and shoved past her, out of the door. I didn't want to be near someone as vile as that. I knew where I was going— Mr. Henderson.

He was sitting at his desk marking work when I flung open the door. He jumped as he took a sip of his coffee.

"Hello to you, too," he said.

I sat down in front of his desk as I usually did. Next year, I knew I would miss these weird therapy sessions. While Mum and Dad were only coming around to everything now, Mr. Henderson was always there for me despite what I did or didn't want to do.

"Cynthia? Seriously?" I asked.

He nodded and set down his coffee. "Yep. Cynthia. You wouldn't have expected it, would you?"

I shook my head. I never would have guessed it was Cynthia. She was always so perfect and always had the most amazing life, so why did she want to ruin mine and everyone else's? Her explanation made zero sense.

"Sometimes it's the people you don't suspect who hurt you the most," he told me.

I looked up at him. "What do you mean?"

"Well, you didn't think Gareth would have hurt you how he did, did you?" he questioned. I shook my head. "You see, but he had reasons. Cynthia... Well, I don't think you can condone bullying your entire year group, but it'll pass, because in a month, you have your exams. That's what you need to focus on."

"I need to focus on getting better," I said immediately.

Mr. Henderson was smiling at me. "I guess you've figured life out, then."

"Not completely. But I've figured out this bit and I'm happy with my decision. I'm happy with not going to university, I'm happy with getting better, and I'm happy with Gareth." He handed me a box of donuts and told me to take one. I took out a ringed donut with white icing. My absolute favourite. I began to eat it as he took out an iced chocolate one.

"Do you always have a donut with coffee before you teach us?" I asked him.

He laughed and nodded. "I need something to cope with you lot."

"Maybe you should give us the same to help us cope with you."

He smirked at me. I would miss our jokes and laughter next year. But I promised to come back and visit. Even if it was a fleeting visit, I would make it there.

The bell rang as we finished our donuts. I grabbed my bag off the ground and put the chair back where I got it from. I smiled at him.

263

"Thanks for everything. You've been an amazing help to me," I told him.

"Don't thank me. It's my job to be here for students. But you're so annoying," he replied, laughing.

I began to laugh too. "That's what everyone loves about me."

He stood up and walked me to the door. He opened his classroom door for me.

"Well, go out there and face the day. Give Gareth my regards."

"You seem to be on good terms with him. But I definitely will. You've no idea how much I love him."

Then Mr. Henderson beamed at me. He told me how Gareth had come to him when I left, wanting to know where I was. That was why Mr. Henderson went to me at Michael's house. He and Lucy worked together to get Gareth to follow me to Llandudno, too.

"Thank you," I said.

He shrugged. "It's nothing. Now scram before you do my head in."

"I'm always doing your head in," I called as I walked out. I heard him laughing as I walked down the corridor.

By lunchtime, Molly had told me that Cynthia had gone home sick. Apparently, she had fallen ill due to "stress." Personally, I think Nurse Erin was just happy to send her home— as we all were. Louise came in and sat with me, but then Lola came over. I frowned as I looked between Molly and Louise. Neither of them would look at me. I didn't understand why.

Lola sat down with Louise on the sofa opposite Molly and me. She took out her lunch and began to eat it.

"I'm sorry," Lola whispered to me.

"Why?"

"For all I've done. It wasn't right of me. I know you probably thought I was behind the gossip page, but I wasn't. Although, your confrontation to Cynthia this morning tells me you know it wasn't me. We all had our fair share of grief from the gossip page," Lola mumbled.

When we finished our lunch, Molly told me that Lola had gotten attacked by the page, too. Lola was apparently failing every single class, caused by tensions in her family at home— Cynthia had somehow found out about it and put it on the page. Lola put on a popular façade to make people like her. All she wanted was love and to be liked by people. I felt sorry for her. That's something depression can do— make you feel unwanted and unloved. I could have been angry at Lola for all the grief she ever gave me, but I just couldn't manage it. I knew what it was like to feel alone, especially with depression. It's like screaming in a crowded room and no one ever hears you. I didn't want anyone to suffer the way I did, even if it was Lola.

Lola went to the bathrooms in the common room. I followed her there. She was reapplying her makeup. Her eye caught mine, and she smiled at me for the first time in ages. I smiled back and closed the door gently behind me.

"Molly told me," I admitted to her. She nodded.

"Yeah," she mumbled, putting her lip-gloss away in the pocket of her blazer. She looked back up at me in the mirror. "I hope you and Gareth worked things out."

I shrugged and took my hair out of the plait it was in. "Kind of. We're taking it slow, but we're back in each other's company again."

"I'm glad to hear it. You two really suited each other." Lola continued to fix her makeup before grabbing her bag from the floor. She turned to me, swishing her blonde hair over her shoulder.

"I know you're having trouble at home. I'm sorry. We haven't always gotten along well, but I'm always here for you. If you need help with classes then I'll help you anyway I can."

That was when she hugged me, something so out of character for her. She never hugged anyone unless they were a man or were part of her crowd. I hugged her back. The whiff of her expensive perfume filled my lungs. I smiled slightly.

"I'm here for you, too."

Lola and I may have had our differences, but I couldn't let someone go through depression alone, as I had. It wasn't fair to experience that alone. Yet, so many did.

I told her about not going to university yet and instead getting help for myself. She handed me the card for her specialist before we walked out to the girls again. My phone buzzed as I sat down with them

@GarethJohnson: Have a good day, beautiful. I can't wait to see you later xxx

@OliviaBernard: You, too. Can't wait to see you and Poppy xxx

The girls were looking over my shoulder as I typed out my reply. A chorus of "awws" went around them all. A warm glow came on to my cheeks as I put my phone away again. As I looked around at the smiling girls around me, I felt like life was coming together. Molly would go to Oxford, Louise and Lola would go to the universities they had dreamt of, and I would spend a gap year getting help. That would be us on the journey called "The Rest of Our Lives." The prospect of it scared me, but I knew things would work out for the best.

The bell rang, and everyone got up. I slung my bag over my shoulder as I stood up.

"Let's go to study room," Lola said as Louise made her way to maths.

I frowned. "Are you with us now?"

"Yeah, I got my timetable changed after some bullying, cause of my depression."

I smiled and held the common room door open. "Let's go then. Come on, Molly."

The three of us sat down in study room. Miss Harshaw came in and silenced us with a glare. I grinned at Molly. I really had missed all of this. If I didn't come back, I would have missed it more. But in my dark thoughts, my mind told me that things would have been okay if I didn't go back to school. I was so wrong.

"Names. And no dirty names," Miss Harshaw yelled, handing out the sign in sheet to the first person in the room. "Except for you, Stiffy."

Everyone laughed until Miss Harshaw glared. Molly planted a load of papers on my desk. It was catch-up work. I knew I wouldn't get away with skiving off school. As much as Mr. Henderson basically acted like a second dad to me, I knew even he would have made me catch up on everything.

"Is Stiffy still with Louise?" I whispered to Molly and Lola who were sitting beside me. They both nodded. Apparently, it had gotten more serious. They were both planning to go to the same university.

"Let's get studying, everyone. Exams and university won't magic themselves into your lives," Miss Harshaw said before beginning to pace around the room.

Just like that, our focus was on exams and getting into university. It was as if no one cared about the gossip page any longer. All that mattered was passing exams. I knew that I had to focus, too. I had to try my best— that was my focus.

SUMMER

"He saved me in every way that a person can be saved."

Titanic (1997)

Thirty

It was results day— the day every student across the U.K. dreaded more than anything. I wasn't concerned. Since I had made the decision not to go to university, I felt less stressed. I might not have made my parents proud like Ava and Harper had, but I was happy with my decision. That's all I cared about.

I was three months into my treatment. When I began, I was made aware that my depression wouldn't go away completely; it never would. But it would help me cope more. Gareth had been so supportive of it all. I couldn't have asked for someone better to have my heart.

My treatment was tailored to my needs, involving mostly creative therapy. People in the same centre as me were doing art therapy and music therapy, but I wasn't that good at either of those. Once my doctor discovered that I wrote a blog, she put me in for creative writing therapy. It was the best decision I ever made.

Every day, good or bad, I would write out bits of my novel, and my anger and sadness would be poured into the pages of it. Somehow it made things a bit more bearable. That was something my parents were relieved about. They only cared that I was getting help and getting better. It was all anyone cared about now.

I sat at the table doing some writing. My phone sat on the table buzzing like mad. I lifted it eventually and read the notifications on the screen. It was Molly, Louise, and Lola telling me their results and where they were off to.

@MollyWilson: I got A*A*A! Off to Oxford!

@LouiseKillen: I got ABB. I got into London. What about you, Lola and Liv?

@LolaMiller: I'm off to Edinburgh with BBB

They were waiting for me to tell them my results. They all knew I wasn't intending to go to university, and they didn't judge me for it. When I explained about my depression and anger problems, they understood the importance of me getting help rather than to suffer another three or four years at university doing something I wasn't loving because of my mental health.

The thing was that I didn't know my results either. My parents had gone to get them with Harper. Ava wasn't at home. She was away on holiday with Michael and his children. After my exams, Michael had asked for my help to propose to Ava. We agreed to take her to a beach at sunset to propose. Michael told her we were going for a walk, making the excuse for me that I wanted to get some photos of the beach before I left for treatment. Instead, I was taking photos of the whole proposal.

If you didn't guess it, she said yes. The wedding was a year away, but Ava was so excited already. Mum had finally welcomed the idea of the two of them together, only after Michael proposed, of course. But the good news was that she was warming up to Michael and Gareth a lot more. She even spent some time with Poppy a week ago when Gareth came over to see me with her.

My phone buzzed with a text from my parents to tell me my results. Immediately, I text the girls to tell them what I got.

@OliviaBernard: ABB! Off to get myself better, who knows if I'll go to uni yet. But enjoy your time at uni, girls. You all deserve it.

I turned off my phone as I felt hands rest on my shoulders. I smiled as Gareth kissed my head.

"Still writing that novel?" Gareth asked.

I grinned. "Yeah, still working on it. Louise, Lola, and Molly got into university. Have you heard about Lucy's results? She didn't text me."

Gareth handed me his phone. It was a video sent from Lucy on WhatsApp. He played it for me. We watched as Poppy babbled while playing with foam letters. The letters spelled "AAA." That had to have been the cutest announcement video ever created. I handed Gareth his phone back.

"Tell her I said congratulations and good luck at Oxford," I told him.

"I will later when I give her a call. Want to go for a walk?" he asked.

I nodded. "Sure, just let me post this blog."

He got his trainers and jacket on while I quickly posted it. I turned off my laptop and grabbed my own trainers. I put on my jacket before going outside. It was a beautiful, sunny day. I couldn't have asked for a nicer day to be here. I got a few weeks off from my treatment to spend somewhere I really wanted to be. Gareth promised to take me home; for us, that was Wales.

"I thought I should let you know, because Lucy's told me to, that she works for a blog and has been promoting yours through that. I know I told you I was telling people, but that was just a cover-up. Lucy wanted to make sure you realised your dream— not your parents' dream for you. I think you finally have."

I smiled at Gareth, unable to believe that Lucy had done that for me. I walked over to him and hugged him as tight as I could muster. Lucy never gave up on being there for me, even before I reconnected with her.

We walked across the road to the promenade. Seagulls were going wild for food that people had left down on the beach and on top of bins. Gareth's fingers interlocked with mine as we walked towards the pier.

With it being the summer holidays, there were loads of families around and children playing on the beach. We walked on to the beach for a bit before walking back up to the pier. Stalls were out in their full capacity to welcome tourists to the shores of Llandudno. There was a genie game, which always reminded me of that famous Tom Hanks film. Gareth thought I was crazy, and maybe I was. Just maybe.

We walked past stalls of CDs from artists that were long dead before my time. It amazed me that people still listened to them, and when I voiced my opinion to Gareth, he had the cheek to walk over and lift not only a Beatles CD but also an Elvis Presley CD.

"Hey! Don't advertise my music taste to tourists," I said. He laughed and scooped me up under his arm as we walked on down the pier. I laughed and kicked my legs.

"Stop!" I screamed in between laughter.

We were more than aware of everyone staring at us. I began to get self-conscious, casually nudging him to put me down, but he didn't seem to care. He was proud of me and happy to carry me around, showing me off to everyone. Gareth put me down and I took his hand. The thing about Wales was that I could come back every time and feel just as inspired as I did when I first arrived. Being inspired and seeing such gorgeous scenery made the journey worth it. It made me feel alive, knowing that there was hope out there. For too long I had been trapped and didn't truly live. But Llandudno was where I began to live my life. Coming back to Wales made me realise that I needed to continue living my life. Every single day of my life, I could feel alive— if only I lived properly.

We walked up to the end of the pier, and Gareth took me into his arms. I smiled up at him, wrapping my arms around the back of his neck. He kissed me gently. I kissed him back, even though some tourists were snapping pictures of the pier and capturing us in it. I guess that gave us a slight feeling of immortality.

Gareth hadn't ever left me, even though I thought he had. He stayed up as late as possible trying to contact me in every which way he could think of. I didn't know anyone, except my sisters and parents, who would do that for me.

I pulled away and looked into his brown eyes. They were the type of brown that would remind you of autumn and winter all in one. They were beautiful.

My mum always told me that you could tell a lot about how a person was feeling from looking into their eyes. As I looked into Gareth's, all I could see was my reflection staring back at me in dark brown monochrome.

"I'm glad I'm here with you," he stated.

Our foreheads touched as we smiled at each other. The sun blazed down on us in the August sky. All around us we were surrounded by summer, yet every season seemed to be placed firmly in the eyes of the love of my life. It was as if God wanted my heart to experience every season ever created all in one place.

"I wouldn't want to be here with anyone else," I told him.

He pecked my lips gently before we walked over to the edge of the pier. We looked at the horizon. The sky and the sea seemed to blend into one. Gareth wrapped his arms around me from behind. I laid my head back against his chest and smiled.

Gareth put his chin on the top of my head. The gentle breeze blew my hair around his face, but he didn't seem to mind.

"So, are you happy with your decision?" Gareth asked me.

I nodded. "More than happy. This is what I needed. I couldn't go to uni and expect to heal while putting so much pressure on myself. It wasn't healthy."

"I'm so proud of you."

I grinned and held Gareth's arms tightly around me. Feeling him so close to me gave me comfort. I knew everything would be okay. If I weren't filled with hope, then it wasn't the end of the road. I needed to keep going, for myself, and for all those who loved me.

Gareth spun me around again. He smiled back at me with a goofy smile only he could own. His parents had gotten a divorce, and due to finding a lot of work down in the south of England, he decided to move in with Sharon. For him, it was closer to Poppy, Lucy, and me. I loved him. I really did.

I wrapped my arms around his neck. His arms went instinctively around my waist, holding me as close as possible. Not a breath of sea air could pass between our bodies.

"You posted on your blog before we came out, didn't you?" I laughed. "I did indeed."

"What does it say? Is it about me?"

I smiled, and we touched foreheads. We kissed gently, eyes closed, bodies close. We were one. We had hope in a future for each other, even if it wasn't together. The most important thing was, I had hope in a future. Even if Gareth and I ended up breaking up, he taught me lessons that I will remember for the rest of my life. Perhaps my life wasn't perfect. But whose life is perfect? No one's is. We just have to make the best of the life we've been given. Right then in that moment, I was making the best of my life. I was making the best of my time with Gareth. The future wasn't something I needed to worry about, not now. I needed to focus on the present. I needed to focus on me.

"Go on, what does it say about me?" Gareth asked again, when we pulled away from the kiss. We smiled at each other.

"You'll just have to wait and see."

Dear readers of my mad, crazy blog,

Well, you've been with me for a full year of school. The last you heard from me, I had taken a break away from everything to discover who I am. Now, I'm getting help for my depression and anger. So often we're told by society that if we have something wrong with us that no one will ever care about us or love us. That's not true, though I thought it was. Life has a funny way of surprising you and showing you what's truly important. As I sit here in Wales writing this, I want to tell you my story.

My depression and anger issues have always been a dark secret in my life and in other people's lives. Being a typical middle child, I felt talentless and unloved— both of which are untrue. But I believed it at the time. It was building up to the depression I would later face. Eventually, when my best friend moved away without a trace or reason, I was left feeling more alone than ever. That was when my depression and anger hit me hard.

My life changed when I met this guy. He'll be reading this, so be nice in the comments! When I met Gareth, I was sinking fast. He helped me to see that the things I liked, who I was, and the choices I wanted to make weren't a bad thing. They're what made me, me.

This was something I couldn't see, yet he never gave up on me. He helped me to keep my blog going, something that was so helpful to my mental health. Granted, we had a huge falling-out, which made me feel alone again.

But still, he didn't give up on me. Being away from everything, in a place that he showed me, helped me to see that I needed help. I was so broken that without help, I would sink further down. No one wanted that for me. If you're feeling like that, no one wants you to have those feelings. They want you to get help, and that's the most important thing.

My parents wanted me to go to university, but that wasn't the life for me. I focused on my mental health instead. With the support of Gareth, Lucy, my family, and my three friends at school, I went to get help.

I'm currently on a break in the place where I first fell in love, back where I first realised that I needed help. I'm still so in love with this place. I'm here with Gareth. There's no one else I would rather spend time here with.

Gareth and I aren't perfect. He didn't take away my mental illness, but he helped me to see that the person I am is good, and that there is hope in the world. He helped me and loved me when I felt like I was beyond all that; I thought I didn't deserve it. I know that I'd be nothing without him— I wouldn't be the person I am today. I love him. I really love him, and I tried to deny it for so long, especially when we fell out. He's probably tired listening to me telling him that I love him.

This might be the real deal. But even if it isn't, there's nothing lost, because for once in my life, I had hope in a world of despair and darkness. He didn't cure me, but he helped me through it. No one can cure you, but they can make your world a little bit brighter.

So, if you see a man with a scruffy-looking beard and beautiful brown eyes with a girl that looks like she has her whole life together, just remember— we don't have anything together. We're making the best of what we've been given in life. The smile I wear is the battle scar of the storms I've been through.

I will get better. I will. I'll get better because there's always Blu Skyes at the end of a dark night.

Blu Skyes x

MENTAL HEALTH RESOURCES

United States

- Emergency Medical Services - 911

- National Suicide Prevention Lifeline - 1-800-273-8255

- Crisis Text Line – Text HOME to 741-741

- SAMHSA Treatment Referral Helpline - 1-877-726-4727

United Kingdom

Republic of Ireland

- National Emergency Numbers – 112 and 999

- Samaritans Emotional Support – 116 and 123

England

- National Emergency Numbers – 112 and 999

- Samaritans Emotional Support – 116 and 123

- Campaign Against Living Miserably - 0800 58 58 58 (nation-wide) and 0808 802 58 58 (London)

- Shout Crisis – Text HELP to 85258

ACKNOWLEDGEMENTS

I would firstly like to thank God for my ability to write these stories and for the opportunities given to me to get them out into the world. To my family, for always supporting me with my writing. No matter what I've needed help and advice with, you all have been there. Especially Mumma, who has given me ideas and opinions on books that are yet to be written. I love you all so much.

To my friends and the people on Instagram that have supported me for two whole years. I wouldn't have had confidence in my writing without you all. Alex and Ruth, you two have been constant rocks to my many writing problems. You have always guided me to help me build my writing community.

To my publishing company who took a chance on me, my dream, and Liv's story in *Not Always Blu Skyes*. Every single one of you have been so supportive, especially when I decided to go under my real name. Thank you to Lauren Johnson who designed my cover and helped me to make this book what it is. It is so beautiful. I adore it. Thank you to my editors who worked tirelessly with me to make my novel the best that it could be. I am so grateful and blessed to have such a supportive publishing company.

Finally, to all those who never thought that I would get this far. I never gave up. You never kept me down, and I'm so proud of myself to have made it this far despite what you all thought.

www.ingramcontent.com/pod-product-compliance
Lightning Source LLC
Chambersburg PA
CBHW020847020726
47497CB00005B/1287